The white powder looked innocent lying there in
the open, but this was the drug of the damned,
the curse of mankind: heroin, what some call
"smack," others "junk," "snow," "stuff," "poison,"
"horse." It had different names but the same effect.
To all of its users—to all of the dopefiends in the
Detroit ghetto—it was slow death.

*Holloway House Classics by Donald Goines*

# DOPEFIEND

## DONALD GOINES

**KENSINGTON PUBLISHING CORP.**
http://www.kensingtonbooks.com

HOLLOWAY HOUSE CLASSICS are published by

Kensington Publishing Corp.
119 West 40th Street
New York, NY 10018

All Kensington Titles, Imprints, and Distributed Lines are available at special quantity discounts for bulk purchases for sales promotions, premiums, fund-raising, and educational or institutional use. Special book excerpts or customized printings can also be created to fit specific needs. For details, write or phone the office of the Kensington special sales manager: Kensington Publishing Corp., 119 West 40th Street, New York, NY 10018, attn: Special Sales Department, Phone: 1-800-221-2647.

\
ISBN-13: 978-0-7582-7319-2
ISBN-10: 0-7582-7319-3

First Kensington trade paperback printing: December 2011

10  9  8  7  6  5  4  3  2  1

Printed in the United States of America

# DOPEFIEND

# 1

The voices inside the flat were loud as the argument continued. Porky, black and horribly fat, stared around his domain with small, red, reptilian eyes. His apartment was his castle. His world consisted of the narrow confines of the four walls that surrounded him. In his huge armchair he would sit watching the drug addicts come and go. They entertained him, not intentionally, but nevertheless they did. When they came to his shooting gallery and begged for credit, it gave him the feeling of power. With the women addicts he enjoyed himself even more. When they were short of money, his fiendish mind came up with newer and more abnormal acts for them to entertain him with.

He set aside the book he had been glancing through, laying it down in such a way that he could glance at the large color pictures of a horse and woman faking an act of copulation. The four addicts who had just bought a fourth of dope from his doorman were deep in an argument over who would use the two sets of works first. The rest of the tools were already in use by other addicts.

"Here, baby," a dopefiend yelled across the room. "One of you can use my works, just as long as you don't stop them up." He hesitated, then added, "Just make sure you clean them out when you finish using 'em." To emphasize his point, he stuck the works back down in a glass of water sitting next to him and drew up a dropper full of water. He slowly skeeted it out on the floor, making sure the needle wasn't stopped up before loaning it out.

"When you return them, Jean, make sure they work as good as they do now." He skeeted some more water out of the needle, showing the woman that his tools weren't stopped up.

Porky watched their behavior without any show of emotion. It didn't disturb him to see bloody water skeeted on his floor, since it was already littered with cigarette butts and bloody toilet tissue. The floor of the apartment had pools of blood on it, from where addicts had tried to get a hit but the works had stopped up and they had pulled the needle out, leaving a flowing trail of blood that dropped down from their arms or necks and settled on the floor. From the accumulation of filth and old dried-up blood, the house had a reeking odor that was nauseous to anyone who hadn't smelled it before.

Jean, a tall brown-skinned addict who looked ten years older than her twenty years, grabbed the works out of Joe's outstretched hand. Her face was still attractive, but one could discern marks of dissipation in it. Her lips were drawn down in a perpetual dopefiend frown.

Porky wet his huge blubberish lips in anticipation. Jean was one of the few female addicts to come to his apartment who had trouble finding a vein to hit in. Because of this problem she hit in the inner part of her thigh. He watched her greedily as she prepared to hit in the groin. She cooked up her dope in a large bottle top, almost burning her fingers when the top became too hot to hold, but not hot enough to make her drop her dope. She slowly rolled up a piece of cotton and dropped it inside the cooker. She drew the heroin up through the cotton. As her fingers moved delicately with the dropper, her eyes came up and she caught Porky's eyes following her every motion. Her small mouth tightened sarcastically. She realized that he would continue to watch until she was finished, but she was far past the stage where she was concerned about such a small matter as a man looking under her dress.

The only concern she had at the moment was whether or not she could get a hit. Without any embarrassment whatsoever, she pulled up her short skirt until it was above her hips, revealing the absence of panties, while displaying the tangled mass of dark hairs on her pubic mound. Anxiously she began to run her finger up and down until she could feel the vein she was searching for. Without hesitation, she plunged the dull needle down into her groin. There was a blue-black scar on the inside of her thigh, which at closer observation was revealed to be needle marks from where she had hit before. In the middle of the track she plunged the needle into what was a small abscess. As she pushed and pulled on the needle, trying to find the hit, pus ran out of the sore and down her leg.

Porky watched the dark fertile thighs with hunger. He had had Jean on many occasions, but she still aroused him with her complete disregard for what other people thought. He remembered the time she had put on a freak show with one of his large German police dogs. She had performed in the front room before everyone without any hesitation. Just the mention of the fourth of dope he was giving her set her right to work. The vivid picture of her and the dog on the floor came to his mind, and he grabbed himself and rocked back and forth. Small sounds of pleasure escaped from him as he imagined the dog between her black thighs.

With an expression of exquisite pleasure Jean sat back in her chair. She worked the dropper slowly, then let it fill back up with blood. When the blood reached the top of the dropper, she backed it up into her veins, working the blood in the dropper slowly as she jacked the works off.

After she repeated this act over and over again, the junkie who had loaned her the works yelled: "I done told you, bitch, not to stop up my works. You keep jackin' them off, they goin' sure as hell stop up." Joe stood up and stared at her angrily. He was tall and thin, with dark features. His hair still held the accumulation of debris from where he had slept.

Jean pulled the needle out slowly. A look of rapture filled her face. She looked up and noticed Porky holding himself and watching her. Her eyes filled with scorn. She opened her legs wide and scratched herself.

"Why don't you come over here, Porky, and let me rub some of this pussy up against your fat, black face." She spoke in a slow tantalizing voice, all the while rubbing the sides of her cunt. The sight was beyond vulgarity. It was grotesque, even sickening, because as she sat there with her legs wide, a stream of blood mixed with pus ran slowly down her thigh.

Porky watched her as though he was in a trance. He licked his lips and moaned. His breathing became heavy and loud in the wide, spacious front room of the apartment. Most of the addicts sitting on the couches watched him with contempt, if they weren't nodding too much to see. To them, Porky was just a fat freak with good dope. They used him the same way they would use anyone else to get their fix. They tried to play on his weakness.

"Bitch," Joe yelled at the woman as he walked over and snatched up his bloody works. "You done let all that motherfuckin' blood dry in my spike." He stared at her coldly. "A dopefiend bitch ain't shit," he stated, then walked back across the room and began to clean his tools out.

A circus, Porky thought as he watched another girl cross the room and sit down on the floor between Jean's legs. She raised her lips and kissed Jean's thigh. Her short skirt rose high on her hips as she nestled between Jean's spreading legs. As she raised her arm to stroke Jean's leg, a swarm of sores were revealed. On closer inspection, a person could see that each of the sores was an open abscess. The sleeves of her light-colored blouse were spotted with dried blood.

As he watched, Porky's eyes began to roll. He reached down inside his pants and rubbed vigorously. The addicts watched Porky, anxiously hoping that he didn't reach a climax too soon. They knew that, at times when Porky felt freakiest, he might set enough dope out for everyone.

Suddenly Jean dropped her skirt and stood up. Her eyes went across the room to Porky. His face was covered with sweat, while his double chin hung down quivering. His cheeks had become so fat that they hung down around his neck.

"Set some dope out, Porky," Jean said in an unconcerned tone. "If you want to watch a freak show, lay it out, baby." Her face was hawklike, with sharp black eyes.

With instant control Porky pulled himself together. His beady eyes glittered with animal cunning. Where before there had been lust, now only cruelty could be seen. "Smokey!" he yelled. His voice seemed shrill for such a huge person.

The bedroom door opened and a slim, dark-skinned woman in her early thirties came out. She had a look about her as though she had seen all the horrors that life could reveal and then experienced them. Her skin was dry and wrinkled, while her eyes had a flat, dead look about them. She moved across the room as though she was floating.

The dopefiends watched Smokey out of the corners of their eyes. They knew it was the end of their thoughts of free dope. With Smokey there, nothing would be given away. The addicts, men and women alike, thought of Smokey as one of the dirtiest-hearted black bitches alive.

Her eyes traveled around the room, missing nothing. Wherever she glanced, the addict who caught Smokey's eye quickly looked away. Smokey had tricked her way out of a cotton field in Georgia when she was thirteen. By the time she reached New York a year later, she was a professional whore and dopefiend.

She took in Porky's appearance with a glance. His hand was still buried inside his pants. She removed his hand as she sat down on his huge lap, put her small hand behind his back, and reached down inside his pants. She manipulated her fingers dexterously as she swept the room with a cold glance. Her shrewd stare took in the blood dropping on the floor as one of the dopefiends nodded with a spike in his arm.

In the corner another addict was lying on the floor while his companion kneeled over him. His cheeks were puffed up as he tried to build up the vein in his neck. Slowly he let out the air, then turned his head as his friend felt his neck, feeling for the vein. Using a size 28 needle, extra long, the addict's friend, Junior, stuck the long needle deeply into his partner's neck. Missing the vein, he removed the needle quickly and felt his friend's neck again. He held the vein with his middle finger and pushed the needle back into his companion's neck.

Suddenly blood began to flow up into the dropper, letting the man know that he had made a direct hit. He removed the dropper from the needle, leaving the needle still protruding from the addict's neck. He squirted the water out of the dropper and drew up some heroin from a top that was carefully placed beside the man on the floor. Gently he replaced the dropper into the needle that was sticking out of his friend's neck, waiting until blood flowed up in the dropper again before releasing the drug slowly. Waiting for the reflow of blood was the only way he had of knowing if the works had stopped on him while he was changing stuff in the dropper.

Twice more Junior refilled the dropper from the top and ran the heroin into his partner's neck. He picked the top up and wiggled the dropper around, using it to suck up the last of the dope in the cotton.

Junior had a good hit because, while the dropper was removed, blood gushed out of the open end of the needle. He stuck the dropper into the needle and ran the last of the dope. When he pulled the needle out, blood ran down the dopefiend's neck as he stretched out on the floor. It didn't disturb the addict though. He just lay there until his partner used some toilet paper to wipe the blood from his neck.

Porky let out a loud groan and his monstrous body jerked uncontrollably. Smokey removed her hand and wiped it on her dirty skirt. She stuck her hand down inside her bra and removed a small package and opened it. The white powder looked innocent lying there in the open, but this was the drug of the damned, the curse of mankind: heroin, what some call "smack," others "junk," "snow," "stuff," "poison," "horse." It had different names, but it still had the same effect. To all of its users, it was slow death.

Smokey stood up and swept the room with her brutal stare. Most of the addicts looked away. She was one of them and they knew there was no story they could tell her because she had heard them all.

# 2

The couple in the automobile was still arguing when the man driving parked in front of Porky's house. From outside, the house looked innocent enough. A small two-family flat, with the downstairs flat boarded up. There were boards over all the windows in the downstairs apartment, giving it the appearance of having been closed for quite a while. Once there had been a fence around the place, but like many houses on the east side of Detroit, the fence had gone first, then the grass had followed. Now, there were only a few fence posts remaining in random spots around the front of the house.

Teddy glanced at the small woman sitting beside him. "Terry, give me those other two dollars, and I'll get a ten-dollar pack for us."

The woman sitting beside him had the looks of

a small doll. She was tiny, just under five feet, with jet black hair that hung down around her shoulders. Her skin had a golden hue about it impossible to acquire unless you were fortunate enough to be born with it. Her eyes, when she glanced up at the man with her, were bright and glittered with the joy of life and the happiness of being a woman in love. All of her features were small, and she had a habit of sticking her tongue out between her beautifully curved lips whenever she was deep in thought. Her smile held the promise of sweet sensuality—and inward delights for the man lucky enough to receive her attention.

At his words, Terry puckered her mouth in a tight frown. "I can't do that, Teddy. I've got to have gas money so I can drive back and forth to work." She crossed her legs, revealing lovely tan thighs. "Besides," she continued, "I already gave you eight dollars out of the ten-dollar bill I borrowed from Momma, and I was supposed to make it last me the rest of the week."

"Aw, baby," Teddy whined. He stuck his lip out like a small child.

Terry squinted up her nose. "Shit, Teddy, you don't need all that dope anyway."

For a moment Teddy was too occupied considering the gas gauge to reply. "You got enough gas, Terry, to get to work and back," he said. "Come on, let's run up to Porky's and get a little blow."

Again she frowned. "Damn, Teddy, you know I don't want to go upstairs in that nasty house. The smell makes me sick, plus that nasty, fat, black bastard always tries to look up under my dress." She made a small gesture with her hand, then continued. "Teddy, you know I hate the sight of all those people lying around on that dirty floor, with blood running all down their arms and legs. No thank you, baby; I can think of one thousand things I'd rather do this day than go up in that funky house. So please, Daddy, don't ask me to go up there with you. I'd rather wait in the car."

Teddy didn't even bother to listen to what she had to say. If she didn't go up, he didn't have to give her any of the dope. But then again, if she went with him, he stood a better chance of hitting Porky up for a little credit. He tossed the idea around in his head. He was well aware of the fact that Porky was interested in Terry, but for that matter, Porky was interested in anything with a skirt on, and that didn't just go for women.

"Come on," he ordered, making his mind up at once. With Terry along, he just might be able to get enough stuff so that he wouldn't have to go out hustling the rest of the day. It was worth the chance. He didn't have anything to lose by trying.

Terry shrugged. She knew that sound in his voice. It was always better to give in when Teddy spoke like that, because if she didn't she ran the chance of getting slapped down; or worse, they would end up arguing the rest of the day, until she went to work. She climbed out of the small compact car, grumbling under her breath, and waited until Teddy came around the car. The look she tossed him was full of anger, but there was no hiding the love she held for her man. They were both just about the same size, with the same golden brown complexions. At first sight, many people would take them to be brother and sister. He flashed his brilliant smile at her when he reached the sidewalk. Sometimes it made her happy just to be allowed to run with him. She didn't really care when he didn't take her anywhere. What she wanted was the enjoyment of just being with her man.

"You black men in Detroit are something else," Terry said as she grabbed his arm. If I can only figure out a way to get him away from all this dope, she thought. She remembered the beautiful times they had had together before Teddy started using.

She wondered again, for the thousandth time, if Teddy had a habit. He claimed he didn't, but she didn't know. For one thing, she didn't know that much about dope to be able to tell if he had one or not. She believed he was becoming strung out, if he wasn't hooked yet. At the rate he was going, it was just a matter of time. If she could figure out some way to stop him from using, things would be just like they used to be. The little amount of heroin she took when she was out with him was nothing. She believed she was too strong to become addicted. Actually, the only reason she took the stuff was that Teddy liked her to turn on at

times when he did, but other than that, she really
didn't like the stuff. Sometimes it made her sick.
She couldn't even hold any food in her stomach.

Teddy took her arm and led her up the sidewalk towards the house. She glanced at him out
of the corner of her eye. Self-consciously she noticed again that she was taller than he was whenever she wore her heels. She made a mental note
not to wear her heels when he picked her up, unless they were going out somewhere.

The thought of going out somewhere made
her smile. They hadn't even been to a movie in
the last month. She twisted around and stared at
him. His thin face with its keen nose, topped off
by his deep, fierce, cold black eyes, was a woman's
dream. His eyes gave him the look of a hunting
eagle.

When they reached the porch steps, she
stopped. "I'll follow you," she said and stood
waiting patiently until Teddy went up the stairs
first. They entered the frame house and went up
the rickety stairway. By the time they reached the
top, someone was already watching their approach out of one of the small peepholes that had
been cut in the door of Porky's apartment.

Terry wrinkled up her nose as the smell from
the flat came to her. It was a sickening odor. Stale
blood, with whatever else happened to be on the
floor. She wondered how the people living there
could adjust to such an odor. She remembered

the first time she had come up these steps with Teddy. The odor had been so strong she had almost vomited.

Before Teddy could knock, they heard someone remove the two-by-four that was kept across the door, and then the door opened slowly.

A feeling of nausea began to invade her soul as she entered the apartment. Terry swallowed, fighting down the sickness. For some reason, it was always this way when she entered this flat, or what she sometimes called jokingly "the room of horror." The doorman closed the door behind them and replaced the large two-by-four across the doorway.

Terry's sharp dark eyes darted around like flying sparrows as she scanned the room. It was the same as usual, the only difference being that the people changed. Other than that, they were doing the same things. It's like stepping into another world, she thought, as she stared around at the addicts nodding and searching for veins to shoot the dope in. The people were strange. Men and women alike scratched whatever part of their body itched, no matter who might be watching.

She stared at two white boys who would have been conspicuous in any other all-black environment. But here the color problem didn't really exist. A dopefiend was a dopefiend, whether he was black or not. If he had the money and was cool with Porky he could relax and shoot his dope.

Teddy grinned as Porky's voice came booming across the room. It was an artificial grin, one that many junkies have complete control of. Always smile when the pusher speaks. Very seldom can he do anything wrong.

"Well well well, look who's finally came and visited little me," Porky yelled from the bedroom doorway. They both turned in time to see Porky waddling out of the bedroom towards them. His fat face seemed to be the epitome of happiness as he crossed the living room floor towards them.

"Teddy, you naughty boy, you. Why have you been keeping this lovely child away from me?" He stopped and wiped the sweat from his brow. "You know how much I enjoy looking at such a cute young thing as Terry." His eyes swept up and down Terry's well-shaped body, stripping her of her clothes with his piercing, piglike eyes.

She managed to fight down a shiver of horror as she returned his stare. There was no way for her to conceal the fear she had of him. It was in her eyes, and she trembled slightly as she looked away from his hungry stare. To her, he was a monstrosity, fatter than any human being had a right to be. In truth, he was a good specimen of a freak of nature. Grotesque to the sight, more fantastic in appearance than the mind could imagine.

With his quick insight, Porky read the fear in her eyes and it only aroused him. He rubbed himself intimately, unaware of the motion. Terry saw it and turned her face away, paralyzed by the thought that he acted more like an animal than the huge dogs he kept in his bedroom.

"Say, Porky," Teddy said in his most persuading voice. "I ain't got but ten dollars, man, you think you can toss in a little gapper for me and Terry?"

Terry glared at him angrily. She hadn't asked for any dope and she didn't want Porky giving her any. Instantly, she realized that this was the real reason Teddy had asked her to come up with him. It was not because he really wanted her company; he only tolerated her with him because he knew Porky liked her, and he was taking advantage of that fact. She could feel herself blushing as the anger welled up inside her. She tried not to let it show as she glared at Teddy, but from the smile on Porky's face, she believed he knew just how she felt.

Amused, Porky stared at Teddy. He realized that Terry was the reason why Teddy asked for more dope than he would ordinarily have done. It would be a cold day in hell when one of these dopefiends started to outthink him, Porky thought coldly.

"You know I'm goin' look out for my little girl, Terry," Porky replied easily. He grinned when he noticed her flinch. Yes, he would give her all the dope she wanted, and then some. The way he had it reasoned out, he didn't believe it would take long to get her strung out, not if she continued to snort the extra-good dope he put her way. And he was definitely going to see that she snorted most of the dope he gave them.

Porky glanced at Terry and smiled, while his mind quickly calculated up what he had in store for her. Just let her keep on chippin'. One of these days she would wake up with a little monkey on her back. That was the day in the future he was waiting and planning for.

"Smokey," he bellowed, "bring me some of that loose stuff." He waddled over to his large armchair and sat down. He waited until Smokey had come and gone before he shook out some white powder on top of a record cover. He pushed a large amount towards Teddy, then pulled it back and pushed a smaller amount towards Terry.

"You know your woman has got to snort all of this stuff up, don't you, Teddy. I ain't about to have her saving none of my dope to give to you," he growled, then added, more in a joking manner, "I know how slick some of you try and be, so don't even try and slick me out of none of my dope. I'm up on you already."

Teddy's hand shook as he reached out for the dope. "She goin' snort it, Porky; you know I ain't trying to put no game on you, man." He stared at all the stuff Porky pushed over to him. He counted up the price the dope would have cost him. It was over two ten-dollar spoons, at the least.

All the time the two men were talking, Terry

hadn't taken her eyes off the large pile of dope that she was supposed to snort. She had never snorted so much stuff at one time. She started to shake her head, but one look at Teddy was enough to make her change her mind. He was staring at the dope as though it had hypnotized him.

This is the last time, she promised herself, as she took the record cover and put it on her lap. She sat back in her chair and pulled out a book of matches. Tearing a small piece off the cover, she made a small shovel and began to snort the dope from the album cover. She frowned when the bitter taste filled her throat. but she continued putting the stuff in her nose. The strong drug began to take effect almost immediately.

Porky began to breathe heavily as he watched her. Before, she had been sitting like a little lady, her legs held tightly together. But as the drug took effect, she slowly relaxed and her beautiful golden brown legs began to open, wider and wider. He stared openly. He could see the neat little slip she wore, as her skirt rose up higher around her thighs.

He whispered hoarsely to himself. The words were incoherent as spit ran out of the corners of his mouth. The slight flashes he saw of golden thighs were enough to arouse him to erection. He wanted to masturbate but was afraid he would frighten her. He stared in fascination. No woman had ever really made him feel as Terry did. She was so tiny yet so well put together. How fragile she appeared to be! Never, never had he met a woman whom he wanted to treat as though she was something rare, or so delicate that she aroused a tenderness inside of him that he hadn't been aware of.

Terry could feel herself drifting off. It was as if she were in a fog, yet she was aware of her surroundings. She noticed Porky staring at her, and she tried to pull herself together. The drug was too powerful, or rather, gave her an attitude of indifference. "The hell with it," she reasoned and drifted off into a nod, as her head slowly dropped down on her chest.

Teddy was too occupied to give them any thought. He rolled up his sleeve and felt until he found the vein he wanted. He removed a rag from his pocket, one that he used to tie up his hair when he got it processed, and tied it around his arm. With slow deliberation, he stuck the needle into his arm, hitting the vein on his first try. Blood backed up in the dropper before he started to run the drug into his arm. A look of peaceful contentment flooded his face as the drug quickly took effect. He removed the dropper from his needle and refilled it with smack, then stuck it back in his arm. The dope invaded his mind, bringing on a false empyrean. For a few hours he wouldn't have any worries in the world. All his problems became insignificant as he fed the insatiable monster known to all users as their personal monkey.

At one time the sight of Teddy sticking the spike in his arm had been repugnant to Terry. Now, as the drug removed all of her unnecessary worry, she watched him out of half-opened eyes. If that was what he wanted to do, it shouldn't disturb me, she reasoned. Everybody was entitled to do his own thing, so who was she to complain?

A slight disturbance occurred across the room. One of the young white boys passed out from too much stuff. As he fell out on the floor, someone yelled for Smokey. As his friend kneeled down over him, his hands moved quickly inside his partner's pockets. As Terry watched, she noticed him remove a small bankroll and stuff it into his own pocket.

"Put it back!" The words were a sharp command. As the young white junkie looked up from the unconscious body of his friend, he saw Smokey bearing down on him. Her words came to him sharp and clear.

"Put it back, you son-of-a-bitch." She yelled, yet it seemed as though she never raised her voice. "The first thing you'll tell him when he comes to is that he got beat up here." She stopped and stood on her heels, hands on her hips. "You don't think I'm goin' let you bring that heat down on top of us, do you?" She stared, not angrily but with a look that let him know she wouldn't take any shit.

"I wasn't going to keep it," the young addict

replied. "I was just going to hold it for him, until he gets himself together."

Smokey held out her hand. "Give it here," she ordered and nodded towards two of her house men who had come over. "Get some salt, or some ice under his nuts or something, but make sure that peck don't die on us up here." She tapped her foot as she waited for the young white kid to hand over the money. "He'll get his money as soon as he's able to wake up enough to know he's got it back, but, peckerwood, I don't never want to see you in here again. You can wait until your friend is together and leave with him, but from now on, honkie, find you somewhere else to go. We don't have no dippin' in this house."

The young boy looked around Smokey for Porky as he pushed the money towards her. His voice had a whine in it as he tried to explain. "For real, I wasn't taking his money, I was just gonna hold it. You believe me, don't you, Porky? You know I wouldn't beat my friend. Look how many times we've come up here together." His eyes held a frantic note. He stared at Porky, pleading, waiting for him to say something that would remove the exile Smokey was forcing on him.

Smokey didn't even bother to wait. She watched her two doormen work over the young kid. As soon as he started to moan, she turned on her heels. She stopped at the door of the bedroom. "Ya heard what I said. Don't let neither one

23

of them honkies back in again. I done told you, Porky, they ain't nothing but trouble. If that wood woulda died, we'd have to close up shop, 'cause the police sure ain't goin' accept no young white boy dying from no overdose at our house."

Porky shrugged his huge shoulders and looked away. Whenever Smokey spoke, he generally listened if it was about their business, because he knew that she damn well knew what she was talking about. He turned his back on the young boy's pleas. There wasn't a junkie in the world who could make him go against something his woman had said.

# 3

Terry walked slowly around her section in the department store as though she were in a dream. For the thousandth time, her mind returned to the dope she had in her pocketbook. No matter how busy she tried to be, her mind would return to the tiny package. She counted slowly on her fingers. It had been ten days since the incident occurred in Porky's apartment where the white junkie passed out. Since then, Teddy had taken her by Porky's place every day so that he could get some dope, and she had ended snorting some stuff each day.

She wondered if it was possible for her to have gotten a habit in such a short amount of time. "No way," she told herself over and over again, but why did she keep thinking about the dope she had in her purse then? "Why, why, why?" The question exploded in her mind. If only Porky hadn't given her that dope today when they had started to leave his place. She silently cursed Teddy and Porky as her mind dwelled on the dope in her purse. If she just took a little blow, Teddy would never know about it, she told herself.

Before the thought had completely evolved in her mind, she found herself slipping away from her sweater counter. It was as though she were standing on the outside watching someone else. She hurried towards the women's rest room and locked herself in one of the stalls. Quickly she removed the neatly wrapped package from her purse and spread it out on her lap. Her fingers trembled slightly as she rolled up a dollar bill, making it into a quill. She stuck one end of the quill in her nose, while she held the other end to the white powder in the package. As if by magic, the white powder disappeared as she inhaled.

After two or three deep snorts, it suddenly occurred to her that there really wasn't enough stuff left in the package to take home to Teddy, so she quickly snorted up the rest of the dope. Her head dropped down on her bosom as she went into a deep nod. She stayed in the toilet nodding until she was awakened by the voice of one of her white friends who worked on the same floor with her.

"Terry, Terry! Are you in there?" The woman's excited voice came to her as though out of a dense fog. "Is everything all right? You're not sick or something, are you?"

Terry lifted her head slowly. She could hardly keep her eyes open. The strong P, "pure," that Porky had given her was enough to bring the worse dopefiend into a dreamlike state. "I'll be all right in a minute. I think I've got diarrhea or something." Her voice was low and she slurred her words as she spoke.

"Is there anything I can do for you?" the other salesgirl asked.

"No, I don't think so. Just let Mrs. Breeding know that I'm not feeling too well. Tell her I'll be out in a few moments."

Terry waited until the sound of the door closing came to her, then her head dropped again as she went into another nod. After what she thought to be just a few minutes passed, she stood up. Half an hour had gone by since the other salesgirl had spoken to her. She made her way to the face bowl and splashed cold water onto her face. While she was standing there, the door opened and the woman in charge of the floor came in.

"My, Terry, you do look a mess, don't you," Mrs. Breeding said kindly. "If you're not feeling any better, you had better take the rest of the day off."

Terry fought back a nod as she stared up at the friendly, gray-haired white woman. "I think I'll do just that, Mrs. Breeding. I'll stop in and see our family doctor before I come in tomorrow." For a moment, Terry's eyes closed, then she continued. "I don't really know what's the matter with me. Maybe it's something I ate?"

Mrs. Breeding stared at her closely. "If I were you, Terry, I'd try and get a little more sleep. You young girls think you can stay up all night and it won't bother you the next day, but you're wrong. You need your rest just like the rest of us, even an old lady like me."

Before Terry could answer, Mrs. Breeding added, "You probably haven't noticed me, Terry, but I've been watching you lately, and I've seen you actually going to sleep on your feet out there."

Terry caught herself going into a nod. She jerked her head up sharply, not aware that Mrs. Breeding was watching her closely. "I have been staying up late for the past few nights," she said lamely, as she thought, you nosy old bitch.

Anxious not to be seen nodding, Terry splashed cold water on her face. She took her time washing until she heard the door close as her department head went out. She peered in the mirror at herself. Her eyes were as tiny as pinpoints. There was plenty of evidence of the drug user in them for anyone knowing the signs of drug abuse to see.

Terry quickly got her coat and left the store before anyone else got a chance to see her. Once outside, she leaned against the building until her conscience got the best of her. What am I doing? she asked herself. Here I am, downtown, nodding against the wall of one of the largest white stores in the city. She tried to shake the drug off. All she wanted to do was find a place where she could sit and nod in peace. Her hair blew down in her face as she stood there nodding against the building. Two young black teenagers walked past and smiled knowingly in her direction.

The effect of the poisonous drug was still strong as she made her way to the nearest bus station. She cursed angrily at herself as she waited for the Woodward bus. If she hadn't been so stupid, she would never have allowed Teddy to keep her car. She waited patiently until a bus stopped in front of her. She climbed on the coach and found a seat in the back so that she wouldn't be under too many prying eyes. Her head became heavy so she just let it drop down on her bosom as she went into a nod. Without being conscious of it she began to scratch. Slowly at first, then without any apparent concern over who was watching, she scratched herself openly. She started on her leg, then went higher while she nodded.

A young married couple on their way home from a theater watched her with amusement at first, but it quickly turned to embarrassment. Terry glanced up and saw them watching her. She tried to pull herself together. With difficulty, she fought off the desire to nod over and over again. Five minutes later, she was back doing the same thing. The light-chocolate-tanned skin on the upper part of her thigh showed long groove marks from where she had scratched herself. Her arms were also covered with the same scratch marks.

I've got to get hold of myself, she told herself. I'm acting just like a dopefiend. Her guilty feeling was quickly forgotten as she began to feel nauseated from the motion of the bus. She reached up and pulled the cord and got on her feet, fighting down the urge to puke.

To the shock of the people on the bus, she started to throw up before it came to a complete stop. When the bus finally stopped, she continued to puke as she went down the steps. People stared out the bus window at her as she jumped from the coach, puking all the way to the sidewalk.

Her stomach seemed to be twisting in knots as she held onto a lamppost for support. She stared up and down well-lighted Woodward Avenue. The more she puked, the higher she became. She finished and stood up, her head feeling lighter, and walked as though she were gliding. Terry found a small handkerchief in her purse and wiped her mouth. The compelling desire to find a nice secluded place to nod pushed her forward. She wanted to get away from all prying eyes and really enjoy her high. Such a feeling of exquisite peace came over her from the drug that the worry over her car and job disappeared.

Terry hesitated on the sidewalk until suddenly everything was clear. When the thought hit her, it became compelling and soon it took complete control. She believed she knew just what she needed. Another blow. If she could get another snort of dope, everything would be all right. Just another snort of stuff. She'd have a place to nod, plus there wouldn't be any funny stares. There was no more fear of Porky's place, even though she had never been there without Teddy. It was now a place of refuge, a place away from the un-enlightened.

The thought of being around people whom she could call her kind came to her—then jolted her wide awake. What did she mean by her kind of people? She wasn't a dopefiend, she was far too strong. The only people who got hooked were weak people, and she knew in her heart that she was too strong to get hooked.

With that thought guiding her, she started to make her way towards Porky's. She opened her purse and counted the few remaining dollars as she staggered slightly down the street. One car and then another pulled up beside her. She didn't even bother to look up at the drivers as she counted the few remaining dollars she had. There was just a little over eight dollars, but it would be more than enough, she told herself, especially if Porky was there.

At that moment she couldn't care if Porky stared at her legs or not, just as long as she got what she wanted. And what she wanted was an-other blow, another blow of heroin.

Porky was sitting in his favorite spot at the window watching the hotel across the street when the cab pulled up. He always took an interest in cabs on his block because dopefiends had a habit of riding up in a cab, leaving it in front of his house with the meter running, never to return. Whenever he caught one doing this, he made the addict go back out and pay the cab driver off. He didn't want any dopefiends burning up his house, even though he paid off the vice squad monthly to allow him to operate.

He grinned when he saw Terry jump out of the cab. Her short miniskirt began to rise as she bent over and paid off the cab driver. Porky opened the window quickly and leaned out, trying to peep as her skirt went higher. He sat down disgustedly as she straightened up.

His agile mind raced over the reasons that would bring her to his house by herself. There were only two, he told himself. If it had been Teddy she was looking for, she wouldn't have got out of the cab. She could see her car wasn't parked outside. The only other reason would be she wanted a blow.

Whether or not it was a blow she wanted, he was planning to make sure she had one before leaving. He counted the days she had been using P. It was close to two weeks now that he had been giving her the best dope he had in the house. If she didn't have a habit yet, he was pretty sure she had a strong yearn. From his past experience with drug addicts, he knew a yearn was just as bad as having a habit. Whenever they reached the stage where the drug became compelling, it was just a matter of time before they became full-fledged addicts.

When they got a yearn, they made all kinds of excuses to themselves to justify using. It was only a short step from mentally desiring heroin to physically needing it.

Terry glanced up and down the street without slowing down. She didn't see her car anywhere, so she knew she wouldn't have to put up with Teddy's begging. She wandered idly as she went up the steps what was happening to her love life. Only a month ago, she would have given Teddy anything she possessed. Now his constant begging grew worrisome. Whenever she saw him he needed money. He looked on her payday as if it were his. It had also been quite a while since he'd tried to take her to one of those cheap hotels he used to love to get her in. Well, that was one problem she didn't have to worry about anymore. The fear of getting knocked up by Teddy was over, because he didn't seem to be interested in her that way anymore. In fact, she thought, he really was interested in her no way, except in finding out how much money he could beg her out of.

The door was open when she reached the top of the stairway. Porky was standing in the doorway grinning.

"Well, now, what brings such a lovely thing as

you to my house this time of the night, all by herself?" he asked as he leered at her.

Her reply was quick and evasive. "I was looking for Teddy. I hoped to find him up here, Porky." She stared up at him and prayed that her nervousness wasn't noticeable.

From constantly dealing with addicts Porky had grown good at judging their behavior. He had difficulty with the hardened users, but as for the younger ones, he could read them like a book. Porky decided to make her squirm a little. "You didn't see your car downstairs anywhere, did you?" Before she could reply he continued, "If you had looked up, I would have saved you the trouble of coming up all them steps. It wouldn't have been no problem for me to yell down and tell you your sweet daddy wasn't here."

For a moment a transitory shiver of fear ran through her. Suppose he refuses to sell me any dope, she thought anxiously. The thought of buying some dope had been just a notion before, but now, faced with the problem of maybe not copping, it became a driving force. She just had to cop some drugs now.

"I was so sure Teddy would be here," she said and turned on her most captivating smile. Her teeth had a dazzling whiteness about them and, combined with her incomparable complexion, the smile was an enchanting weapon that had captured stronger men than Porky.

"Really, Porky, I didn't even bother to look for my car," she added. "I was so sure he was here."

Porky had seen the anxiety in her eyes though. Before his knees gave him away, he stepped towards the door and pretended to get ready to close it on her. "If he comes by, Terry, I'll tell him you stopped by lookin' for him."

Now the idea of having a blow became all-consuming. The very thought of being turned away without being allowed to buy some stuff filled her with dread. She clutched at the door desperately. She had never entertained the thought that he might not sell her a blow.

She blocked the door with her small body. "I was thinking about wasting a few dollars on a blow for myself, Porky." She wet her lips and rushed on, "Unless you have some reason for not wanting to sell me some dope?" She stared up at him and moved closer, not really aware of what she was doing.

Though he had expected it and waited for this minute, the words coming from her sounded like a dream come true. Porky could hardly believe his eyes and ears. This was what he had been waiting for. At long last Miss High-and-mighty had been brought to her knees. All her ladylike behavior from the past would now be shattered and he'd have the opportunity to watch her fall.

With difficulty he managed to conceal his pleasure. "Why, by all means, girlie. You should know your money is good at my house. Ain't I been giving you a blow whenever you wanted one these past few days?" He stared down at her as though he were a confessional preacher. His face was full of compassion and understanding.

A few of the addicts sitting around the apartment glanced up. The byplay of words hadn't shot past them. All of them knew just what Porky was working out of. Minnie, a thin, short, brownskinned dopefiend in her late twenties, watched Porky with anger. She was well aware that he was playing with Terry. It seemed like a replay out of her past. The only difference was that it was a different pusher but the same technique. Once they realized you really had a yen for the stuff, the free samples began to come to an end.

When she had first started using, the pushers used to call her up so she could come over and sample the dope they had just got in. They used to ask her to test it for them, as though she really knew what she was sampling. Minnie stared at Porky, her eyes glittering. She knew he wasn't stringing Terry out for the sake of another customer, either. When it concerned a young, attractive girl, sex was the hidden key in the background of his warped mind.

"Don't just stand there, girl, come on in," Porky ordered, standing in the doorway in such a way that she would have to squeeze against his huge stomach if she wanted to come in. He could feel her softness as she went by. He tried to press against her tightly, while he reached out and rubbed her ass, making it seem as though it was a friendly pat.

"How much money was you planning on spending?" he inquired as he walked closely behind her. Her short, light skirt fitted her tightly across the rear, and her legs were bowed enough to give her a very sexual look when she walked.

Terry opened her purse and counted the few dollars there, pushing back the five-dollar bill so that he wouldn't see it. "I got about three dollars, Porky, counting the little change I've got. Damn!" she cursed. "I thought I had more than that!" she said sweetly, playing on his lust. She could still feel the impression of his hand on her butt, and she planned on making him pay for that free feel.

He grunted. "You know that ain't enough money to get no stuff with, girl." He sat down and patted the arm of the chair. "Come over here and sit down, Terry, while I try and figure out what we can do for you, short money and all."

His fertile brain began to scheme. He didn't want to push it too fast, but this was an opportunity that didn't come to his house every day. Actually, this was the first time she had ever come to his pad without Teddy, and he didn't want to blow it. In the back of his mind a small voice kept warning him not to rush. He had all the time in the world, because if she came once alone, she would come back again, if she wasn't frightened too bad. He wet his lips slowly, trying to decide what course to take.

Minnie spoke up before he could make up his mind. "I'll put in the rest of the money with you, Terry, if you don't mind sharing a pack of stuff with me."

Porky shot her a villainous glance full of the promise of vengeance. He couldn't quite succeed in masking his anger at being temporarily thwarted, but he managed a slight grin. "By all means, you get together and pool up on one of those ten-dollar packs." He stared at Minnie meaningfully. "I guess you know we done run out of five-dollar bags." He grinned ruthlessly; he knew Minnie hadn't planned on buying anything higher than a five-dollar pack.

Minnie reached in her bra and removed some crumpled one-dollar bills. She counted the money out to Terry. With her back turned to Porky, Terry removed the five-dollar bill and showed it to Minnie. Both girls grinned at each other. After they pooled up the money, Terry took the money over and dropped it in Porky's fat lap.

Porky stared at the money in his lap as though it were a snake someone had tossed on him. "Smokey!" he yelled, his voice ringing loudly in the flat. "Bitch, don't you never put no money on me no more!" he yelled harshly at Terry, his voice carrying a note of fear. Like many pushers, Porky made it a point never to sell any drugs directly to an addict. Either his woman or one of his doormen always made the sale. Porky even refused to touch any of the money, believing that, if a bust went down with phony money, his hands would not light up if they ran tests on him at the police station.

Smokey came slowly into the room. She was wearing only a short half-slip and bra. She picked up the money quickly and counted it, making sure Minnie hadn't tried to short-change them. She stared coldly at Terry out of half-closed eyes. There was contempt in her look. She despised women like Terry. She considered them as pampered bitches, never having really experienced any of the hardships of life.

She remembered how it had been when she first met Porky. He was a small-time pusher, and she had come to his house broke and sick. He had taken her in, given her a place to stay and enough dope to get her drug sickness off, then enough money to go to the doctor the next day. It had taken two weeks before the female trouble she had disappeared, and in all that time, Porky supported her. It was the first time in her life anyone had ever been kind to her.

"Is it all there, baby?" Porky asked, hoping in his heart that they were short. When Smokey nodded, he removed two ten-dollar bags from his shirt pocket and gave one to Smokey.

Smokey counted the money again, then took the pack and held it out to Terry. Before Terry could take the dope and walk away, Porky grabbed her arm and pulled her close. His breath was strong and hot as his yellowish teeth grinned up at her.

"You take this other pack, Terry, and use it to wake up on." He pushed the other package of dope into her hand as she tried to pull away. He rubbed her arm slowly. A feeling of revulsion shook her as she felt his sweaty fingers caressing her arm intimately, but it didn't occur to her to refuse the heroin.

"Let's go over to my place and do this stuff up, Terry," Minnie said as she stood up. "That way we can get comfortable and relax without worrying about some freak trying to look under our skirts." Her open scorn had a strange effect on Porky. Instead of becoming angry, he became aroused. His breathing became heavy and he stared at her with open hostility.

"One of these days, bitch," he stated meaningfully, "you're going to overload your smart ass, and I'll be there to see it happen." The thought of Terry leaving before he could see her nod made him angry.

There was genuine hatred in Minnie's eyes as she stared back at him. "Not living, nigger. As long as there are tricks in the street, I'll never put myself down so low as to have to ask you for any kind of favor." She continued, her voice dripping venom. "And if you think I give a fuck about buying my dope from you, forget it. I spend fifty dollars a day, every day, so I don't have to kiss no-body's ass to get them to accept my money. You know as well as I know, there are too many deal-ers in Detroit for me to have to get down on my knees to your fat ass, so whenever you feel as if you don't want my business, don't bite your tongue."

Smokey had started back towards the bedroom but stopped to listen to Minnie. "Tell that wise-ass bitch to take her business somewhere else, then," she yelled to Porky. "Like we really give a fuck about her funky fifty dollars."

Porky hesitated for a brief minute. He didn't want to say something while he was angry that he would regret. She was a good customer, true enough, but fifty dollars didn't mean shit to a man who had the business he had. If he put her out for keeps, he'd never have the chance to see her when she became sick, and he had no doubt about her one day having to come to him for help. Not if she kept using, and he was sure she'd con-tinue using until the day she was arrested, or the day they put dirt on top of her. He had put up with her sharp tongue now for over a year, so it shouldn't be too hard to put up with it for at least six more months. With her being pregnant, it shouldn't take that long. When the day did come, when she came begging him to take her to bed, he'd laugh in her face and then make her perform with one of his dogs. The very thought of it was enough to cool down his anger.

"Take care of your own damn business, Smokey," he yelled, but there was no anger in his voice.

Terry stared at his scowling features. The very thought of him putting his large blubbering lips on her was enough to fill her with revulsion. She stared at Smokey's departing back and wondered how the woman could possibly live with such a man. It only went to prove that what they said was true. There was someone for everybody.

"How far do you live from here, Minnie?" Terry asked.

"I stay at the hotel across the street," Minnie answered and started towards the door. "If Porky don't act funny and stop us from taking our stuff out, we can go over there and do up."

The doorman opened the door for them after Porky gave him a nod. Both women gave a sigh of relief as they left the shooting gallery. Terry stared at the old hotel curiously as they crossed the street. The front of it was sagging as though it would fall over if a strong wind blew its way. The only thing that informed the passerby that it was a hotel was an old sign hanging from the dilapidated porch that read "Transient Rooms For Rent."

A sharp blast of wind almost lifted the short skirt Terry wore as they hurried across the street. She clutched her short, stylish coat around her and followed Minnie. They entered the hotel and she glanced around. The inside was just as bad as the outside. Just past the entrance, on the right, was a check-in office. Actually it was just a room, only the door was different. The top of the door opened, while the bottom part could be kept closed. Sitting behind the closed part of the door was an old woman who looked as if she were part of the building. Her face was covered with wrinkles and her head a ball of knotted gray hair. When she leered at them she revealed a mouth completely empty of teeth. There were two or three snags that might have once upon a time been called teeth, but now there was nothing but yellow stumps inside her mouth.

She waved a withered hand at Minnie. "My, honey, you ain't working tonight, huh?" she inquired in a voice that was much stronger than the frail body it came from.

"Maybe later on tonight," Minnie replied over her shoulder as she led the way up some stairs. Once upstairs, they went down a narrow, dimly lit hallway. Minnie stopped at a door without a number on it. "I use this room for my tricks," she said in answer to Terry's surprised glance.

"That's about all this hotel is used for, Terry. If you got a john who ain't got too much money, you can bring him here and the old bitch downstairs won't charge you but a dollar for the use of a room." Minnie opened the door as she talked and they went in.

"The only thing really wrong with the damn place," she continued after closing the door behind them, "is the toilets. You have to use the one at the end of the hall. Ain't none of the rooms got a private john, but you get used to it." She tossed her light summer coat on the bed. "Sometimes it pays off. If a trick pays you beforehand and you can get out of the room with the excuse that you're going to the toilet, well, it's just too damn bad for the trick. If he's that damn dumb, he needs to be took off."

Terry examined the room as though it were an alien spaceship. Her upbringing had not prepared her for such poverty. Being from a middle-class black family she had never seen the inside of such a place as this. The neighborhood she grew up in had been an interracial one since she was a child, and since most of the people in the neighborhood kept their homes and lawns up, no one was in a hurry to move. There were no deserted homes on her block, nor any bars or pawnshops in the immediate district.

Terry's flashing eyes took in the tiny face bowl with the cracked mirror over it. An ancient dresser leaned against the wall and, as she stared in its direction, two roaches ran from behind it and crawled into the wall. The only light in the room was given off by a small light bulb that hung down from the ceiling on a chain. Besides the bed and small chair, there was no other furniture in the bleak-looking room.

Minnie took out her small package of heroin and opened it. She shook its contents onto an album cover. With a knife she removed from her bra, she split the white powder into two piles, pushing the smaller of the two towards Terry. Terry took the smaller share without complaint. Minnie walked over to the dresser and removed a small bundle wrapped up in an old sock. When she unwrapped the bundle, a large top plus a dropper and needle fell out. She came back to the bed and pushed her pile of dope into the cooker. Her fingers shook as she removed a piece of cotton from the mattress and rolled it into a tiny ball.

"How about taking that glass and filling it up with fresh water for me, Terry?"

Terry got up as though she were in a dream and did what she was bid. Her mind was beginning to reel under the impact of what she had done today. She came back to the bed and set the water down in front of Minnie. She picked up the album cover with her small amount of dope on it. With the end of a match book cover she made a small shovel and picked up some of the dope and snorted it, all the while her eyes following Minnie with fascination.

Minnie removed her shoe and started to rub her foot. She examined it closely, searching for a vein. She put water in her dropper after cooking up the heroin. She raised her foot onto the bed and stuck the needle into it.

As Terry watched, she could feel herself starting to blush. She couldn't imagine herself sitting in front of another woman with her skirt up and her legs wide open. It was not because she was overly shy, either. When she was in high school it was nothing for her to undress in gym class with the rest of the girls. But this seemed vulgar and indecent.

Minnie pulled the needle out and pushed it into another spot. Each time she withdrew it a tiny stream of blood would flow from the spot she had just left. Blood began to fall onto the dirty sheet, then run down to the floor. As Terry watched, her eyes became large as saucers. She stared at her new friend in horror.

Cursing, Minnie snatched the needle out of her foot and began to rub her arm, searching desperately for a vein. Her eyes filled with anguish. Suddenly she stopped and balled up her fist. She took an old stocking and tied up her hand. She made a small fist, then jabbed the needle into the back of her hand. She waited impatiently for the telltale mark of blood to back up into the dropper. When she didn't get any results, she pulled out the needle and tried another spot.

In minutes, her hand was full of running blood. The blood dripped down on her bare legs and onto the bed and floor. She was becoming so frantic that she was almost in tears. She jumped up from the bed and rushed to the mirror. She ran back to the dresser and searched around until she came out with a long needle. She changed spikes on her dropper.

Terry had almost forgotten the dope in her lap

as she stared at Minnie in horror. Blood was everywhere—the floor, the dresser—and now the face bowl was covered with it, as Minnie stood over the bowl staring into the mirror. Her fingers ran along the side of her neck, feeling for her jugular vein. Blood ran down her upraised arm as she plunged the extra-long needle into her neck.

As she watched, Terry began to fight down the desire to puke. She jumped up from her chair, knocking over the album cover with the dope on it. She clutched her mouth with her hand, desperately trying to hold back the vomit, but before she could flee the room, vomit began to bubble through her tightly-gripped fingers like a boiling liquid.

# 4

The warm sun came through the partially open window, tossing silhouettes on the wall. The sound of an angry fly buzzing around his head yanked Teddy back from his drug-ridden sleep and brought him wide awake. At first he tried to cover his head under his sheet, but the fly continued to buzz until he sat up and stared around his room in a daze. For a brief moment he couldn't remember where he was. The sound of his mother knocking pots around in the kitchen and his sister's three kids playing loudly in the front room brought him to his senses.

Teddy sat up in bed and reached over for a cigarette. He blew smoke through his nose as he began to plan his day. The first thought that came to him was getting his morning blow. He relaxed as he remembered that Porky had told him last night that he had given Terry a ten-dollar pack to take home. He smiled as he thought about Terry. She would have taken it home so that he would have something to wake up on. How faithful a square bitch could be at times. I'll have to take the bitch to a motel pretty soon and give her some dick, he thought. For a minute, he tried to remember how long it had been since he had taken his woman anywhere, let alone to a motel. Oh well, the bitch should be happy just to be in his company, he decided, tossing his legs over the side of the bed and sitting up.

With his morning fix already taken care of, Teddy started to plan the rest of the day. It would be nice to have a bowel movement, he thought, since he hadn't had one in over ten days. After calling Terry, he decided he'd go into the toilet and make himself have one, even if he had to use his sister's douche bag and give himself an enema. He shivered; the sight of that long stem and the thought of having to put it in his own rectum sent goose pimples up and down his spine. But the idea of staying constipated any longer was out of the question. He had to have a bowel movement, and as long as he kept shooting dope as soon as he woke up, he'd never have an ordinary one. Somebody had told him that the longer his bowels stayed locked, the more dope it would take to make him high.

He cursed, picked up the phone, and dialed Terry's number. After the third ring Terry's mother answered the phone. "Hello, Mrs. Wilson. Could I speak to Terry?" He cursed inwardly as she inquired about his health, his mother, and his sister's children. The goddamn woman would take all morning just asking about people's health. Finally she yelled upstairs for her daughter. There was a long delay before the sound of Terry's sleepy voice came over the wire.

"Terry!" he ordered. "I want you to get up and come over here as soon as possible, baby." He remembered suddenly that he still had her car but decided the hell with picking her up. It was warm outside, and she always kept a few dollars in her purse so she could catch a cab.

"What for?" she asked, her voice no longer filled with sleep.

"What for!" He cursed. "I want you to bring me that package Porky gave you for me." He yelled more harshly than he had planned.

Terry hesitated for just a second. Her eyes went to her purse and back. The shock of Minnie's self-abuse had worn off, and now the thought of parting with that small package was disagreeable. Suddenly her mind was filled with a fierce desire to keep the small amount of dope. An unspoken warning ran through her and she knew she would need it before the day was out. She wet her lips, thinking about taking a small blow now that she was awake.

"I don't know nothing about a package Porky gave me for you. He gave me some stuff, but he sure didn't say anything about it being yours. And besides," she added, "Minnie and me snorted it up last night."

"What?" Teddy asked, not wanting to believe what he had heard. When she repeated it, he could only hold the phone dumbfounded. Finally it dawned on him that she didn't have any dope. Before the words had completely worked their way into his consciousness, his body began to react to the news. His nose began to run. He sniffed twice and slammed the receiver down as she started to inquire about her car. He cursed loudly.

It was that goddamn dopefiend-ass bitch Minnie. A dopefiend bitch wasn't shit, he swore. He planted his feet firmly on the floor. All thoughts of trying to have a bowel movement had disappeared. His only thought was where could he get the money for a fix. He stared stupidly at the closet. He had pawned his last suit a week ago, so there wasn't anything left to pawn. He began to dress hurriedly. Something would have to be stolen and sold real quick. His knees began to feel stiff and he knew he was becoming boogy. His mind raced feverishly. He had to have a fix.

Suddenly his sister's voice drifted through the thin bedroom wall. Something in the back of his mind clicked. Bessy was inquiring about the mailman. Instantly it came to him—today was the day for some of the ADC mothers to get their checks, and his sister was one of them. He thought about stealing the check but just as quickly tossed the idea away. His sister was too sharp to let him beat her to the postman.

Teddy stumbled out of the bedroom into the front room. They lived in a small three-bedroom frame house. There were six of them, his mother, his sister and her kids, and him. He couldn't begin to remember what his father had looked like. When he was four, his father was stabbed to death in the neighborhood bar. Since then, his mother and sister had worked, always making sure there was enough food in the house and that the place stayed clean. Sometimes he would steal enough stuff from various stores and bring some of the stolen meat home. Ham, lunch meat, steaks, it didn't matter, whatever he stole there was always some use for it at home. Though his mother would complain about his stealing, she always accepted the food. She knew if she didn't accept it, he would only take it out and sell it to one of the neighbors, who were always looking for some kid in the neighborhood to stop off with some hot meat.

His sister Bessy stared at him. "Look what the cat drug in," she said coldly. "You better watch your purse, Momma; his nose is running, so he's looking for something to steal."

"Why don't you shut your goddamn mouth?" Teddy yelled angrily, glaring at his sister.

"You just shut your filthy mouth up, boy," his mother ordered from the clean little kitchen. "I done told you, Teddy, I ain't goin' have you swearing around these little kids like you ain't got no sense. You better get your mind right, boy, or either get out in the streets and stay with them bums you run around with."

Teddy stared at his mother. For a moment he wanted to cry, to be able to lay his head on her huge bosom and beg for help, for understanding. He needed someone to understand the hell he was caught up in. He stared at her short, squat figure and knew she would never understand. Her wide face would fill with concern, because she loved him, but she would never be able to understand his being strung out on a habit. Anything you couldn't control, leave it alone, she would say. She had once liked to drink, but after getting religious, she had quit. She believed firmly that that was all you had to do, quit. On many occasions she had tried to get him to go to church with her, believing that once he found God the desire for dope would just disappear.

He turned to his sister. "Bessy, I got to have five dollars. How about loaning it to me when your check comes?"

Bessy snorted. "Huh, that's what you said last check day, and I ain't got my money back yet." She glanced out the window for the mailman. "You keep up with my check day better than I do." Bessy looked like a younger version of her mother. She was short and plump, with a round face. The only difference was that she had the same golden brown complexion Teddy had, while their mother was dark.

"Why don't you ask that Miss Fine you're always running around with? She got a job downtown and all them pretty clothes. That's where you ought to be trying to get your money from," Bessy stated, putting her hands on her hips. "I got three kids to support and I sure can't take care of no dopefiend."

"You got that winehead nigger to support," Teddy yelled, losing his control. "You just keep on and he's going to put another baby in you."

"It ain't none of your business what me and him do," she answered angrily, "and at least he ain't no damn dopefiend."

Their mother came into the room tossing her arms in the air. "You two kids is going to be the death of me yet! Always arguing about nothing. Why, you carry on worse than the little ones, and that's a fact." She spoke to her daughter. "You better pay heed to what he said, too, Bessy. I don't want you coming up with no more babies." She remained silent for a moment. "And you ain't got no money to be giving that man, either. If he comes sitting around here today, I'm sure goin' tell him about it." She turned on Teddy. "Ain't you got Terry's car out front? I seen it when I come back from the store," she said, not giving him time to answer. "Bessy Mae, you pay that boy something to take you and them kids to K-Marks, so you can buy them some shoes and pants. Why, them boys of yours is running around with their feet on the ground."

Bessy squirmed. "Aw, Momma, you know I can't keep them in shoes. They just run outside and kick cans with them, and a week from now they'll be done ran so much that the soles will be coming off."

"I don't give a damn," her mother said unyieldingly. "You had 'em, and you goin' damn well take care of 'em, you hear me, girl? You ain't got too big for me to take a strap to, and don't you give me no sass."

"You always startin' something," Bessy said, turning and taking her anger out on Teddy.

Their mother walked to the window and looked out. "You get them kids ready, 'cause the mailman will be here any minute."

"Damn you," Bessy said, softly, so that her mother couldn't hear. "I ain't goin' give you but five dollars to take us shopping, Teddy," she said loudly over her shoulder.

"Give me the money now," he ordered. "I'll be back by the time you get the kids ready."

Her mocking laughter drifted back to him. "I wouldn't give you the time of day. You must think everybody in this world is a damn fool but you, don't you?" she asked harshly.

Teddy started to pace up and down the small living room. His nose continued to run. Every two minutes he would yell at his sister to hurry up. Finally he walked into her small bedroom and started to help her dress the children. He dressed both the little boys while she dressed the girl.

Bessy watched him, amused at his discomfort. "I don't know why you keep rushing, fool. We can't go nowhere until the mailman comes." She added sharply, "What's wrong, Teddy? That little monkey you got on your back done turned into a full-grown gorilla?"

He wiped his nose on the back of his hand. "Don't worry about my thing. I can handle it," he replied arrogantly.

She stared at him closely, her eyes suddenly filling with compassion. "Teddy, why don't you commit yourself to some hospital? You should be able to get help somewhere. You ain't doing nothing but throwing your life away now. Look at you! I used to be so proud of my little brother. You used to stay sharp, and people used to talk about what a sharp dresser you were. But now, since you been using that dope, you ain't nothing but another dopefiend. You done pawned all your clothes, or sold them. You don't keep your hair done anymore. All you want to do is fill your arm up with some of that dope and sit around scratching and nodding."

"It ain't none of your business what I do," Teddy answered angrily. "You ain't nobody's prize either. All you do is keep your goddamn legs cocked up in the air. Every time some man looks at you hard, you come up pregnant."

She flinched as though someone had struck

her. For a moment it seemed as though she would cry. Teddy swallowed and wished he hadn't said what he had, but it was too late. She was hurt and getting madder every moment. The children stared first at one grownup and then the other. They hadn't understood what had been said, but they knew something was wrong.

The sound of their mother calling them interrupted what could have become a very touchy affair. "Bessy, here come the mailman, girl."

They both rushed out of the bedroom with the children running behind. As young as the children were, they had come to realize that, on a certain day, the mailman became very important. It was a day in their lives when they knew they wouldn't be denied when they asked for candy money. Maybe a pop later on when they had dinner. Because of this, they looked forward to the mailman, too.

After the mailman dropped the check off and left, Teddy went out to the car and waited. It wasn't long before he was blowing the car horn, trying to rush his sister up.

She finally came out of the house, closely followed by the children. "God damn it, Teddy," she yelled as she climbed in the car. "You ain't got to wake up the whole neighborhood just because you want five funky dollars."

Teddy didn't reply. He knew that, now they were out of the house, he had better be careful about what he said to her. If she got mad, she would get out of the car and find someone else to take her out to the shopping center. And that would be the last he would see of that five-dollar bill. He removed a piece of toilet paper from his pocket and wiped his nose. He began to sweat under his arms. The sweat ran down inside his shirt and he knew that it would have a rank odor to it. If he didn't hurry and get a fix, he would be too sick for a five-dollar pack to help him. He wasn't worried about getting high; what he wanted was a fix so that he could feel normal again. Later in the day he would try to hustle enough money to get high, but for the moment he had only one concern—to get the sickness off.

Teddy pulled up and parked in front of the neighborhood store. The white merchant inside cashed all the checks for the women in the neighborhood. He had been dealing with the black people in the neighborhood for the past thirty years. When the city had rioted and people were burning out the white businessmen in the slums, the black women of his neighborhood had surrounded the store and wouldn't allow the men to loot. Teddy and his crowd of friends had been there, wanting to take off all the meat, but his mother and sister were in the front of the crowd of women. They stayed up in shifts protecting the store. The wineheads, who wanted the cheap wine free, and the dopefiends, who wanted whatever they could get to sell, called the women "honky lovers" and whatever else they could think of, but it hadn't done any good.

The next day when the owner came, expecting to see his store burned down or looted out, he cried when he found the women sitting out front joking. The women had displayed more sense than most of the men. They knew he was the only one they could turn to when their check money ran out. He carried them until the end of the month, and longer when some of them had trouble out of their men over their checks. It was not surprising for some of them to owe as much as sixty or seventy dollars out of their checks at the end of the month.

Bessy went in and cashed her check. When she came out, she gave Teddy five dollars. She had been mad at him before, but she knew she couldn't help herself. She had grown up in the neighborhood just as he had. She had seen junkies all her life. Her brother was sick, and she knew it. When she gave him the money, she also knew he would go to the nearest dope house before taking her to the shopping center.

Teddy's hand shook as he reached for the money. "Thanks, baby," he said with genuine emotion in his voice.

He drove away from the curb without bothering to look. A beer truck almost hit him. "Goddamn it, why don't you look where you're going," he yelled out the window at the rear of the truck.

When he parked in front of Porky's house he prayed that Porky wouldn't be out of stuff. He met two addicts coming down the stairs as he ran up. "Is Porky all right?" he asked breathlessly.

"Yah, man, he got some stuff," one of the addicts answered.

Bessy waited impatiently in the car. After half an hour, she thought about blowing the horn, but she knew that it would be wrong. It would probably get Teddy in trouble with the dope man if she blew the horn in front of his house. When she had just about made up her mind to blow the horn anyway, she saw him coming down the steps. He came over to the car grinning. The drug had made another man out of him. He was almost like his old self, friendly and easy to joke with.

He slid in under the steering wheel. "I'm sorry, Sis, if I stayed too long, but I had to wait until he had cut up some stuff."

She sighed; it wouldn't do any good to complain. He had given his excuse, and he probably thought that anyone would be able to understand why they had to wait almost an hour.

The shopping center was crowded when they pulled into the parking lot. Teddy found a spot to park, not too far away, and they all climbed out. Bessy led the way into the store. Just like most women, once she entered the store she lost all conception of time.

Her eyes brightened and she became obsessed with shopping. After an hour, she was still walking from counter to counter. After the second trip around the store, Teddy began to grow restless.

"I thought you was going to buy the kids some shoes, Bessy?" he asked. "We been around this dress counter for the last five hours," he complained, exaggerating the time.

She glanced over her shoulder at him while she and another woman both tugged at the same dress. "In a moment, honey," she said as she got a tighter grip on the dress.

Teddy snorted, eyeing the dress rack coldly. They were too cheap to steal, unless he could get away with the whole rack. He watched the other woman's purse and wondered idly if he could dip on her before she noticed him. He disregarded the idea; ever since entering the store he had been looking for something to steal, but whenever he got the opportunity, the merchandise was always too cheap to bother with. He promised himself that, before he left, he'd take something to get another blow off of.

As soon as the woman turned loose her end of the dress, Bessy lost interest in it and turned away from the dress counter. It occurred to Teddy that women enjoyed shopping more for the sake of snatching something out of each other's hands than for really shopping. The P.A. system announced a sale on children's clothes. The mention of sale immediately caught the women's attention, and before the speaker had finished there was a small stampede toward the children's department.

Teddy watched his sister, amused. She was like a racehorse coming out of a stall. With a firm grip on each of her sons' arms, she was off and running in the wake of many of the faster women shoppers. When they reached the sale counter it was too crowded, so they walked over to the children's shoes. After new tennis shoes were put on the boys' feet, they didn't want to take them off. They started to cry when Bessy ordered them to take the shoes off. To prevent the children from crying, she let the boys keep their new shoes on. The little girl decided she wanted to wear hers, too, so again she relented. She gave Teddy the old shoes to carry. They started for the check-out counter, but Bessy spotted an opening where the sale was going on and made a beeline for it.

"Give me the money for the shoes, Bessy," Teddy said quickly. "I'll take the kids up front so we won't still be at the end of the line when you get there."

Without giving it any thought, she removed a ten-dollar bill from her purse and gave it to him. "I'll catch up with you shortly, Teddy. I just want to get a few new outfits so the kids will have something to wear when school starts back."

Teddy took the money. As he stood in the crowd of women, he dropped the boys' shoes on the floor, out of sight. He kicked them towards

the front of the crowd of women. He pushed the
kids up the aisle in front of him. When he got to
the front counter, he stood on the side, not bothering to get in the line. He glanced around him casually. The old pair of girl's shoes were stuck down
inside his shirt. With his jacket on, you couldn't
even see a bulge. Without any apparent hurry, he
started the children toward the nearest door.

As soon as they reached the sidewalk two white
men stepped up beside him and grabbed his
arms. Without any hurry they ushered him and
the children back in the store and led them to an
office in the rear of the building. It had been done
so neatly that very few people realized what was
going on. A little later, when Bessy paid for her articles, another woman approached her as she left
the check-out counter. They spoke briefly for a
few moments, then the woman led her toward the
office in the back of the store. When Bessy entered the office she saw her children standing
around crying, while her brother leaned up against
the wall as though nothing had happened.

More ashamed than frightened, Bessy removed
all of her sales slips and showed that she had paid
for all of her purchases. "It must have been a misunderstanding," she pleaded. "Teddy must have
thought that I was going to pay for the shoes."

The store detectives watched her closely. The
crying of the children was beginning to get on
their nerves. "We don't have the slightest doubt in

our minds about whether or not your brother was planning on stealing those shoes, miss. If he had intended on paying for them, why would he have bothered to conceal the old ones that the kids took off?"

Bessy shrugged her shoulders. She felt like crying herself. Nothing like this had ever happened to her before. She was angry at Teddy, but she didn't want to see him go to jail. "Couldn't you let him go this time?" she pleaded. "I'm sure if you do, he'll never come back in your store again." She stared from one detective to the other, anxiously.

The woman who had shown her the way to the office spoke up. "Could you pay for the shoes?" she asked.

Bessy fumbled awkwardly with her purse. She snatched it open. "Here!" she said and held out a twenty-dollar bill. "This should be more than enough."

The detectives glanced at each other. The older one spoke up sharply. "We'll give him a break this time, but if we ever see his face in here again," he said as he stared at Teddy, "we'll lock his ass up so fast he won't know what happened."

Teddy sneered as Bessy followed him and the children out of the store. She believed that everyone in the store was watching them and she blushed furiously. Before they had reached the car, her shame had turned to anger.

"Give me my money!" she demanded sharply. Her voice was full of scorn and anger.

Teddy felt the ten-dollar bill in his pocket. "I lost it," he stated coldly and continued on towards the car.

# 5

It was a hot, muggy day and the sun was shining brightly through the windows. Terry put the vacuum cleaner in the closet and went back into the front room. Their home was a lovely house that ran in the twenty-thousand-dollar bracket. Her father kept the lawn beautiful and her mother kept the inside of the house immaculate. The living-room and dining-room floors were covered with light brown wall-to-wall carpeting and boasted matching dark bronze French provincial furniture and golden drapes. The dining-room table had a matching china cabinet. All gave the appearance of utter good taste.

"Terry," her mother called from the kitchen, "have you finished yet?"

"Yes, Mom," Terry replied as she flopped down on the couch.

"You want me to make some chicken sand-
wiches for your lunch today?"

"Don't worry, Mom. I'll probably buy something to eat at work. Lately I haven't been having
any type of appetite."

"You can say that again," her mother replied.

Again and again her mind returned to the dope
upstairs. She had got out of bed and come downstairs to get away from the temptation, but the
yearn for the drug was getting too big. All the
while she had been cleaning up, her mind kept
returning to the heroin. It was becoming a fixa-
tion she couldn't quite get away from. Never before in her short life had she ever had such a
desire. It was a nagging, constant thought, something she couldn't just dismiss. She sniffed and
wondered if she was coming down with a cold.
For the past half an hour she had been sniffling.
She promised herself that she would absolutely
refuse to snort any dope for the next week, yet before the promise had left her mind, she found
herself climbing the stairs towards her bedroom.
Her mother's voice drifted up the stairs.

"What is it now, Mother?" she asked sharply.
She couldn't keep the irritation out of her voice.

Her father's voice reached her, even though it
was muffled by the walls of the bathroom. "When
did you start talking to your mother in that tone
of voice, Terry?" he asked mildly.

"I'm sorry, Father. I just have this awful
headache today, and everything seems to annoy

me." She yelled back down the stairs, "I'm going to lie down for a few minutes, Mom. If you want anything, I'll be in my room." She added, "My head is killing me."

Before she could hear her mother's reply, she was in the bedroom. Terry locked the door behind her and rushed over to her purse. Her fingers shook as she took out the heroin and poured it onto a small face mirror. Quickly she rolled up a dollar bill and made a quill. With trembling hands, she began to snort the poisonous white powder. She made a face as the bitter taste came up in her throat, but it soon passed and she began to feel the soothing effects of the drug. Terry lay back on the bed and put her feet up. She slowly lit a cigarette. Her eyes closed and the cigarette dropped from her hand. Her head jerked up as the fire burned through her thin blouse. She caught the cigarette as it fell to the floor.

Suddenly there was a sharp knock on the door. She flinched at the sound. "Terry, are you in there? What's the idea of the lock? Are you dressing or something?" Her father sounded concerned. "You're not sick, are you?"

"No, Daddy. I was just changing my clothes," she lied easily. Terry took off her blouse and opened the door in her bra. "Ain't it kind of early for you to be up, Daddy?"

Seeing his daughter half dressed caused Terry's father to hesitate in the doorway. He had on a T shirt and an old pair of work pants. His hair was turning gray in spots, while his brown eyes showed crinkles in the corners. He was a pleasant-featured, middle-aged man who looked as if he found a lot to smile about. His complexion was the same as his daughter's while his physique was that of a man in his late forties, just beginning to gain a pot gut.

Terry sat down on the edge of the bed. "What do I owe this pleasant surprise visit to, Mr. Wilson?" she asked teasingly.

He smiled at his daughter. His eyes were mild. The sight of his lovely grown daughter filled him with delight. He had always been a frugal person, more from nature than from economics, so he had been able to give his wife and daughter anything they might want within reason. He was proud of his home, car, and most of all, his little family.

"Your mother wanted to know if you would have time to drive her to the supermarket," he asked.

Terry bit her lip. "I'm sorry, Daddy, I let Teddy have the car so that he could go job hunting this morning," she answered, knowing that Teddy would never bother looking for a job.

He frowned. "That's something I've been wanting to talk to you about, young lady. Do you think it's wise to keep allowing Teddy to have your car?" Before she could reply, he continued. "Even though the car is in my name, I've always treated it as though it was yours, Terry, but lately I've been having second thoughts about the matter. I just received two tickets in the mail this week, parking tickets, and I know they weren't yours, unless you've started hanging around down on Brush in those slums."

"I meant to pay for those tickets, Daddy," she replied, lying again. "But they just slipped my mind. I was down there waiting on Teddy and left the car sitting in a no-parking zone too long."

Her father stared at her curiously. "There's one more thing I want to bring to your attention, Terry. I told you when I signed for that car that it was your responsibility to pay the car notes on it, yet I've got a notice in my room that says you are overdue on a payment." He continued, "Now I don't want to get in your business, but you don't even have to pay rent, so I can't imagine what you're doing with your money unless you're starting to take care of that lazy young man you run around with."

"I'll take care of that note this week, Daddy," she answered angrily. "I don't know why you and Momma always think I'm giving my money away. I happen to be buying some winter clothes, and I just forgot the car note."

Her father turned away from the doorway and started down the hall to his room. "Just make sure you don't forget it this week, or I'll make sure you don't have to worry about it anymore," he answered her loudly over his shoulder as he continued on his way.

Dammit, dammit, dammit, she swore as she slammed the bedroom door. I lost my high listening to him complain, she rationalized to herself as she picked up the mirror and raked up the little bit of dope left on it. After snorting it, she sat back on the bed and tried to recapture the high, but it was no use. I can't even get a decent nod in this house without someone bothering me, she thought.

Terry began to pace the floor, thinking of where she could get the money to buy another blow before going to work. She picked up the phone and dialed Teddy's house. After talking to Teddy's mother she hung up the phone, more angry than she had been at first. There was one thing she was going to do, she decided. The loaning out of her car every day would have to come to an end. If she kept the car, it wouldn't be any problem running down a quick blow, she thought coldly.

Terry jumped up and walked over to her closet. She removed a pink miniskirt with matching blouse and laid them out on the bed. She debated over taking a quick bath, but the dope had her feeling lazy, so she just dressed quickly. Downstairs in the living room she found her mother waiting patiently for her father to come down and take her to the store.

Terry wrapped her arms around her mother's plump neck and kissed her. "Moms dear, won't you loan your only daughter five dollars without Daddy knowing it. I got to get to work and Teddy's got my car."

Her mother stared at her fondly. She was the kind of woman who would always be friendly and courteous to strangers. It was a rare occasion when she lost her temper around anyone, including her family. Frequently in the past, Terry had wondered if anything could shake her mother's decorous behavior.

"Terry, I don't know what's your problem, dear, but I just gave you ten dollars the first of the week, and here you are back again, asking for more." She tried to look sternly at her daughter but failed. Both of them were small-built women, and the mother looked more like an older sister than a mother.

"Moms sweet, I'm buying the sharpest outfit. I just had to pay down on it. Now if you want me to be the poorest dressed girl at work I'll just start wearing blue jeans."

Her mother sighed. It was hard to say no to her only daughter. "Here, girl, but don't you let your father know about it. He's having a fit about that car already, and if he finds out you keep spending money, well."

She opened her purse. The only small bill she had was a ten. Terry reached over and removed it from her hand. "I'll give this back to you this weekend, sweets. Don't worry about a thing."

"Don't worry about me, Terry. You just be sure to get that car note in the mail so your father can sleep."

With a backward wave of her hand Terry ran for the door. "Don't worry, Moms, I'll take care of everything."

Once she reached the sidewalk she began to breathe more easily. She walked swiftly, keeping one eye open on the street, watching for someone she might get a ride with. The young boy who lived down the street blew his horn at her and she waved him down. She ran over and jumped in his car, not giving him time to say no.

"Billy Banks, I ain't seen you since last winter," she said quickly, giving him her most charming smile.

He smiled back. "Hi, Terry. I've been busy working midnights and going to college in the daytime." His voice was full of pride.

"How come you ain't in school today?" she inquired, endeavoring to keep the conversation flowing.

"I had to get the brakes fixed on this old wreck so I just took the day off. I need it too bad to get me back and forth to work to take a chance on having an accident." Billy lit a cigarette and then added, "I saw your father out to the plant the other day, and he was telling me that he hadn't missed a day in the past three years."

"That's just like him," she replied. "He hasn't

too much to brag about, so it's a big thing for him to keep a good record out at that damn plant."

Billy glanced at her curiously. "That's a funny remark, Terry. I think your father has a lot to be proud of, and besides, he's just about the best-liked man out there." Billy hesitated. "Did he tell you they made him the leader on the midnight shift?"

"Big deal!" she answered sarcastically. "The next thing you'll be telling me is he's a foreman."

"That sarcasm doesn't become you, Terry. You really have changed in the past few months. I suppose you would like for your old man to be more like your boyfriend, Teddy," he said coldly.

"Do we have to argue, Billy? All I wanted was a lift to the east side, but I guess with your new opinion of me, that would be asking too much."

Billy drove silently for a minute, staring straight ahead. "No, I'll take you," he answered sharply.

Terry crossed her legs and began to scratch her thigh slowly. She lit a cigarette and settled back against the seat. As they drove smoothly along she found herself nodding. Her head would slowly drop on her chest, and then she would snatch it back up.

The quietness of the car had a drowsy effect on her. Billy's voice came to her suddenly. "If you keep scratching your leg like that you're going to start it to bleeding." His voice had the keen edge of a razor.

She glanced down at her leg. Without knowing it, she had ripped through her stocking and put long scratch marks on her thigh. "You don't miss a thing, do you, Billy?"

"Not when an old friend of mine has started to turn herself into a tramp by the quickest route possible. Of all the things in the world you could have been, Terry, I never thought you'd end up being a dopefiend."

Her head snapped up. "What the hell are you talking about, Billy? I don't use any dope." Her denial was weak.

He laughed harshly. "You tell that lie to fool-man-shoe, or somebody who doesn't know any better, Terry. I been watching you ever since you got in this car, and all you been doing is nodding."

Terry snorted. "Noddin' hell. I'm just sleepy from staying out all night. You been reading too many books at that college you go to. Man, you better come back down to reality and get out of them damn clouds."

There was nothing but pity in the look he gave her. "You aren't fooling anyone but yourself, Terry. My older brother used to be an addict before he got killed trying to stick up a store. I can remember as though it was yesterday the way he used to act when he got high. We used to sleep in the same bedroom, and I used to watch him cook up that stuff before he shot it." Billy slowed down for a light, then continued. "Every time he got high off it, he acted just like you're doing. Nodding and scratching all over the place." His voice filled with scorn. "You tell Teddy the first time I catch up with him, and I don't give a fuck where it's at, I'm going to jump off on his ass and break one of his legs for putting you on that stuff."

"You ain't none of my daddy," she answered with as much sassiness as possible. "And don't you go bothering Teddy just because you're bigger than he is. I don't know nothing about what you've been talking about, Billy Banks, and if you say something to my father, I'm just going to tell him you lied." She stared up at him and then added, "I'm going to tell him that you hit on me, and I wouldn't give you none."

"Give me none!" Billy laughed coldly. "All I got to do is wait six months and then ride down on Brush or John-R and pick you up off the corner and spend three dollars with you."

"You just try waitin' six months, Billy, and see what you get." She turned her back on him and said, "If that's all you can talk about, I don't think we have anything else to discuss."

As they continued on in silence, she debated whether or not to have him drive up in front of Porky's house. She decided to have him drop her off two doors away; she reasoned that he wouldn't know the difference between Porky's or Joe Blow's.

When they got to Porky's street, she saw Teddy parking in front of the dope house. She grabbed

Billy's arm. "Don't you start nothing with Teddy. Please, Billy?" She held his arm, waiting for an answer.

She knew Billy's reputation as a fighter from their high-school days. It wouldn't be anything strange for him to get out of the car and knock Teddy down.

Billy glanced at her and saw the fear in her eyes. He had been in love with her ever since their early school days. They had ridden the same school bus, and he used to wait in the snow just for the chance to walk to their bus stop with her. When the other boys his age had started to date he had been too busy working after school selling papers, then later working in a supermarket.

All the while he worked, he had kept one burning idea in mind. Make a success of his life, and one day she would be his. In the past half an hour, he had seen his daydream destroyed. Once he became aware of her use of drugs, he knew that there was no room in his life for her. He had watched one life ruined because of heroin, and he knew he could not stand to see another person close to him go the same way.

The sight of Teddy, and the idea of his having made an addict out of her, was almost too much. He fought to control himself. He realized that, if he got out of the car now, he would lose everything he had worked for. All the nights he had spent in the factory, all the sleepless days in school. There was no doubt in his mind that, if he got out of the car, he would end up killing Teddy. He smothered the black rage that consumed him.

Billy reached across Terry and fumbled the door latch open. "Okay Terry," he managed to say, fighting back the lump in his throat. "It's your play, honey, just be sure to take care of yourself."

She stepped from the car. "Okay Billy, and thanks for the lift."

"Terry!" he called, her name bringing tears to his eyes. "Terry, if you ever need something, or someone, call me. Don't forget, now. I'll come to you wherever you're at, just call."

She forced a smile. She wanted to leap back in the car and lay her head on his large shoulders and ask for help. She looked up and saw Teddy bearing down on them, so she quickly closed the car door. "Thanks, Billy," she called after him as he pulled away from the curb.

Teddy glared angrily at Billy as he drove past. He grabbed Terry brutally by the arm and snatched her around. "What the fuck was you doing with that square-ass Billy?"

She jerked her arm loose. "If you'd leave my car alone, I wouldn't have to bum rides."

Before she knew what was happening he slapped her upside the head. "Don't you talk to me in that tone of voice. You save all your smart-ass answers for your square-ass friend."

Without thinking about it, she looked down the street to make sure Billy hadn't seen Teddy strike her. It wouldn't do at all for him to see that.

If he had, she doubted she would have been able to stop him from whipping Teddy.

Teddy slapped her again. "Bitch, don't be looking for that nigger. Ain't nothing he can do but get both of you killed out here in the street."

Teddy glanced in the direction Billy had gone. For all of his threats, he didn't really want to see Billy coming back. After making sure Billy was nowhere in sight, he slapped her again, then wheeled on his heel and walked towards the dope house.

Terry rubbed her palm over her cheek and followed docilely behind him. "Your days are numbered," she murmured softly under her breath.

# 6

The department store was just about empty. The doors had been closed for the last twenty minutes and most of the salesgirls were getting rid of the slow shoppers. Terry glanced at her watch nervously. It was a quarter after ten, so it wouldn't be too much longer before she could get away. For one of the few times she had loaned Teddy her car, she wasn't worried about him not picking her up. He had told her to steal something to sell, and she had taken two Kimberly Knit dresses earlier in the evening and put them in her large pocketbook.

It was the first time she had stolen something and her nerves were acting up. After she got rid of her last customer she rushed to her locker and slipped on her fall coat. She removed the purse and started towards the door. She hadn't stolen the garments because of Teddy's constant nagging. She had taken the dresses because she wanted a blow as soon as she got off work. Her anger was still aroused over Teddy's slapping her earlier that evening, but for now she knew there wasn't much she could do about it.

"Good night, Mrs. Breeding," she called as she waved at her supervisor. Her legs trembled slightly, but she knew she had gone too far now. If she was busted, it would be before she left the store. She reached the door and began to breathe more easily. As soon as she stepped outside she saw Teddy double-parked, waiting for her. He blew the horn loudly as soon as he saw her come outside.

Terry bit her lip in frustration. What in the world had she ever seen in him? He was loud, he cursed all the time. She wondered what it would have been like to have a man like Billy for her boyfriend. Terry ran between two parked cars and stopped. The front fender of her car had a large dent in it. She stared at it surprised.

Before she could move, Teddy's voice came to her. "Come on, goddammit! We ain't got all night." He glared at her angrily from behind the steering wheel. The passenger door opened and Snake, tall and dark, stepped out. For the first time she noticed that he was not alone. The back-seat held a couple of other dopefiends. They stared at her curiously.

Terry hurried towards the car. She glanced over

her shoulder to see if any of the other salesgirls had come out. The last thing in the world she wanted was for them to see the car full of men waiting for her. She blushed furiously and jumped in the car.

Snake got back inside, squeezing her in the middle. She stared up at Teddy. "I see you finally got around to tearing the car up," she said, her words dripping with sarcasm.

"Damn all that," Teddy replied arrogantly. "It ain't about that. I had an accident, as you can see, so that should cover that shit. What I want to know," he began, "is whether or not you took care of that business I told you to take care of." He pushed the gas pedal down to the floor, trying to catch a yellow light, and ended up running through a red one. Two of the addicts in the back-seat turned around to see if any police cars were behind them.

"Take it easy, man," Snake said in his easy drawl. "We got that hot record player in the back-seat."

"Don't make me ask you again, bitch," Teddy said loudly, more for his friends' benefit than Terry's. "Did you swing with that stuff like I asked you?"

Terry shook her head, afraid to take the chance on speaking. She was so angry that she knew if she opened her mouth, he wouldn't like what he heard.

"Let me see what you got!" he ordered loudly.
"I got to make sure you ain't brought some of that
cheap shit out."

"What you thinking about, Teddy?" Snake asked
lightly. "Terry probably knows more about expensive clothes now than you'll ever know. Ain't you
forgettin', man, that she works with the stuff every
day?" He rubbed his leg up against hers. If Teddy
should end up blowing, he thought, he couldn't
think of a better man to get Terry on the rebound
than himself. The more he listened, the more sure
he was of Teddy losing her. A man didn't treat a
woman like Terry like a dog—not if he wanted
her. You had to baby them, keep them interested,
and never go out of your way to embarrass them
in front of anyone, even dopefiends.

Teddy took the express and drove over to the
west side. He was too busy driving to examine the
dresses Terry pulled out of her purse. The other
addicts in the car quickly gave him their opinion
of the clothes. From their admiration, he knew
that he could get good money off of them. He left
the freeway at Grandriver and turned right. He
parked a block away from Linwood and climbed
out of the car, taking the clothes with him. When
Terry started to follow, he waved her back. "You
wait in the car, baby. We'll be back shortly. The
fence don't like too many new faces coming up."

Snake pulled the record player out of the back.
"You can wait, too," he said to the other two addicts.

"Bullshit!" Red and Tiny Tim both said together. Both addicts climbed out and followed them down the street.

For a brief moment, Terry was tempted to go. She was quite aware that Teddy was planning on playing on her for the dresses. She stayed in the car and sat staring out of the windshield with unseeing eyes. Her mind was too occupied with the problem of trying to figure out what she could tell her father about the car. If she told him Teddy had wrecked it, he would go through the ceiling. It would be better to just say that she had left it parked, and when she came back, someone had backed into it.

It wasn't long before Teddy and his group reappeared, arguing amongst themselves over the money. Teddy got in and started up the motor.

"How much did you get for the outfits I gave you?" she asked curiously.

"I had to accept one-third of the original price," he said quickly. "But since the man had some dope, I just took a fourth of dope for my share."

"You know I told you this afternoon, Teddy, that I would have to have some money because I had to pay the car note." She glared up at him.

"How many times I got to tell you, Terry, you don't tell me anything. I'm the man, and as long as I'm your man, you'll stay in a bitch's place."

She tried another approach. "I know you're the man, Teddy, but you use the car as much as I do, and you know it's in my daddy's name." She hated the whining sound in her voice. "If I don't come up with some money this week, he's going to take the car away from me until I show him I know how to pay my bills."

"Use your paycheck, bitch," he replied facetiously. "You get a check every week."

"Pimp hard, nigger, pimp hard," Tim said loudly from the back.

Terry remained silent the rest of the trip. She was consumed with blind anger. All right, big shot, she told herself coldly, just have your fun. Every day ain't the same, and I'll bet I'll be around to see better days than this.

He pulled into a motel and parked beside Snake's old car. "We might as well go in your joint and split up the skag," Teddy said.

Snake opened the car door and got out. "You might as well come in, Terry, since we goin' be a while." He grinned and held the door open for her. As she climbed out he stared straight in her eyes. It was all there for a man to see. The handwriting was on the wall. Teddy had over-sported his hand.

That's the last thing I want is another dope-fiend, she thought as she saw the look in his eye. He took her arm and led her towards the motel. Teddy, watching the little byplay, smiled. He was too confident in his hold on Terry to distrust her. They had been together so long he had begun to think he controlled her completely.

Snake opened the door and they all marched in. They sat around and shot up their shares of the dope, while Terry snorted the pile Teddy had given her. When everyone was finished, Snake got up to leave.

"If it's cool with you, Snake, me and Terry will lay up a while. I still got some stuff, so I'll lock up when we get finished."

"Just don't mess up my sheets," Snake said and led his friends out of the motel room.

After they left, Teddy pulled his clothes off and sprawled out on the bed in his shorts. "Take that shit off, Terry. Ain't no sense in you gettin' it wrinkled up before we leave," he ordered.

As she slowly undressed, she watched him measure out two piles of heroin from the fourth of dope he had. He made one small pile and held it out towards her.

She could feel her eyelids growing heavy from the earlier drug. "Is it all right if I take that home for in the morning, Teddy?" she asked sweetly.

"If I want you to have something for in the morning I'll give it to you. If you don't want this, just say so. I can just as easy put it in my cooker." He stared at her coldly as she removed the last of her clothes. "Take them panties and bra off, too."

She hesitated briefly. "I'll keep this, Teddy," she replied, moving the small pile of dope out of his reach. She stretched out on the bed and set the dope on the night stand. She wiggled out of her panties and twisted around so he could unsnap her bra. This would be the last time Teddy would have a chance to do anything to her or for her, she told herself coldly. She gritted her teeth. It had already become an unpleasant task.

Teddy cooked his dope and shot it up before turning to her. He ran his finger slowly down her body, starting at her neck, and followed the path his finger took with light kisses. She lay beside him passively. When he drew his head back up and kissed her, he found her lips cold and unresisting. Her coldness aroused his anger, so he mounted her with the intention of riding her roughly, but he couldn't get a hard up. The heroin had taken effect; he lay between her legs and moved slowly. His hips rotated in a grinding motion. He continued until he believed he had an erection. He reached down and tried to force his limp penis inside her. She remained still, as though she were a corpse. For a moment he nodded, the strong drug taking effect. He allowed his head to drop between her tits. Her stillness aroused his anger further. He began to run his tongue down over her body intimately. Before he could perform cunnilingus on her, she squeezed her legs together.

"Bitch! Open your goddamn legs!" he ordered.

She shook her head angrily. "You ain't about to do nothing like that to me, Teddy," she replied sharply.

"If you'd act more like a woman than a fuckin' piece of wood, it wouldn't be necessary," he yelled. He climbed back up. "I know what you need," he said and sat up on her chest with his penis aimed at her mouth. She twisted her face to the side, trying to avoid being forced into an act of fellatio.

Teddy slapped her viciously across the face. "Open your goddamn mouth, bitch!" he yelled.

"If you force me," she replied, her voice muffled by the pillow, "I promise you one thing, Teddy. When I get through you won't ever stick it in anyone else's mouth, because I'm going to bite that motherfucker off."

"Bite it off!" he screamed, and slapped her ruthlessly. "I'll teach you to tell me what you're going to do."

She screamed and jumped from the bed. Terry covered her head as he punched at her face. He hit her twice on the neck and a couple of times on the top of the head, but she managed to avoid any facial blows.

"Get the fuck out of my eyesight, dopefiend-ass bitch!" he yelled, beside himself. "When a bitch gets so sorry she can't even make her man get his dick hard, she ain't no use." His anger was directed more at himself than at Terry. To cover his shame at not being able to function as a young man should, he exploded in a blind rage.

Terry grabbed her clothes and ran into the bathroom, locking the door. After she dressed, she waited a few moments before coming out, and when she reentered the bedroom, Teddy was busy shooting dope. She stared at him coldly. There was really no anger over what had happened. She was too happy that it had ended. She knew that this was really the end.

"I need the keys to my car, Teddy," she said as she opened the door leading to the street.

"I ain't giving you nothing," Teddy replied slowly, nodding all the time.

She stared at him silently for a minute. "I know you ain't crazy, Teddy. Ain't no way for you to take that car and get away with it. When I go home and tell my father what happened, he ain't goin' hardly come out in the streets looking for you. All he goin' do is call the police station and report it stolen. Do you want that to happen?" she asked as a last resort. "You done took my money tonight, Teddy. What else do you want to take, my father's car, too?"

He didn't reply. He just continued to sit on the bed nodding. She eased back in the room and picked up his pants. She found the key in his pocket. She felt some money but was too frightened to take it. She slowly backed out of the room. Terry slammed the door behind her and ran to her car. She locked both doors after jumping in and rolled up all the windows.

She didn't begin to breathe easier until she drove away from the motel. She debated with herself as to whether or not she should go get Billy but decided to be thankful the affair hadn't ended any worse than it had.

# 7

Teddy sat in the front seat of the car staring out of the window. He was in a black mood. Things had changed for the worse these past two weeks. He silently cursed the night he had been so high he'd forgotten how nice it was to have the use of Terry's car. He also felt the loss of the ten- and twenty-dollar bills he used to take for granted every time she got paid. Actually, he believed it hadn't really been his fault. The real problem was that Terry had gotten strung out, and that was the reason she had quit him. He told himself this so often that he had actually come to believe it.

Snake grinned as he glanced around at Teddy. He knew just what was eating at him. "I got a sell for some record albums if we can get some," he said to no one in particular. "That tight sonofabitch who owns the record shop on the east side said he would give us two dollars apiece for every new record we bring him."

The group in the car rode on in silence. All of them were dopefiends, and all of them were looking for something to steal. There were four of them in the car, and all of them had the same thought racing through their minds—they all needed a fix.

Dirty Red, sitting in the backseat with Tim, spoke up. "I got a sale for two lawn mowers that ain't got to be new." He added, "Just as long as they run on gas, we got a sale."

They were just beginning a morning of hustling and the first thing they had to get together on was what did their customers want. All of them had regular customers to whom they sold hot articles every day, and many of their customers requested certain items. Almost any good thieving addict will follow this policy, because if he knows what he can sell and where he can sell it, he'll save a lot of time. People ordered anything from a good dopefiend, anything from a bedsheet up through stoves and refrigerators.

Tiny Tim, a short, stocky, dark-skinned addict, spoke up. "I need twenty-five steaks and two hams for Miss Bee. She says she having a party this weekend and she needs the stuff so she can make some money off of dinner. She payin' half price and it's cash money."

"What about you, Teddy?" Snake asked, turning sideways to glance at his silent partner.

"You know what I need," he replied coldly. "I still got the same customer waiting on that portable TV, but it don't look like we're going to come up with it."

"I don't see nothing wrong with your arms or legs," Dirty Red said harshly. "They got televisions sittin' down in the basement at Sears, but I ain't seen you walk in there yet and come out with one."

"Shit, Snake," Tim said. "Your sister got a nice one sitting in her bedroom. It would be a hell of a lot easier ripping that one off than walking out of one of these stores with one."

"Your mammy got one sittin' downstairs in her house, too, only it just ain't colored," Snake replied loudly, with no apparent anger.

Tim thought it over for a minute before replying. "I'll tell you what I'll do, Snake. The day we cop your sister's, we can stop by my house and I'll swing with my mother's."

The men in the car rode on in silence, waiting for Snake's reply. If he decided to steal the televisions, they wouldn't have to try their luck in the stores. They all prayed quietly that he would go for it.

"If the day ever comes when I need a fix that bad, I'll see if you really mean that, Tim. I'm going to sure find out where your heart is at, 'cause your mammy is going to kick your goddamn ass when she finds her TV gone," Snake answered.

Red yelled suddenly, "There's a wine store,

baby; let's chip in and get a couple bottles of grapes." He added, "Maybe we can swing with some whiskey while we're in there."

No sooner did he mention it than Snake pulled over to the curb and parked. Everybody piled out but the driver. Red stuck his hand back in the car window. "Give me some change to help out on the wine."

Snake shook his head. "I bought the goddamn gas, the least you can do is buy the motherfuckin' wine."

Red walked away from the car and followed the other two into the store. He hadn't really believed Snake would give up the money, but it never hurt to ask. He caught up with them and broke the sad news. They both cursed over Snake's tightness, more from habit than anger.

After giving Red the money for the wine, they all split up inside the store, each man taking a different aisle to go down. Teddy walked slowly up and down the aisles, searching for something worth stealing. Not finding anything he deemed worth his skill, he walked over to the counter and joined Red. While the druggist waited on them, they watched Tim in the mirror behind the counter. Tim had found the stocking rack and, with his back towards the mirror, he began to load up. He opened the shirt under his light jacket and pushed handful after handful of stockings inside his open shirt. When he finished, he zipped up his jacket and walked slowly up the aisle toward the door. As Red paid for the wine, Teddy walked away, heading over to the stocking rack. He opened his jacket and shirt as he walked. When he reached the rack, he noticed the counter girl busy with another girl customer, so he took two handfuls of stockings and continued towards the door. Before he reached his destination, he made one smooth motion and the stockings disappeared under his shirt.

When Red joined them at the car, they were counting pairs of stockings. Between them, they had removed fifty-two pairs of seamless stockings from the rack. They each put up their loot in one of the empty shopping bags lying in the back window of the car. Each man kept count of his and his friends' merchandise, because it was no surprise if at the end of the day one of his buddies came up with merchandise that belonged to another addict. "After we get another small sting," Snake said as he pulled away from the curb, "we can stop and get a little blow." He grinned at his friends. "I been feeling boogy ever since this morning. I didn't do but a five-dollar pack when I woke up."

"If we listened to you, Snake, we wouldn't never get no hustling done. Between you and Teddy, you stay boogy. It don't make no difference how much dope you shoot in the morning, either," Tim said harshly from the backseat.

Red poured all the cups full of wine. "They got a five-and-ten-cent store right down the street, but the floorwalkers are hip to me and Tim." He drank down his wine in one gulp before continuing. "If we go in the store first, we can pull the two floorwalkers that work on the main floor, and you and Teddy, Snake, can cop the record albums they got settin' out."

They argued back and forth on how to swing with the LPs. Snake wanted to use the shot box they had in the trunk of the car, but Red argued that they didn't need it. They decided to try and swing with the records with an over-the-shoulder shot, draping their jackets over one shoulder while holding the stolen records in the crook of their arm. That way, it was decided, they could steal more albums than they would be able to get away with using their shot box.

Snake parked almost in front of the dime store. "I'm leaving the keys in the ashtray, here," he informed the group. He glanced up and down the street. "That little short street over there," he said as he pointed over his shoulder. "If we have to run, whoever reaches the car pull over there and look in the nearest alley. You'll find us somewhere down in it."

All of the men glanced at the escape route. It was very important to them because they never knew when they would need it. It was best to know which way you were running before you came out of a store with detectives running behind you. With no hesitation, they always had a good chance of getting away. The floorwalkers wouldn't have any car, and once the pickup was made, it was smooth sailing unless they stumbled upon a patrol car.

Red and Tim got out first and ambled towards the store. The other two waited until they had entered the building before following. Then they got out and went in by another door. Before Red and Tim had even got in the door, the floorwalkers, a man and woman posing as a couple shopping, began to follow them. They walked slowly towards the counters in the back, acting as though they didn't have a care in the world. By the time Teddy and Snake entered they had drawn the floorwalkers as far away from the album counter as it was possible for them to go.

Snake's dark face was gleaming with sweat. Out of the group, he was the worst thief in the bunch. His hands shook and he broke out sweating whenever he was called on to do any stealing. He was tall and thin, and he had a cadaverous look about him. Teddy hated to work with him because he seemed to draw the floorwalkers as though he were some kind of magnet.

From the directions they had been given, Snake and Teddy walked straight to the rack that held the albums. There was no one behind the counter. Quickly they sorted out the jazz albums and latest rhythm and blues records. These were the ones they knew they could sell. When both of them had a large stack of albums in front of the rack, they made their move. Teddy glanced around him casually. He waited until two women shoppers had ambled past, then picked up an armful of records and put them under his jacket, which was hanging off one shoulder. Snake followed suit. Without looking back they walked swiftly towards the front of the store. From the rear of the dime store, Red watched them leave.

Tim caught his eye and laid down some women's articles he had been fingering. He turned towards the two floorwalkers who had worked up beside them. "If I were you," he said pleasantly, "I'd shop down the street. This store seems to carry some of the worst merchandise in town." He slapped Red on the back and they both walked away laughing.

Back at the car Snake and Teddy waited impatiently for them. It had been a good sting. Teddy had eighteen albums and Snake had fifteen. The morning was starting off nicely. When Red and Tim returned to the car, they were both still laughing, more from the release of tension than anything else.

As soon as Red got in the car he poured out the last of the wine in the first bottle and opened the second one. "Man, we damn near got enough stuff to go and buy us an eye-opener now. We can cop the rest of the stuff later on this afternoon."

They kicked the idea around, back and forth, until Snake spoke up. "You niggers is a bitch. You know goddamn well if we quit now, you ain't goin' want to steal nothing later on, until all the dope is gone."

"That's the truth!" Teddy testified loudly. "And then after you get high you goin' be noddin' all over the fuckin' stores. We better get the business taken care of while we're able to handle it."

They drank the wine without speaking. Tiny Tim broke the silence. "Suppose we just cop the meat or the lawn mowers, then call it a day."

"That sounds sweet," Snake replied. "We'll run out to the Westgate shopping center first and check it out. We ain't been out there in over a month, so that goddamn manager they got out there done just about forgot what we look like."

Teddy put his cup on the top of the seat for a refill. "They got a mirror system out there now. Me and Red went out last week and played for some steaks."

"It ain't shit, though," Red said knowingly. "They got a blind spot right at the milk and egg department. All you got to do is carry your meat over there and make your shot under the mirror so they can't see you." He continued, "That new market that opened up next door ain't got nothing but an old guard about eighty years old, so he ain't no problem. I guess they hired him to scare away the housewives that do a little stealing, but he ain't shit for anyone like us."

"We'll give it a try, then," Snake said and turned off on the closest street that led to the freeway.

The shopping center was full when they pulled in and parked. They all climbed out of the car at the same time, then split up into pairs. In less than ten minutes Teddy and Snake were back from the first market. They climbed in the front seat and put their meat in a shopping bag. They had stolen five steaks apiece. Before they could get out of the car, Red and Tim walked up and jumped in the backseat.

"How did it look in there?" Teddy asked quietly, as he watched them remove steaks from under their armpits and from between their belts and pants.

"Sweet, baby, sweet!" Tim exclaimed loudly. "The old cop is helping fill bags at the check-out counter. When you go in, slide under the rail and he won't even know you're in the fuckin' store. We came out that way. His back was turned towards us the whole time we was in there."

"Mellow!" Snake replied and got out. Teddy followed him closely. They entered the store, slipped under the rail, and slowly walked to the back of the market, where the meat was kept. Both men took their time picking over the steaks. They only wanted the most expensive meat they could find. All the three-dollar steaks they came across they tossed back as too cheap.

Since both of them were counting on an easy sting, they loaded up. Teddy picked up nine steaks. Five in one hand, four in the other. Snake followed right behind him, as he went up the aisle nearest the door. Teddy opened his shirtfront wide. First he put four steaks up under one armpit, then pushed the rest up under the other one. His light fall jacket was bulging at both sides. It would have been impossible for him to go through one of the check-out lines, so clearly could the outline of the meat be seen.

Teddy glanced back over his shoulder at Snake. The first thing that caught his attention was the woman who worked on the meat counter. She was standing in the back watching Snake. Before he could give Snake a warning, the meat disappeared under his jacket. The woman stared after them for a moment with her mouth open, then swiftly turned and vanished.

"Quick, baby, the woman saw you swing," Teddy yelled. The women shoppers in the aisle glanced up at them. Surprise spread across their faces as they watched the two young men break and run. Teddy reached the rail and went under it quickly, Snake one step behind him, stepping on his heels. Before the alarm was given they were out of the supermarket and running for the car.

Red and Tim, already at the car, saw them coming. They jumped in and, before the runners could reach the car, the motor was humming. Both men jumped in the back and hugged the floor. Red pressed down on the gas and raced for the nearest exit. In his rearview mirror he saw two men run out of the store and look up and down, but they hadn't seen which way the thieves had gone. A woman standing on the sidewalk pointed at the speeding car, but it was much too late. In a matter of minutes they were on the freeway, heading back to the heart of the city. Again their wild laughter filled the car. It hadn't even been close. To them, it was all in a day's work. In the run of a month they had many experiences like this. In another month they would be back in the same store, trying their luck again.

"Which way should we go?" Red asked sharply, watching his rearview mirror. "I doubt if they had enough time to make it to a phone, but ain't no sense taking any chances."

"Get up off the expressway, baby," Snake ordered. "Then find the quickest route to get us to the east side."

They made it across town and stopped at the record shop. Snake and Teddy went in and sold the albums. Next, they stopped off and sold the meat and stockings, letting the women's nylons go for less than half price. They had made off with over fifty prime steaks altogether. The money off the meat alone was over one hundred dollars. For the albums they settled on seventy-five dollars, and for the stockings they got twenty-five. After taking out for the gas and wine, they still cleared over two hundred dollars for a little over an hour's work.

Snake stopped at a dope house on the east side. All of them chipped in twenty-five dollars apiece. He was gone about ten minutes before he returned with another man. They climbed in the car.

"He ain't got nothing but pills," Snake responded to their unspoken question. "So I didn't cop none." He nodded towards the man who had gotten in the car with him. "Lee here says he knows where to cop the bomb at. We can get a half a piece of stuff for one hundred."

All of the men in the car stared closely at the new man. They had hassled too hard to allow another addict to come along and burn them for their money.

Tiny Tim said what they all were thinking. "Man, I wouldn't allow Lee to look at my money too long, let alone take it somewhere and cop. He ain't about to leave me sittin' out in front of some apartment building while he runs out the back door with all my bread in his pocket."

"Ain't that the truth!" Red muttered. "I wouldn't trust Lee in a shit-house with a muzzle on."

Lee was a short, balding man, turning to fat in his late twenties. He listened to them without any apparent concern. What they had said was just about true. No matter how close friends they might be, one hundred dollars would be a lot of temptation.

"What's the matter with you? You think I'm a fool or something?" Snake asked hotly. "Whenever my money goes out of sight, I'm going with it."

Teddy spoke up. "What's Lee goin' get out of it, since he's so willing to take us to cop?"

"Nothing!" Snake replied bluntly. "All he wants for me to do is take him by his wife's house, so he can pick up his TV to pawn."

He didn't wait for any replies but started the car and pulled away from the curb.

"Man, I'm sick!" Red exclaimed loudly. "I thought we were going to cop some stuff, and now here we are running all over town."

"It ain't but a couple of blocks away," Lee said. "What I need is some help lifting the damn thing, 'cause it's a floor model."

Lee pointed out the directions and in a few minutes they pulled up in front of a small frame house. Lee got out, with Snake following him. They went up the front steps and Lee walked in without knocking. In the front room, five little children were sitting on the floor watching cartoons on television. Without bothering to speak, Lee unplugged the TV set and began winding up the cord. The children let out a yell, and their mother came running in from the kitchen.

She stopped at the sight of the two men and put her hands on her hips. She was a tall, very light-skinned woman, thin to the point of being frail, with freckles covering her nose. Her large bosom heaved up and down with controlled wrath. Her eyes narrowed, glittering with disgust.

"You done took everything else out of the house to sell, you lowdown bastard, so now you done decided to take the only thing the children got they can enjoy." She sat down and put her arms around two of the children. "Don't you worry, and quit that crying." She pulled the children closer in an attempt to stop their tears. "Just get out, Lee. If you don't never come back, we can consider ourselves lucky."

Snake picked up his end of the television. He was in a hurry to get away with it. He hated to see children cry, but the ten dollars he was getting for helping smoothed over his small concern. They carried the floor model television out to the car. The sound of the kids crying followed them outside. The set was so large they had to put it in the trunk of the car and leave part of it hanging out.

The rest of the men grumbled until they reached the pawnshop. They worried over the possibility of the police stopping them. If a police car should happen to pass them and see the TV, it was an automatic search. They didn't stop talking about it until after they had pawned it and reached the dope house.

Snake went in with Lee, and when he returned he stared up and down the street closely before walking to the car. From his behavior, the men in the car knew he had reached the man and made a score.

# 8

---

The rain was still falling in an infernal down-pour. Terry tossed the magazine down on the couch and got up. She paced up and down, wondering where she could put her hands on ten dollars. She sniffed suddenly; her nose was leaking again. "Goddamn it," she cursed quietly, "I've got to have ten dollars." She quickly rejected the idea of trying to borrow it from her mother. "That's out," she muttered and ran up the steps. The sound of her father's loud snoring came to her, and she hesitated outside his room. She fought down the temptation to slip into his room and try to remove ten dollars from his pocket.

Suddenly a new idea popped into her head. She rushed over to her dresser and searched wildly until she found her address book. She flipped the pages until she found what she was looking for.

Holding the page open with one finger, she quickly dialed the number. "Hello," she said as soon as the receiver on the other end was picked up. "Could I speak to Billy?" she asked, annoyed by the sound of a feminine voice on the other end of the line.

"I'm sorry, but he's in school. Could I take a message?" The voice was kind and pleasing.

Terry slammed the phone down, not bothering to answer. She stretched out on the bed, fighting back the tears. "Tears won't help you now, girl," a small voice inside her warned. She twisted over on the bed. A hot flash ran through her, followed quickly by sweat running down her armpits. She rolled over on the bed, her legs beginning to feel stiff and heavy.

"What am I going to do?" she cried silently into the pillow. She sat up quickly as cold chills shot through her body. She stared at the tiny portable radio sitting on her dresser. "It's useless," she told herself miserably. "It didn't cost over ten dollars when it was new." Terry jumped up and ran to the window and stared out, her mind racing frantically. She trembled from a chill and hugged herself tightly.

She retraced her steps and snatched up the phone. She dialed a number, tapping her foot impatiently. "Porky!" Her voice was almost hysterical. "I got to have a favor from you!"

"You don't have to have anything, young lady, but first of all, who do I have the pleasure of speaking to?" His voice was low and sweet.

"Porky!" She almost screamed. "This is Terry! I got some money coming tonight, Porky. Porky, are you listening?" she asked frantically.

"Yes, dear Terry, but I'm not interested in anything you might have tonight. Money, honey, that's the new magic word in the Seventies, ain't you hip?" He laughed uproariously.

She began to plead. "Listen, Porky, please. If you won't give me no credit, how about letting me bring you my winter coat? I just want to pawn it to you, until I get off from work tonight."

"Listen, Terry," he ordered, his voice brittle. "You already owe me twenty dollars, dear, so I don't think I can allow you to go any deeper in debt." Suddenly his voice became sweet again. He started to sing. "It's raining outside and I'm in the mood for love."

Terry sobbed and slammed the phone down. "You dirty, dirty bastard," she muttered as she fought back the tears in the corners of her eyes.

The sound of her father's snoring came to her. Her addict's mind quickly came up with another idea. Snatching up a piece of Kleenex she wiped her nose as she ran out of the room. She knocked lightly on her father's door. When there was no answer she pushed open the door and stepped in. He was still sleeping.

She grabbed his arm. "Wake up, Daddy, wake up."

He rolled over and sat up, rubbing his eyes with the back of his hand. "Terry. What you want, girl?" He glanced at the clock on the table at the side of the bed. "My God! It ain't nowhere near time to get up." He slipped back down between the covers and would have pulled them up over his head if it hadn't been for Terry.

She grabbed the sheets and pulled them back down. "Listen, Daddy," she said in desperation. "I got to have you do something for me."

He glanced up at his daughter. "Well, what is it, girl, so I can go back to sleep."

"Daddy, they got a sale on at the store, and I got the most beautiful coat picked out for Momma."

He grunted and tried to grab the bedcovers. "Ain't that nice," he managed to say.

She sat down on the bed, determined not to give him any peace. "Daddy, the sale ends tonight, and they won't let me put it in the layaway, unless I put up ten dollars."

"Your momma already got two winter coats, Terry," he answered, more awake now.

"Aw, Daddy, them things is all out of style. You don't want Momma going to church with them old things on this winter."

He grunted again and made as if to roll over.

"Please, Daddy, please," she begged, a slight sob catching in her throat.

"How much do you need, Terry?" he asked finally, wishing his daughter were elsewhere.

"Just ten dollars, Daddy. That's all," she answered quickly. She sniffed and wiped her nose.

"Get it out of my pants, then, but don't come in here waking me up no more, girl, about no damn money." He growled and rolled over, attempting to go back to sleep.

Terry got the money and ran from the room. She stopped and snatched up a fall coat and her large pocketbook. When she got to the front porch, she put the coat over her head and ran for her car.

When she reached Porky's, she had to wait until he finished having fun with Jean. Jean stood in the middle of the floor in agony. Because of the heavy downpour, the tricks had stopped riding, or rather, she hadn't been able to catch one. Her nose was running also, and she was a pitiful sight. Her hair had gotten wet, and the natural she wore was out of shape. She had removed her spring coat to allow the water to drip from it, and the abscesses on her arms were oozing pus. The yellowish fluid was running down slowly from the open sores on the back of her hands and on her forearms.

"If you need stuff, Jean, I done told you what you'd have to do. If I wasn't scared of you giving my dogs the syphillis I'd have you put on a little floor show for the folks, but you look so nasty I don't even know if my dogs can get their bones up for you." He waited until all the sycophants sitting around the apartment laughed on cue before continuing. "If you really want some dope, baby, just start making the rounds." He pointed at all the addicts sitting around. "Just give them a lick or two on their bones. When you finish with them come on back around to me, and I'll let you polish this knob until it spits."

Porky glanced at Terry. "If you ain't got no money, you just get on your knees, too, and follow her around the room." There were a few snickers and some of the male addicts glanced at her expectantly.

Jean, too sick to care, stopped at the first male addict. He unbuttoned his pants and grinned foolishly at the rest of the people in the room.

Terry watched in disgust. She removed the ten-dollar bill from her bra and walked over and gave it to Smokey. Jean left the first man, and he rebuttoned his pants. She stopped in front of a junkie drawing up some dope. He waved her away angrily. She continued on around the room, stopping in front of all the men, giving them a chance to put their penis in her mouth. Most of the time she was flatly refused. The addicts were more interested in putting dope in their arms than in being part of a show.

She stopped in front of Porky, who removed an enormous penis from his pants as she dropped to her knees. Terry turned her head away, sickened. She staggered to the couch and sat down, keeping her face averted from the sight that was going on in the room. She could still hear the animal sounds coming from Porky, as he directed Jean's efforts with a detachment that belied his enjoyment.

Without any show of emotion, Smokey got up and walked into the small kitchen. When she returned, she was carrying a small pan full of water and a clean rag. She waited patiently until Porky reached his climax, then walked over as Jean got up from her knees and washed him off, her face expressionless.

Porky grunted. "Give the hot-headed bitch a half a fourth," he ordered loudly. "If any of you other bitches happen to want a blow, you better speak up now. If you wait till later, I might not be in the mood to watch no show."

The few dopefiend women in the room ignored him and continued to finish whatever they were doing.

Jean walked over to the couch and found the largest cooker she could get her hands on. She shook out most of the dope in the package Smokey gave her. Her fingers shook as she lit a match under the Vaseline top. As soon as the dope melted down, she took a set of works out of her bra and drew up a dropper full of dope.

"You goin' fuck around and kill your ignorant ass, bitch," Porky said loudly as he watched her prepare to shoot all the dope.

She didn't bother to reply as she stuck the needle down into one of the many sores on her hand. She got a hit and slowly closed her eyes and ran the dope in.

Terry shuddered as she noticed the open sores. It was really a house of horrors, she thought.

Jean ran the dope in, then removed the dropper from the spike, leaving the needle still in her hand. She drew up the rest of the dope and ran it in quickly. Before she could take the spike out, she fell over on the floor.

"The bitch done had an O.D.," a few of the junkies yelled together.

Before Jean had hit the floor good, Porky's doormen and Smokey went into action. "Get some saltwater," Gee Gee yelled.

Smokey came out of the kitchen carrying a tray full of ice cubes. She knelt down beside the stricken woman and raised her dress. She began to insert the chilling ice into Jean's womb, while another girl put ice cubes around her neck and bosom.

Gee Gee drew up a dropper full of saltwater and shot it into her veins. They worked on her quickly and professionally. Porky watched silently. As soon as she moaned and got propped up, he stood up and walked over.

"Big Ed," he yelled, "as soon as that bitch gets awoke enough to hold up, you get her the fuck out of here. I don't care where you take her, the nearest alley is good enough, just see to it that she ain't nowhere near this house."

He turned and glared at the addicts watching him closely. "If I hear word of her having had that O.D. anywhere near this house, don't none of you come back, 'cause my doors will be closed." His voice was sharp; it was a deadly threat he had given. To a dopefiend, it was no small matter to be able to cop from Porky. He always had dope, and it was the best in the city.

Terry watched silently as the two men half carried, half dragged Jean from the apartment. "I wonder what they'll do with her," she said quietly, not even aware that the addict next to her had heard.

"They'll take her to some alley and drop her in it, if she don't wake up soon," he offered quietly.

She shuddered at their ruthlessness. A slow awareness of what she had become involved in forced her to ask, "But suppose she dies, then what?"

The dopefiend shrugged his shoulders. "So what! Another dead dopefiend, that's all! You goin' lose any tears over it? If you ain't, the police sure in the fuck ain't, you dig?"

"I guess not," she muttered and took another snort of her dope. As the heroin quickly took effect, she began to drift off, the episode almost forgotten.

# 9

———

The rain was still falling as Minnie hurried towards the department store. It had been a wonderful opportunity for her, she reasoned, when she and Terry had started working together. With Terry working on the inside of the store, it was almost impossible for a floorwalker to bust her, because Terry knew them all.

She clutched the bag she was carrying in her arms, trying to keep it from getting too wet. Inside the bag were two expensive sweaters she was taking back for a refund. With Terry's help earlier, she had been able to steal them. Instead of selling them for half price, Terry had told her to bring them back and she would refund them, giving her their full value plus tax.

She entered the department store, wondering idly if Terry had heard the latest news about Jean.

"How many times have I told that bitch not to be so greedy," she thought. "Well, she won't have to worry about it anymore." They had found her slumped over a cup of coffee in a restaurant, dead. That was a hell of a way to die, but when you left here, there couldn't be a better way to go than high, Minnie thought philosophically.

Terry paused briefly, then continued waiting on the customer she had been taking care of when Minnie walked up. In a few minutes the customer left, and she began to make out a refund slip for Minnie.

"Did you bring that blow for me?" she asked anxiously. Although she didn't really need one, the thought of having a hit on the way filled her with anticipation. Her hands fluttered nervously as she waited for Minnie's answer.

Minnie watched her closely. "You got it bad, ain't you, honey? You better cut down on your blows, Terry, or you're going to end up with a oil burner." As she spoke, she removed a small pack of heroin and slipped it under the bag she had laid on the counter.

The sight of the drug caused Terry to break wind loudly. She blushed, snatched up the small package, and hurried toward the rest room. She clutched at her stomach; the closer she got, the more compelling it seemed that she was about to have a bowel movement.

Minnie watched her leave with concern. It would have looked better if Terry had waited until after she had left the counter. She waited until Terry disappeared from sight, then turned and made her way toward the refund counter, un- aware that she had been under surveillance ever since she entered the store.

Terry found an empty stall in the rest room and went in. No sooner had she entered it than another woman came through the rest room door. The sound of someone washing her hands came to her, but Terry paid it no heed. She cursed silently. She had forgotten to stop and get her purse. Now she didn't have anything to make a quill with. It would have been too inconvenient to go back for the purse, so she just opened the tiny package and held it close to her nose and snorted. Doing it this way caused her to waste a small amount of the dope, but it didn't disturb her. The only thing that mattered was that she get most of it into her system. It didn't occur to her that the drug didn't make her high anymore unless she had a large amount of it. She just knew the drug made her feel normal again, and that was what she so desperately sought. The drug had become a temporary relief from the terrible desire that ate at her mind and body every day until it had been appeased.

After the drug brought on its mellowing effect, Terry again thought about going to a doctor for help. But it was always this way after she had satisfied the nagging hunger of the habit. When she was sick, there was but one thought on her mind:

where could she get a fix? She had promised herself time and time again that she would seek out a
doctor, but when she awoke in the morning crav-
ing a fix, the only thing she would seek would be
the nearest dope house.

Terry opened the door and stepped out. The
woman standing at the faucet watched her in the
mirror. Terry nodded her head in a form of greet-
ing, and walked over and looked in the mirror.
The first thing she noticed was a small amount of
white powder on the edge of her nose. With the
back of her hand she removed it and, telling herself the other woman wouldn't know what was
happening, snorted it off her hand.

Something in the back of her mind rang a bell;
she tried to place the woman next to her. Suddenly it dawned on her: the woman was one of
the extra floorwalkers the store hired to help
keep down their loss of merchandise from
shoplifters. She washed up quickly and left the
woman in the rest room.

After picking up the refund for the two
sweaters, Minnie came back to Terry's department. She fingered some dresses as she waited for
Terry to return. It had been a good day's hustling
for both of them, she reasoned. Both sweaters
had sold for over thirty-nine dollars separately.
With the tax money added on, each sweater had
brought over forty dollars on the refund. Eighty
dollars wasn't a bad day's work, and with her
stomach getting larger every day, she would have

to find some other way of hustling other than whoring.

She glanced around casually as she waited for Terry to come back and wait on her. The department store was one of the largest in Detroit. It carried a full supply of almost any kind of merchandise a woman could want. The departments on the upper floors carried furs and expensive jewelry, while the basement held a full range of furniture, from couches to wall-to-wall carpets.

Under a cheap dress she had picked out Minnie placed three Kimberly Knit two-piece outfits. She glanced around casually. There was no one shoppng near them but two elderly women, so when Terry approached she held the bundle out to her.

Terry accepted the clothes and walked over towards her counter. She stopped at the cash register. After taking a brief glance around to satisfy her fear, she began to write up the order. Intentionally she left out the three expensive Kimberly Knits. Her hands trembled slightly as she folded up the dresses and put them all neatly into a white box.

Casually Minnie gave her a ten-dollar bill.

Terry took it, rang up the cash register, and gave Minnie a few dollars back as change. Minnie picked up the box and started walking slowly towards the door. As soon as she reached the exit two women came up beside her and took her by the arms.

"Just come with us quietly, dear," one of them said softly.

From her dress counter farther back in the store, Terry watched the arrest going on. A stab of fear jolted her. It suddenly entered her mind that she might get arrested, too. Before she could react, she saw her supervisor approaching in the company of two other women.

"Terry, we would like to see you in the office. Please follow me." It was a request but it had the sting of an order behind it. Mrs. Breeding waited until Terry came from behind her counter, then led the way towards her office as the other women dropped behind and brought up the rear. The other salesgirls standing at their counters watched the procession curiously.

When they reached the office and stepped in Minnie was already there, standing against the wall looking as though the world had come to an end. Her head hung down and she refused to meet the eyes of any of the women detectives in the room.

A stout, heavy-faced woman was behind the desk, removing the knit dresses from the box. "Well, would you look at this? What in the world could these be?" she asked with pretended innocence.

Mrs. Breeding, the supervisor, stared at the dresses as though she couldn't believe her eyes. "When I was informed about this, Terry, I didn't believe it. I thought that a grievous error had been made. In fact, all the while we were walking toward this room, I was trying to figure out how I could apologize to you for bringing you here. But now, I'm just about shocked out of my senses."

She sat down behind her desk in a daze. She picked up the clothes and felt them, as if trying to prove to herself it was not a bad dream.

"This is utterly unbelievable," she murmured softy. "Why, I've known this child's parents for over twenty years. She has no reason in the world to steal." She spoke to the other women in the room, but actually she was speaking to herself. "I don't know what to make of this. There's the evidence right before my eyes, yet I still don't want to accept it." She picked up the sales slip and slammed it back down on the desk.

Her eyes fell on Minnie leaning against the wall. "Now that," she said, pointing an angry finger in Minnie's direction, "that I wouldn't expect anything else out of. But you, Terry! This is disgraceful. What will your mother think? How will she feel? Did you ever give it a thought?" The questions came fast and hard. "Not even to mention the disgrace you've brought upon yourself, Terry. That's nothing compared to the shock and hurt your parents will receive from this. Didn't you even consider that you could end up in jail for stealing?" Mrs. Breeding shook her abundance of graying hair and glared angrily at Terry.

The door opened and the woman who had been in the toilet with Terry came into the office.

She walked straight over to Minnie and picked up one of her arms. The tracks running up and down the veins stood out in all their sinister implications.

"This girl here is on some kind of drug, Mrs. Breeding. I believe it's heroin." She dropped Minnie's arm. "I don't know for sure, but when I went into the john, I think Terry was using some kind of drug also," she said coldly.

Mrs. Breeding came out of her chair as though shot from a cannon. "Is that true, Terry? Have you been foolish enough to get yourself involved with some kind of addicts?"

"No ma'am," Terry answered in a timid voice. She had been high when she entered the room, but the fear of arrest was like a splash of cold water on her face. She searched frantically for a lie that would get her out of this trouble. If there was any hope of salvation, she had to find it. The very thought of having the store press charges against her for shoplifting was stupefying. If she would have to appear in court in front of all the people just like a common criminal she would just die. The thought made her turn crimson.

Mrs. Breeding, seeing her blush, thought that Terry was ashamed of just being accused of using drugs. There was no possible way, she thought angrily, that a nice girl like Terry could actually be on anything like dope. She couldn't bring herself to think about it, let alone believe Terry guilty of it. She called two of the women detectives over to her desk. They whispered quietly among themselves for a few minutes. Every once in a while one of the women would shake her head vigorously.

"Not the other one," Terry managed to hear as she leaned forward trying to catch snatches of the conversation.

Mrs. Breeding came around to the front of her desk and leaned against it. "Terry, because of your mother's honesty and goodness, I can't be the one to cause her a broken heart. She worked for me for over twenty years, so I owe her something more than heartache. Because of this, young lady, we're going to give you a break. You don't deserve it, but I'm doing it because of my deep respect for your mother." She paused for a moment, walked behind the desk, and opened a drawer. "Here," she snapped, taking out a check and tossing it on the desk. "We have decided to keep this among ourselves. This is your last check, Terry. What you have coming next week, we will keep to pay for the articles you and your friends have stolen."

She glared at Terry, hurt and bewilderment in her eyes. "If for any reason you're ever seen in this store, you will be arrested on sight, Terry. Now if you don't like us keeping your other check, you can get ready to go to the nearest police station and take it up with a judge in the morning. It's your decision." Her voice had grown harsh. "Speak up now; what do you want to do? It doesn't make any difference to me."

For a brief moment Terry couldn't believe what she was hearing. Then it dawned on her that they were really going to let her go. She was really going to get out of it. Relief flooded through her. "Yes, ma'am. I understand," she managed to answer. "You won't have to ever worry about me coming back in the store anymore, either." She hesitated for a moment, then asked, "Is it all right if I leave now?"

Mrs. Breeding just glared at her. There was so much she wanted to say, to find out; but it wouldn't do any good, she reasoned. "Yes, you can go now. Just be sure to take that with you." She pointed her finger at Minnie.

Before Terry and Minnie had even left the room, Mrs. Breeding picked up the phone and dialed Terry's home number. Terry's mother answered the phone and Mrs. Breeding broke the bad news.

There was the sound of someone trying to stifle a sob, then silence. After a few moments' wait, Mrs. Breeding asked with concern, "Are you all right, Mrs. Wilson?"

Mrs. Wilson sat as though she were dead. The phone dangled down from her lap, hanging like a dead limb on a tree. Mr. Wilson stared at his wife in surprise. He walked over and picked up the hanging receiver. After listening to the voice on the other end of the line, he thanked the woman for calling and hung up the phone gently.

His wife stared at the wall, dazed. It was not

just the phone call. She had been dreading something like this for the past month. She couldn't put her finger on it, but she had sensed something happening to Terry that was out of the ordinary.

Mr. Wilson sat down on the arm of the stuffed chair and put his arm around his wife's plump shoulders. His voice was low and tender. "Now, dear, don't take this too hard. There has to be a reason behind it. Terry is no thief. You and I both know that. There must have been some kind of misunderstanding that we don't even know about. Let's not judge Terry until we hear what she has to say about it." His voice was firm and full of confidence in his daughter.

Leona Wilson snatched at her husband's words the way a drowning person would grab at a piece of driftwood. "You're absolutely right, Herman," she said. "I don't know what I was thinking about. We must wait and hear what Terry has to say. It's just that Mrs. Breeding mentioned the use of some kind of dope. I didn't understand just what she was getting at, but she mentioned some other girl with Terry who used dope." She stopped and thought for a second, then added, "Why, I don't even think that Terry would know what dope looked like if she saw it. I know I wouldn't."

She laughed self-consciously at her own ignorance. She continued, "The idea of it is so preposterous that just for a moment it threw me off. Nowadays you hear and read so much about young kids getting hooked on all these awful drugs that, for a minute, it just knocked me off my feet." She smiled up at her husband, trying to find assurance, hoping that his defense of Terry would ease her anxiety about her daughter's peculiar behavior.

Herman had no doubts whatsoever about his daughter. Dope was something you read about, not something that came home and hit you in the face. Not if you were the kind of man he was. He worked hard so that he could give his family everything they wanted within reason. Dope was something the kids in the slums used, not a girl like Terry. She had everything a young girl could want.

Dope! He had to laugh at the thought. He had given Terry more than the average white child received growing up. No, dope was one problem he didn't have to worry about.

He leaned over and kissed his wife's cheek. "Now don't worry, Mother. We don't have anything to worry about. As soon as Terry comes home, she'll explain what happened. I know she's feeling bad about losing her job, so we won't say too much to her about it. All we want is an answer to why she let herself get involved with that other girl. Mrs. Breeding said there was no doubt about it, the other girl was a drug addict. More than likely, Terry was probably trying to help her out." He smiled at his wife reassuringly. "I'll be willing to bet that it was probably one of her old school friends who turned out bad, and Terry was just trying to help her." In his attempt to comfort his wife, he began to believe his own excuses. The more he talked, the more he began to believe it had to be the other girl's fault.

# 10

Terry walked out of the department store in a daze, followed closely by Minnie. Her mind was in such turmoil that Minnie had to lead her to her car, parked at the curb.

"You can always find another job, Terry. It ain't nowhere near as bad as you think it is."

She remained silent until after she got behind the steering wheel. She stuck the key in the ignition. "It ain't the idea of losing the job that I'm worried about. It's what my parents will say about it," she replied softly.

"Ya, I guess you got a point there," Minnie answered offhandedly. She opened her purse and removed the money they had made on the refund. "Well, at least they didn't take back the money we made off the sweaters. If they'd did that, we'd sure be in a hell of a fix now." She spoke in a matter-of-fact voice.

Terry pulled away from the curb and slipped into the slowly passing traffic. "I'm in enough of a goddamn fix now without worrying about some damn dope," she said bitterly. She was just beginning to realize the significance of what had happened. "I'm going to stop using," she declared loudly.

"Sure, honey, I know all about it. Every dope-fiend I know is going to stop using one day," Minnie answered coldly. "The only thing is that, when they do stop, they're usually in jail or someone is tossing dirt in their face like what's going to happen to Jean now. She just kicked, she ain't got to worry about the Chinaman no more. No sir, as soon as she gets her face full of dirt, it will be just another dopefiend gone, honey."

Terry drove on, listening to Minnie's chatter, nodding her head perfunctorily. The handwriting was on the wall, she thought coldly. She knew that she would have to do something about her drug problem, and "problem" was the understatement of the year. How she had ever allowed herself to get into such a condition was beyond her comprehension. Her mind shied away from the naked reality of her addiction. Her hands began to clench and unclench on the steering wheel as she screamed silently over and over again: No! No! No!

Minnie pushed her share of the refund money across the seat. "I don't know about you, Terry, but I would like to stop and get a blow."

The mention of a fix had a psychological effect on Terry. Immediately she began to have a slight yearning for some dope. She tried to put the thought out of her mind, but it kept coming back. Without actually realizing what she was doing, she had started to drive faster. "I won't even get out of the car," she promised herself quietly. "I'll just drop Minnie off and keep on going."

A small voice in the back of her mind started to laugh. The sound grew until it was a roar in her head. The laughter was cruel; it made a mockery of her pretensions. A flash of insight came to her, cold, revealing, and brutal. Behind all this scorn for herself, there lurked a truth too revealing to be openly inspected. All of her problems had been conveniently forgotten while her thoughts dwelled on one subject—dope.

Terry snatched her share of the money from the car seat and clutched it tightly in her fist. Before she realized where she was, she had pulled over to the curb and parked in front of Porky's house. She moved as though she were a sleep-walker. When Minnie got out of the car, she followed behind her, unable to control her own will. She felt a genuine desire to put an end to this self-punishment, but the urge for the drug was too strong to fight alone. She needed help, needed it desperately and knew she needed it but was unable to reach out for it, wherever it might have been.

Terry followed Minnie up the stairs like an obedient child. The closer she got to the door of the dope house, the more demanding grew the desire for a fix. She began to pray that Porky would be home and not out of dope.

Her prayer was answered; Porky opened the door slightly as they reached the top of the stairway. "Well, well, what have we here?" he asked in a husky voice. He stood in the middle of the doorway so that both of them would have to squeeze past him. His huge stomach pressed Terry against the door frame as she inched by. She plunged into the room.

She stopped suddenly and stared in surprise. Two women were lying in the middle of the floor side by side, naked as on the day they came into this world.

Porky put the large two-by-four back across the door, making it virtually impossible for anyone to kick in his door without giving him enough time to throw away his dope. His back door was barred the same way, in case the police should try that entrance.

"You girls are just in time," Porky said lightly. "Those two ladies were just about to begin entertaining us." He added as an afterthought, "If either one of you would like to join in the show on the floor, why I might just find it entertaining enough to put out a fourth of dope for your disposal."

The two women on the floor looked at them anxiously. "Come on, Minnie," one of them called. "It ain't about nothing," she said and winked her eye.

Minnie stared at the women. She knew what they were going to work out of. With four women twisting around on the floor, all it would really boil down to was letting the men see some bare ass. They would end up faking most of the oral sex the men thought they were seeing. All she would have to do was put her mouth down between another woman's legs, and the men looking on wouldn't know if she was doing anything or not. Actually, Porky was the only one who would really be watching them. The male addicts would be too busy nodding, and the few women sitting around couldn't care less.

Minnie glanced at Terry. The way Terry was staring at the women on the floor was enough of an answer for her. With her pregnancy facing her, the last thing she could afford to do was antagonize Terry. She realized that the bigger her stomach became, the more she would be forced to depend on Terry's good will. With the car that she owned, Terry would be indispensable. Give her a couple more months of steady using and a sight like this would be the last thing in the world to shock her. More than likely, Terry would be participating in the shows herself.

"No, honey," she replied to the woman on the floor. "I think we'll just watch."

Terry fumbled in her purse and brought out ten dollars. "Here, Porky," she said, holding the money toward him nervously.

Smokey got up from the couch and came over and removed the money from her outstretched hand.

Porky grinned at her. "You know you ain't got to spend no money, Terry. All you got to do is join the other ladies on the floor."

She stared at him, astonished. "You hold your goddamn breath, nigger, until you see me laying on the floor making a spectacle of myself for one of you freaks." Her small bosom swelled with anger, while her eyes glinted with unconcealed fury.

Her violent reaction worked as a stimulant on Porky. He could feel himself beginning to have an erection. His hand slid down to his penis and he unconsciously began to stroke himself. His breathing became heavy, while his reptilian eyes closed and unclosed in ecstasy.

Terry was overwhelmed with repugnance as she watched him. The fleeting thought that such a man held power over her filled her with dread. She made a silent promise that this would be her last fix. After today she would find some way of getting help; somehow she would find the strength.

Minnie spoke up. Her voice was harsh and sarcastic. "Whenever you finish jackin' off, Porky, we would appreciate it if you would take care of your business." She held out a ten-dollar bill towards him.

Porky stared at her coldly. His small eyes glittered with open scorn. Minnie brought to his mind all the rejections he had received from girls while going to school. They had all talked to him as if he should be thankful they allowed him to breathe the free air. In truth, he had a deep hatred for humanity. He could never forget the horror of his school days. He had been very sensitive about his abnormal size, yet time and time again he had tried to reach out across the span that separated him from the other children, desperately wanting to be accepted.

The only time the other kids would allow him to play was when they felt like ridiculing him. Pig had been his nickname then, but when he got older and began to realize the power a dope bag brought to the pusher, he quickly put an end to being called Pig.

He had always been grotesquely fat, no matter how much he tried to lose weight. Their family doctor had told his mother it was a gland problem, so not to worry about it. Some people were just meant to be large. As he grew older he realized that many people feared him just because of his features. He even admitted to himself that he resembled a gorilla. What he really enjoyed, though, was the fear that he inspired in women. When he saw that, it aroused him the way nothing else could. There was nothing he enjoyed more than sleeping with a woman who was petrified by fear. Many of them became paralyzed, practically statues of stone, when he started making love to them.

Smokey took the money out of Minnie's hand as Porky lumbered over to his overstuffed chair and sat down. "Don't get beside yourself, bitch," she warned Minnie as she gave them each a pack of dope.

"You bitches ain't gettin' paid just to lay on the floor," Porky yelled loudly at the two women on the floor.

Minnie rolled her eyes at Smokey but didn't reply. Smokey resembled a robot, a walking zombie. Porky kept her so high that, most of the time, it seemed she wasn't aware of where she was. Whenever the addicts discussed her abnormal habit, they spoke in voices full of awe. She was completely at the mercy of Porky's whims. If he were to put her out, her chances of staying alive would be small. Her daily use of heroin would cost an addict on the street over five hundred dollars a day. In the run of a week she used the retail value of over three thousand dollars worth of dope.

Smokey headed back towards the bedroom, stepping over the two women on the floor. She stared past them, her dilated eyes not even seeing them. She lacked the slightest interest in what they were about to do.

As Minnie and Terry took their dope and sat down beside each other, the two women on the floor began to perform. More for their own benefit really than for anyone watching. Each woman stretched out with her head pointed towards the other's feet, while their legs interwove intimately. They were using the scissors position, a favorite of professional lesbians, and as they rubbed cunt to cunt, it became apparent that there was nothing faked about this. Both women were thoroughly enjoying themselves to such a degree that no other person seemed to exist in the apartment for them.

Terry found herself blushing as she watched the women. My God, she thought, this can't really be happening. Not in a room full of people and most of them men. She cautiously glanced out of the corner of her eye to see how the men were reacting to this grotesque display. To her astonishment, very few of the male addicts were actually watching. Most of them were too involved in trying to find a vein to shoot their dope in, while those who had already shot up were nodding as though nothing at all strange were going on.

Here and there, Terry could see a person looking on curiously, but on the whole only the women addicts were interested. Many of them moved their legs unconsciously as they watched the act build up to its climax. Porky stared at the women hungrily, saliva running out of the corner of his mouth and dripping down on his huge chest. After watching a little longer, Terry began to find the show repetitious, so she opened her small pack of dope and began to snort it up.

When the women finished, they sat up on the floor and began to snort some dope off an album cover Smokey had set out beside them.

Porky got up and waddled over to the bedroom door. He came back leading one of his huge German police dogs. He held the dog between his legs as he spoke to the women. "I'll tell you what I'll do," he began, his voice thick with desire. "I'll give either one of you half a fourth of dope if you'll freak off with Butch in front of everybody." He patted the dog on its back.

Both of the women stared up at him angrily. Tess, the larger of the two, replied viciously, "I'll tell what I'll do, you fat, black son-of-a-bitch you. I'll give you a fourth of dope if you let us watch your dog fuck you in your fat, black ass. What about that, you freaking motherfucker you!" she spat out at him.

For a brief moment, Porky felt a jolt of fear. He knew Tess was one of the most dangerous lesbians around. He searched the faces around the apartment until he saw one of his doormen watching them closely. He relaxed slightly. "Just because you done time for cuttin' up a nigger, girl, that ain't shit," he said with renewed courage. "If that nigger had been a man, he'd have kicked you in your ass and took that little funky whore you cut him up over."

Tess jumped up and began to put on the men's clothes she wore. Porky bit his lip nervously. He didn't want to lose her business. Between her and the prostitutes she kept, they spent quite a bit of money in the run of a week. Ever since she was released from prison, she had been using. He was sure that she was strung out now. If she kept using drugs, the day would come when she wouldn't find the thought of having one of her girls copulate with a dog repugnant.

Porky's common sense cautioned him to be patient. He grinned suddenly. "Goddamn, Tess baby. You know I was just jokin' with you, girl. I didn't think you'd take me serious and get rocks in your jaws, baby." He removed a ten-dollar pack of dope from his pocket and tossed it to her.

Tess caught the pack and bit back the acid remark she had been about to make. "Yah, Porky, just so long as we understand each other," she said and smiled a knowing smile.

Porky glanced across the room at Terry, who was nodding off her dope. Her neat little dress was pushed up around her thighs, revealing golden tan skin just above her stockings. As her head dropped down on her chest, her legs parted slightly, causing Porky to catch his breath. He stared in fascination. Sliding down in his seat, he tried to peep up higher under her dress. His feverish mind began to undress her, until he could visualize her completely naked. He pictured his dog's large head stuck up between her beautiful thighs. As the dog became excited he imagined Butch biting and growling, his shaggy head shaking from side to side, as blood from his bites came running down her legs. Her screams of pain then turned to moans of pleasure as he snatched the dog away and stuck his huge head in its place.

Tess punched her woman in the side. As the prostitute turned to see what she wanted, she pointed over at Porky, who was deep into his vivid fantasy.

Suddenly becoming aware of his obscene stare, Terry closed her legs and blushed. "Damn," she said to herself, "you're beginning to sit just like some common whore. Legs gaped all open for any man to look under your dress." Perversely she thought, "Well, the bastard sure couldn't see nothing, no matter how hard he was trying. I should open them real wide, maybe then the son of a bitch will see enough to get his kicks off."

She turned to Minnie. "Honey, I'm going to have to be gettin' on. I know I got a lot of explaining to do, so I think I better get on home." She stood up and opened her purse. "Porky, how much is a half a fourth?"

"Thirty dollars, Terry, but for you, baby, I'll let you have it for twenty-five."

Terry counted the money out slowly. Remembering the promise she had made herself earlier, she justified her behavior by telling herself she would slowly cut down her wage until she could buy some medicine to help her kick.

Porky disappeared into the bedroom. After closing the door behind him, he removed a small piece of tinfoil and began dumping a measured amount of dope into it. Then he took some pure heroin, uncut, and sprinkled it on top of the amount he had already measured out, making it extra strong.

Smokey, sitting on the bed staring into space, watched his movements indifferently. She knew what he was doing and why he was doing it, and had she attempted to think about it she would have known what girl he was fixing the potion for.

When he finished, he pointed towards the dope. "Don't collect but twenty-five dollars for it. It goes to Terry."

Smokey carried out the dope and gave it to Terry. Terry turned around to call Minnie but changed her mind. With the help of another addict, Minnie had got a hit up under her armpit, and now she was too involved in shooting the heroin to be disturbed.

After paying for the dope, Terry started towards the door. Big Ed, one of Porky's protectors, got up to let her out. The gun resting under his left arm swung conspicuously as he leaned down and peeked through a peephole in the door before allowing her to leave. Big Ed was only one of the gunmen that Porky hired to protect him from the addicts. Without protection, the addicts would have stuck him up every day without fail.

Most of the time, his gunmen would be addicts who were known for being vicious and who had the nerve to shoot if so pressured. He kept them supplied with drugs and enough money to take care of their personal needs. Most of the time they just stayed there with him, not bothering to go elsewhere to sleep. None of them worked regular hours. They would just rotate as the mood hit them. Whenever they felt like it was getting time for a fix, they would trade places with one of the gunmen who had been up all night. That was the main thing about Porky's dope house. It never closed. Dope was sold twenty-four hours a day.

Terry made her way down the stairs. She staggered when she got to the bottom. "Damn," she murmured, "this sure is a good blow." She made her way to her car and pulled away from the curb slowly. As she drove towards home, she continued to reject one lie after another. Finally she decided to play it by ear. The dope in her system gave her not only courage but also a feeling of not really caring what her parents thought about her losing her job.

She stopped at a red light and lit a cigarette. Before the light changed, she had dropped the cigarette in her lap twice. Her eyes tried to close, but she fought the desire to nod and drove slowly on. She parked in front of her house and climbed out. There was no worry now, only a desire to get an unpleasant chore over with.

When she entered the house, her parents were sitting in the front room waiting for her. They stared at her curiously. She leaned against the wall and stared back at them. Her father had a solemn look on his face, while her mother seemed to be on the verge of crying at any moment.

Her father cleared his throat. "Terry, we want you to explain what the hell is going on. Mrs. Breeding called and told us some very unpleasant news, and we'd like to hear your side of this."

"I knew it, I knew it," Terry shrilled. "Before you even hear my side of it, you've taken Mrs. Breeding's word for what happened."

"Now, honey," Terry's mother said soothingly. "Your father hasn't accused you of anything, dear. All he did was ask you your side of it."

Cold and calculating, Terry stared at her parents. She knew she had her mother won over already, and she could see in her father's face that he wished he were at work or anywhere else except facing his daughter down at this moment.

She changed her tactics. Her voice became wheedling. "I didn't do nothing but try and help this girl I used to go to school with, Daddy. She came in the store and I could see she was sick, you know; I think she uses that stuff. You know, what they call it, dope."

Terry could tell by their faces that they were buying it wholeheartedly. "Well, anyway, Mother, the girl was pregnant, and I felt sorry for her, so when she put these dresses in her box, I couldn't bring myself to call the floorwalker on her, so I just let her go." She stopped to catch her breath. Her parents' faces were shining with hope. They wanted to believe her so badly that for a moment she felt regret. She had never before resorted to lies when dealing with her parents. But then, she had never before been strung out on dope. For a moment she felt like throwing herself in her mother's arms and telling her all of it. How she wished she were a young girl again so she could lie in her father's protecting arms with no worry in the world.

Her mother spoke up hesitantly. "Mrs. Breeding gave us the impression that it was a little different, Terry."

A flash of anger shot through her. For a second she really believed she was the injured one. "Mrs. Breeding, huh." Terry caught herself in time, she had almost said shit. "I'll tell you about Mrs. Breeding. Do you know how many times I've seen her catch white girls stealing and let them go?" She stared at her mother and saw her nod her head in agreement. "You know about that, don't you, Mother? I know she's told you about it, when you're on the phone gossiping."

Her mother came to Mrs. Breeding's defense as Terry knew she would. "Now, Terry, you know she lets young colored girls go, too, if she believes they've been scared enough."

Terry snorted. "Well, she didn't want to let this young pregnant colored girl go today." She turned to her father. "Anyway, Daddy, you know what I mean. You run into the same thing out there where you work. White people do what they want to do, while you do what they tell you to do."

Her father nodded his head. You would have to go to another planet to find a black person who didn't know about discrimination. For the past fifteen years he had been trying to get the crane operator job in his factory, but he was always refused. He had been complaining for the last ten years that it was because of his color.

"Well, that about covers it, Daddy. If I had been a white girl, instead of just some poor black nigger, they wouldn't have done anything—just chewed me out about it."

With the timing of a good diplomat, she had used the one word she knew would make her father angry enough to change the whole subject.

"Terry, you know what I have told you about using that word," he said, his neck muscles swelling from anger. "Don't nobody but common-ass Negroes use that word in regards to themselves. It takes the lowest form of humanity to be stupid enough to call themselves something that the dictionary defines as low life."

Suddenly ashamed at having cursed in front of the two women he loved more than life itself, he walked over and patted his daughter affectionately but clumsily on the shoulder. "Don't worry about a thing, Terry. You can find another job whenever you get ready, and if you don't want to work, we'll make out."

She turned quickly and started for the stairs. She didn't want them to see the tears that sprang up in her eyes. As she stumbled up the stairway, she felt disgusted with herself. How could she deceive them like that? When she reached the top of the stairs, tears were running down her cheeks unchecked.

Terry sat on her bed, her head bowed, completely ashamed of her behavior. As if with a will of their own, her fingers began to move toward her purse, and before she was fully aware of it, she had taken out her package of heroin and opened it. Using a fingernail file, she scooped up a large amount of the white poison and snorted it. She seemed to be watching her motions from a distance outside her body. It was as though someone else were snorting the drug and she was just an innocent bystander.

She failed to notice the opening of the bedroom door as she continued to snort the dope. She drifted into another world, free of worry and responsibility. Her eyes had become small pinpoints, while her spirit took off in a flight of euphoria.

Her father's shocked voice brought her back to reality. "What is that stuff? What in the world are you doing? Terry, Terry, my Terry. You can't be using dope!" He continued, seeing it before his eyes but not yet wanting to believe what he saw. "My God, this can't be you, Terry. Why, some kid brought up in the slum, yes, I could understand that. But not you, Terry. Not you! Why, you ain't never wanted for nothing. I used to work two jobs so that you and your mother could have anything you wanted." Tears began to run down his face. His voice became hoarse, and then finally anger came. "Give me that stuff, Terry. Give it here!"

Terry moved as though her world was crashing down. She jumped to the end of the bed, clutching the heroin to her bosom. Her eyes were dilating with fear, while her nose seemed to expand with each breath.

Her mother stood against the door, staring dumbfounded, her hand clutching at her heart. She repeated over and over, as though it were a song, "It ain't true, honey. Not my little girl, tell me it ain't true."

Consumed by anger, her father snarled at her. "You no-good little bitch! Then it was all true, every goddamn word of it was true and you come in here telling your goddamn lies and we believe every word of it."

Father and daughter stared at each other across the room. Terry, out of fear of losing the small amount of heroin that promised her she wouldn't wake up sick, didn't even think about trying to use reason with him. All her mind could grasp was the danger to her heroin. She knew that, once her father got hold of it, she would never get it back.

Her father's voice became low, filled with disgust. "Either you give me that dope, Terry, or get out of my house. I'm not going to have anyone living under my roof who takes that stuff."

The words were like ice water in her face, but she knew beyond a shadow of a doubt that she could not part with her drugs. "Well, if that's the case," she said slowly, "I hope you will leave me some privacy while I pack."

Before the words were even out of her mouth, her mother slumped over and would have fallen if it had not been for her husband. He caught her and held her up. "I'm going to take your mother to her bedroom. When I return, Terry, I want you out of my house."

Terry grabbed a few things and tossed them in a suitcase. She knew she would have to move fast, before her father returned, because there was the possibility of his asking for the car keys. With the thought of losing her car in her mind, she raced around the room, gathering up only the things she knew she must have. In a few minutes she was finished and on her way down the stairs.

# 11

Teddy and Snake sat in the car waiting impatiently for Dirty Red and Tiny Time to come out of the department store. The store closed at nine o'clock and they both knew their friends would have to come out before some of the doors were locked.

Teddy glanced at the cheap watch he wore. "They got five minutes to make it, Snake."

"I don't like it," Snake replied. "They should have been out of there twenty minutes ago. I told them before they went in that the store had private cops and all of them wore guns."

"You know how they feel about private cops, Snake. A goddamn store cop ain't no different than nobody else. If you goin' play, you got to be able to play on floorwalkers and private cops alike."

Snake snorted. "There's one hell of a difference, Teddy, and that's that fuckin' gun the cops
wear. With cops on the scene, man, if you run,
you're taking your life in your hands. With a floorwalker, you got a chance of knocking the sonofabitch down and gettin' away."

Both men became silent as they worried over
what was keeping their friends. It was in the air;
they could almost smell it. Their senses were so
sharp from stealing every day that they could feel
a bust. On entering a store, they could read roller
in the most innocent-looking floorwalker. Now,
both of them had just about reached the conclu-
sion that their friends had been busted.

Suddenly there was some commotion in the
front of the department store. From where they
sat, they could see everything that happened. Tiny
Tim had come out of the store first, clutching
something under his coat. At his heels was a white
man. As soon as they reached the pavement the
man grabbed his arm. Dirty Red, coming out of
the store behind the white man, made a blurring
motion towards his pocket, causing both of the
men in the car to groan. The floorwalker never
knew what hit him. Red shot him in the back
twice. As the man slid down to the ground, Red
and Tim broke and ran, a box falling from under
Tim's coat.

Snake cursed. "The damn fools, they're heading straight for the car." Before he could get over

his astonishment, two men in blue uniforms rushed from the store with drawn guns.

Their yells of rage filled the night. "Halt, halt, or we'll shoot!" Before the words had cleared the cop's mouth, his partner had aimed and shot.

Red staggered, then tried to regain his balance, but another blow in the back hurled him to the pavement. As Tim passed his fallen body, he seemed to tumble. Two more shots rang out, and Tim pitched over on his face.

"Good God almighty," Teddy moaned. "They done both went and got killed."

Snake jumped out of the car and rushed towards the crowd of people that was gathering beside his fallen friends. From the fringe of the crowd he could tell that both his friends were dead. Neither man moved, and from the murmuring of the people nearest the bodies, he knew they wouldn't have to worry about any more fixes. Teddy joined him and they stood silently. They waited until after the ambulance had come and gone before returning to the car.

"Well," Teddy said, breaking the silence. "At least Red did kill him a peckerwood before going."

"That ain't worth a shit," Snake growled. "Dirty Red is gone, and killin' a peckerwood ain't goin' make no difference. When you dead, you're done."

They drove for a while in silence. Finally Teddy

spoke up. "We ain't got nothing to sell, Snake. What we goin' do about a do? My nose is already running, man, and we ain't got a slug."

"Your nose is always running, Teddy. So that ain't nothing new." He remained silent for a while, but his next words let Teddy know that he was thinking about the same thing. "Porky ought to give us a blow on credit after we tell him the news."

"Ya, man. He ought to give us one free. All the money Red and Tim and us done spent with him, I know it should at least be worth a free do when we tell him he done lost two customers."

With the thought of a free fix in his mind, Snake began to drive a little faster. The money they had spent already that day with Porky should have been enough for a fix on credit, Snake reasoned. He desperately tried to find grounds to support his argument in case Porky turned them down. Among the four of them, they had already spent over two hundred dollars that day.

As they pulled up and parked in front of Porky's, Teddy noticed Terry's car parked in front of the hotel across the street. He cursed under his breath. One of these days, he thought, I'll get a chance to fix her little red wagon, and I'll fix it damn good.

"That your ex-girlfriend's ride parked over there, Teddy?" Snake asked coldly.

"Ya, that's the bitch's car," Teddy answered shortly.

"Why ya break up, Teddy? If I'd had me a sassy little piece like that, I might even have given up shootin' stuff."

"Nigger, you ain't goin' give up shootin' dope till you're as dead as Tim and Red," Teddy replied harshly.

Snake tossed back his head and laughed loudly as they started to climb the stairway. "My, my, man. You still got your nose open for that young bitch, ain't you? She sure must have some good lovin' to keep a dopefiend's nose open." He laughed again, then added more seriously, "It's really your fault that you blew her, Teddy. I don't know what you was thinking about, making a dopefiend out of her. You knew she was going to become a motherfuckin' dog once she got strung out."

"That's all right," Teddy replied hotly. "I fixed her smart ass up properly. I put something on her ass she'll never forget. Every time that bitch gets sick, she'll think about me being the cause of it."

Snake stopped at the head of the stairs and looked back at him strangely. "I guess you did fix her at that, but you made a snake out of her, and damn if you wasn't the first one she bit."

Gee Gee, one of Porky's doormen, opened the door. He watched them closely as they entered, then closed the door behind them.

"Where's Porky at?" Snake asked quickly.

Gee Gee nodded towards the door. "I think he's sleeping, Snake."

"We got to see him," Teddy said, with fear

balling up in his stomach. The thought of Porky not being available had not entered their minds.

Without any apparent concern, Gee Gee stared coldly at them. "I don't see how you goin' see him, dig, if he 'sleep. I ain't about to wake him up over nothing, dig? If you want something, Smokey can take care of it, dig. If you don't want nothing, you might as well let the door hit you in the ass, 'cause Porky done said all that laying out around his dope house has got to cease, dig."

Teddy stared up at Gee Gee. Gee Gee was a touch hot. He liked to fight. It really didn't make any difference to him who it was either. He didn't pick his people.

Snake came in with that smoothing ability of his to sway anyone. "Dig, Gee Gee. We got some bad news for Porky, man. All of us was taking off a joint, and the fuzz busted down on us and shot Dirty Red and Tim. Now we need someone with the knowledge to call them white folks and find out did they do any talking before they died, or are they dead. Can you dig that?"

This rang a bell with Gee Gee. From living in the narrow world of a dope house he was starved for gossip. Most of the time they talked about what other addicts were doing, who was doing time, and who just got busted. News about anyone just getting killed or taking an overdose was always exciting enough to kick around for the next week or two. The room full of addicts had started buzzing over Snake's comment. The only person who didn't seem excited was Smokey. She was sitting in Porky's chair with a king-size cooker, full of dope, trying to find a vein.

Gee Gee spoke to her. "You want to tell Porky, Smokey?"

She looked up at him with eyes that had seen everything. "So what, two fuckin' dopefiends got killed. Big deal. They die every fuckin' day. Now what you want me to do, run all over the house shouting the news?"

Teddy stared at her surprised. It was the first time he had ever heard Smokey say that many words before. Her reply had struck him dumb; he was at a loss for words to make her do what he so desperately wanted.

Taking her reply in stride, Snake spoke to her coldly. "Get on up, bitch, and wake Porky up. When you come back, I'll hit you in the pocket."

"I don't want no shit out of you when I get back, Snake. You done promised to hit me, and I'm going to hold you to it," Smokey said as she got up and walked towards the bedroom. It was hard for her to get someone to hit her, because most of her veins were shot out. Sometimes it took better than an hour before she could find a vein to hit in.

Snake walked over and stared down at her cooker of dope. The dope was covered with blood from where she had tried to find a hit. He pulled the spike out. On the arm of the chair beside the cooker was a package of dope. He started to reach for it, but Big Ed's voice stopped him.

"You can find something easier to steal than that, Snake. All you got to do is look in a better place. Say somewhere that ain't connected with this house." Big Ed smiled at him from the couch. "I know you dig what I'm talking about."

"Ya sure look out for Porky's stuff, don't you," Snake replied sharply.

"If you was to ever pay us as well as he does, we would look out for yours the same way," Gee Gee said, not wanting to be outdone.

Smokey came out of the bedroom, followed closely by Porky, who was dressed in a white bathrobe large enough to be a tent. His small piglike eyes were red from lack of sleep, and from his expression you could tell he didn't like the idea of being woken up.

"This bullshit Smokey was mumbling about better be the real deal," he growled as he crossed the room. "I don't want to find out ya tricked her into waking me up just so you can hit for some stuff."

Snake quickly explained what had happened, wording it to give the impression they had been in the store, too. He gave Porky the name of the department store so he could call and find out what had happened. Knowing that Porky loved gossip, he gave him just enough information to

get him aroused. Porky disappeared into the bedroom.

After about ten minutes he reappeared. "God
damn almighty!" he exclaimed. "Both them dopefiends done went and got themselves killed." He
seemed about to burst with the news. "And that
ain't all. Them fools went and killed a honkie, the
people just told me the whitey died on the way to
the hospital. They wanted to know who the hell I
was, so I told them I was Tim's daddy." He
stopped to catch his breath. "They didn't seem to
know anything about nobody else being there. I
asked if anybody else was with them, but they
went to nut city on me." He stared at Snake and
Teddy as though he had just noticed them. "I
don't know what you goin' do now, them stores
goin' be hot as hell from here on out."

Smokey took off her blouse and raised her arm
so Snake could try to hit the vein under her
armpit. The brassiere she wore was black around
the edges from constant wear. Her breasts were
so tiny, her brassiere fitted her the way a woman's
bra would have fit a child of ten.

Without taking his eyes off what he was doing,
Snake spoke out of the side of his mouth. "We
ain't worried about tomorrow, Porky. What we
need is a fix, now. We'll be able to get out in the
morning and do some hustling."

"I don't know," Porky said as he became alert.
"How much are you on my books?"

"I don't owe you but fifteen dollars," Snake replied slowly. He clamped down on his jaw to keep it from shaking.

Teddy, seeing a chance to cop a blow even if his partner didn't, spoke up quickly. "I don't owe you nothing, Porky; I paid my bill up when I sold you them bedsheets."

The subtle inference wasn't lost on Snake. Teddy's eagerness to cop, even though Snake might not get anything, didn't anger him; he knew he would have done the same thing if circumstances had been reversed.

Blood gushed up into the works Snake was using as he hit a vein in Smokey's armpit. He cursed as he applied pressure and the works refused to function. For a minute he was afraid the tools were stopped up, but just as quickly as they had stopped they began to work. He pressed down on the bulb. Slowly the dope ran out of the dropper and into her vein. He held the needle between two of his fingers tightly as he removed the dropper from the end of the needle. Keeping the needle firmly embedded in her vein, he refilled the dropper and stuck it back on the spike.

"Give them both a ten-dollar pack, Gee Gee," Porky ordered, finally breaking the silence. "I don't know what you goin' do next time and don't give a fuck. If your mammies both die before you pay me, don't come asking for no credit." Porky started to walk back towards the bedroom and stopped. "I don't know if you know it or not, Teddy, but your woman's old man caught her with some dope tonight and put her little smart ass out."

For a brief moment, anger at Terry's father invaded Teddy's selfish thoughts. Deep down, he knew he still cared for her, but the way they had parted made him want to take a petty revenge on her. He wanted to hurt her, not because she had hurt him but because he still loved her and couldn't admit it.

On the end table beside the couch was a glass of water filled with works. Teddy picked out a set and skeeted water out of the needle. The water came out slowly so he picked up another set. He continued until he found a set that was open; when he skeeted the water out the needle was unclogged.

Teddy cooked up all of his ten-dollar pack and drew it up in the dropper. He found a vein, hit, sat back, and cleaned up the works before Snake had even finished hitting Smokey. He sat and nodded, waiting patiently for Snake.

Snake hadn't spent his time in vain. When he finished helping Smokey, he begged her out of a little girl—cocaine—and mixed it with his horse after he cooked up the heroin. He dropped the cocaine down on top of the heroin, and it quickly dissolved without the aid of heat.

"Goddamn, baby," Teddy drawled. "I wish I knew you was goin' fix up a speedball. Why don't you leave the cotton wet for me?"

Snake flexed the muscle of his arm until one of his veins began to stand out. From the muscular contours of his arm it was easy to tell he had once been a powerfully built man. His constant use of dope had caused his large-framed body to appear undernourished. He pushed the needle deep into a vein on his first try. A dark flow of blood filled the dropper. He loosened the tie around his arm and slowly pressed on the dropper until the blood and heroin in the dropper disappeared.

"You hoggish sonofabitch," Teddy yelled, disgruntled. "You done shot up all the coke."

The shot quickly took effect. Snake sat back and relaxed as though he didn't have a care in the world. He grinned over at Teddy. "Damn, baby," he drawled slowly. "I really forgot about you, man."

A while later both men left the apartment. A freezing rain had begun to fall. They clutched their collars around their necks and ran for the car. It was early morning and a chilling wind had begun to blow along with the rain, announcing the coming of winter.

Teddy waited until Snake had started up the car and turned on the heater. "I don't know about you, Snake, but I'd like to see if we can ride down on a sting before we call it a night. It ain't no later than two o'clock, so we got plenty of time to see if we can rip something off before daylight."

"I been thinking, Teddy, about what happened today. I think I done had enough of boostin' to

162

Donald Goines

last me a lifetime." Snake lit up a cigarette. "If we could take off a big enough score, we could buy some dope and start dealing. The way we're going now, it ain't nothing but a matter of time before something happens to us."

"That sounds sweet as a motherfucker," Teddy replied quickly, "only I ain't got the slightest idea where we goin' find a sting big enough to put us in business." He thought about the idea a little more, then continued. "If we had the money, I know where we could cop some good stuff at, but the man don't do nothing but wholesale, so we'd have to have at least a bill before coppin' from him."

"A bill!" Snake exclaimed. "I ain't talking about no funky hundred dollars. I know where a joint is at that we can take off, man, that's got big stuff in it. If you got the heart to get down with me, Teddy, by morning either we'll have big stuff, say something like six or seven hundred dollars, or we'll be in some fuckin' precinct station."

Rain splattered on the windshield in a continuous downpour. "If we can get our hands on just five hundred dollars," Teddy replied, trying to keep the excitement out of his voice, "we'd be able to support our habits with no problem at all."

"We would be able to do a whole lot better than just support our habits, baby," Snake retorted while his fingers beat out a rhythm on the steering wheel. "The way I got it figured, Teddy, if

Porky can support that oil burner Smokey got, we should have no problem taking care of ours, plus making a few ends."

"Shit, Snake, that bag Porky got is so big he could take care of five habits like Smokey's and still make money."

"That's where you wrong," Snake said as he drove slowly through the deserted streets. He made a right turn and hit the John Lodge Freeway. "Porky's got a big bag, true enough, but it ain't that goddamn big. Where he makes his money at is on his ability to never run out of dope. You can make money with a small bag if you don't allow yourself to run out of stuff."

"Man, you could always rap," Teddy said loudly. "If a man listened to you, you could make him believe shit don't stink. Here I am, two o'clock in the morning without fifty cents in my pocket, and you got me believing that in the morning all we goin' have to worry about is where can we cop at."

Snake grinned. "If that connect you're talking about is any good, we'll have plenty dope to shoot up this time tomorrow." His voice was full of assurance. In his mind he had reached the point of either taking off a big score or ending up in prison. There was no middle road. Being a dopefiend he had to have it.

Teddy was a willing partner; he too had reached the point of do or die. "What we goin' take off, Snake? We goin' B-E a joint this morning?" There was no hesitation in his voice. There was only curiosity as to what kind of crime they were going to commit.

For a few minutes Teddy thought Snake hadn't heard him. He continued to drive without answering until he pulled up the ramp leaving the expressway. "We goin' crash a joint this morning, baby. Crash, crash, crash!"

Without warning Teddy's stomach started to act up. He could feel butterflies taking off inside him. For a moment he feared he might lose his dinner. It wasn't really fear even though he had never crashed a joint before. He was too much a dopefiend to have an actual fear of breaking the law. It was the idea of the rip. He was up on what he had to do, he had been around too long not to know what a crash meant. He was aware that, when you crashed, the whole thing depended on speed, if you didn't want to get caught in a freak bust.

He watched the neighborhood closely as Snake drove slowly through an all-white suburb. Snake turned up into a shopping center that was well lit but deserted. He parked in front of an appliance store with a large display of portable television sets and radios.

After furtively glancing around, both men stepped from the car. There was no hesitation in either of them. They had come for a purpose and now they moved toward it professionally.

Snake carried a tire iron he had taken from

under the front seat. "As soon as that goddamn light changes and that car pulls off, I'm going to take care of business, Teddy. When you go in the window, man, don't hand me nothing but portable TVs, baby." His voice was hoarse with excitement.

With a quick nod Teddy agreed, never taking his eyes from the street and the car at the light. As soon as the light changed and the car pulled away, he heard a crash. Most of the front window of the store began to fall out. With three quick blows Snake had the window clear of glass. Before the sound of falling glass had diminished, Teddy was through the window. He returned almost instantly and pushed two television sets towards the waiting hands. When Snake returned from the car, there were two more waiting for him. He rushed back to the car with them in his arms. Quickly the backseat of the car filled with the sets.

"No more room, Teddy," he yelled, taking two more television sets and running for the car. He was still trying to find room for them in the front seat when Teddy joined him, carrying four transistor radios.

"Hurry, Snake, hurry!" Teddy screamed as he frantically climbed over the televisions in the front seat. "A car stopped out front and it's backing up fast!"

His urging was not necessary. Snake had seen the car when he ran around the front of his own.

It only added wings to his feet. There was never any thought of not running.

Snake leaped in the car and put it into gear. He had never cut the motor off. As he sped away from the store, he saw the other car pull into the shopping center. He raced for the exit, his foot glued to the gas pedal.

The other car pulled up in front of the store and stopped. Teddy, leaning out the window watching, yelled, "Take it easy, baby. It was just some ofay kids. I think they're gettin' in on the action."

"You sure, Teddy, you sure?" Snake asked anxiously as he pulled out onto the street.

"Slow it down, Snake. We got it made," Teddy replied as he twisted around in the seat and resumed a normal position. "I saw a couple of them 'wood's come out with televisions."

Snake slowed down and began to breathe easier. Teddy turned and examined their loot. "We got it made, baby," he exclaimed happily. "We got four color TVs and six black and whites."

"We ain't got no problem, then. We got enough to buy the dope, plus get a flat to deal it from," Snake answered softly.

# 12

Porky walked up and down his flat. He would pace a while, then sit down, but before ten minutes had passed he was back up again. He stared out the window, hoping he would see his Cadillac pull up. He couldn't remember ever having seen it like this before. Ever since the bust in New York of over a hundred kilos of dope, the problem of copping dope bad gotten worse and worse. His connection had been out for over a week now, but he had been managing to hold on somehow.

Porky stopped his pacing again to stare out the window impatiently. Smokey had been gone since early morning with Big Ed driving, trying to run down some dope. He wasn't worried about the five thousand dollars of his money she had. What none of the addicts knew was that Smokey was really his legal wife in addition to being his connect. She took care of all his personal business. When he sent money to the bank, she took it. The thought of the fifty thousand dollars he had soaked away didn't bring him any satisfaction. Porky didn't deal for the money anymore. It was nice, true enough, but he loved the power it brought him. The life or death power. He held the future of every dopefiend who came through his door in the palm of his hand. If he wanted to kill them, all he would have to do was give them some strychnine. To give a drug addict a hotshot was the simplest thing in the world.

He saw two carloads of dopefiends pull up in front of his house. His lips pulled back in a sneer and he turned from the window in disgust. Everywhere he looked there were dopefiends. His apartment was full of them, sitting around waiting, more impatient than he was. They were on the floor, sitting against the wall; the room was full of them.

Tess was sitting near the door on the floor with one of her girlfriends. "Tess," Porky snarled, "go down and tell them fools ain't nothing happening."

She got up from the floor and did as she was bidden. She was well aware that now was not the time to get smart. Like most of the other addicts, she figured that, if any of the pushers scored some time soon, it would be Porky. They all knew Smokey was out trying to get down, and with the oil burner she had on her back there was little doubt about her taking care of business. If there was any dope in the city, she would find it.

Before the addicts could reach the front porch Tess stepped out of the door in front of them. "Y'all might as well save yourselves a trip, 'cause Porky ain't got no stuff." As they stopped and stared up at her stupidly, she quickly added, "He also said to tell you he ain't got no room for y'all to lay around and wait, so keep on pushing."

As the crowd of junkies turned around to leave, someone in the crowd called her a bitch. Tess just stared without anger. She knew how they felt because she felt the same way. Her nose and eyes were running, while her bowels had become undependable. When she sat down, she felt like getting up, and as soon as she got up, she felt like lying down. Hot and cold flashes ran through her, while under her skin it felt like small insects were crawling around.

As the junkies piled into the car to continue their endless search, Tess noticed the look of desperation on their faces and knew that it was a mirror image of her own. They would continue searching for the rest of the night and the following day until they found what they sought. They were now at the point where they would shoot morphine, take yellow jackets, or Nembutal capsules, anything to take the edge off. Paregoric would help those who knew how to cook off the alcohol and strain out the camphor. Then it would be fit to inject intravenously. Many of those upstairs had already bought cough medicine with cocaine in it, while the few fortunate ones had come with some delaudid, and others had some precious dionine. Methadone pills were selling for three dollars a pill, number tens, while number fives were bringing two dollars.

Tess's stomach lurched as she gaped at the long midnight blue Cadillac pulling up out front. "Oh God," she murmured under her breath, "let it be them."

Before the car had completely stopped at the curb, the back door flew open and Smokey came hurtling out. The chilling winter wind whirled around her, tossing light snowflakes over the front of her dress. Her thin fall coat spread out behind her like a cape as she ran toward the front of the house. There was nothing slow-moving about her now; she moved with the speed of a young doe.

A car full of addicts pulled up behind the Cadillac. They had seen Big Ed driving Porky's car up on the main street and had followed, in the blind hope that Smokey had been lucky enough to break the panic. If anyone could, they believed it would be one of Porky's connections. Big Ed and the other doorman riding shotgun hurriedly followed Smokey toward the house. The sight of so many addicts only clinched the idea in the other addicts' minds. Drug addicts didn't make it a point to run unless something really important was up.

Tess spotted the package Smokey clutched in her hand, then turned and ran up the stairs, one step in front of the rushing Smokey.

The occupants of the two cars had been seen by Porky from the front window. He cursed as he motioned towards the door. "Goddamn dope-fiends running all over the street like they're crazy. One of you get the fuckin' door open before the foolish sonsabitches break it down."

The sound of thundering footsteps running up the stairs was a rarity, because at any other time Porky would have had a fit about someone running up his stairway. Because of the panic, though, he realized it was impossible to restrict such abandoned behavior. The addicts in the apartment looked as though someone had given them a new lease on life. Before they had been sprawled out on the floor listlessly. Now, as the news spread that Smokey was back, they all sat up, losing their bewildered look, caught up in the anticipation of drugs being plentiful again.

Terry, sitting on the couch beside Minnie, asked in a hushed voice, "Do you really think they copped?"

They had been waiting for over thirty hours now, neither woman leaving her spot on the couch, afraid that if they left they couldn't get back in. Minnie had been hoping and praying that

Smokey would cop, but she was afraid now to become too excited, aware that if Smokey hadn't copped, she would have to commit herself to a hospital or kick cold turkey.

Smokey came through the door and headed straight toward the bedroom. The addicts surrounded Tess, asking questions. The word spread through the room that Smokey had copped. Big Ed made his way across the room and entered the bedroom, closing the door behind him.

Inside the bedroom, everything was already laid out on the bed. A large mirror with a sifter lying beside it was already in place for use when the time came. Small amounts of milk sugar had been meticulously measured out and placed out of the way on the edge of the mirror.

By the time Big Ed entered the bedroom he had to step over Smokey's coat in the middle of the floor, where she had dropped it in her hurry to reach the bed. She was propped up on the edge of the bed sifting heroin through the sifter. She ran the drug through until there were no more lumps in it. She continued to strain it until she had it just the way she wanted it.

As Smokey worked, her mind was busy. It had been a long time since they had allowed themselves to get caught like this, but it was one of the hazards of being a drug user. Whenever a really big bust went down, the users in the streets paid dearly for it. The panic had reached nationwide proportions. She smiled to herself as she thought how lucky she was to have a man like Porky. He had made sure she would have some kind of dope to keep her sickness off.

"How many will it take?" Porky asked impatiently from the side of the bed.

"It won't take much more than a four cut and still be anything," Smokey replied, not stopping her hands moving smoothly. Porky opened the envelope she had given him, quickly counted the money, then counted it again. "Hell, it ain't but three grand left in here, Smoke."

"The bastard charged a grand for each piece, Porky," she answered, not bothering to look up. The thought never entered her mind that he would doubt her, and he didn't.

"Goddamn, that's twice as much as this pure is worth." Porky quickly calculated up the price he had paid for the dope. "Ed, you go out there and tell them junkies that I ain't selling nothing but twenty-dollar packs. You can also tell them that, if they ain't but one goddamn penny short, they can't cop."

His barrage of words didn't surprise Smokey in the least. She knew him so well she could have bet he would raise the price. It was all a matter of business, though. They had had to pay double price for the junk, so quite naturally they would have to up their price.

"Send Dave in here to pack up this shit, too," Porky yelled at Big Ed as he went out the door.

Smokey finished cutting the dope, walked over

to the dresser, and took out her works and cooker. She removed a small spoon from the drawer. "You goin' use the ten-dollar spoon, Porky, to measure up the twenty-dollar packs?"

"You goddamn right I am," he growled. "What did you think I was going to use, bitch, a quarter spoon?"

She ignored his outburst and went back to the bed to fill her cooker up with stuff. Dave entered the room without knocking. He was short and thin, a brown-skinned man nearing fifty. His hair was almost completely gray, while his thin mustache was speckled with gray.

Porky picked up two album covers and dropped them on the bed. He sat down across from the pile of dope. "I want you to pack up all that stuff, Dave, and I'll give you a blow when you finish. Don't let your fingers get sticky," he added, " 'cause I'll be right here on the case."

Big Ed stuck his head in the door. "You want me to start collecting some of this money, Porky? Everybody out here keeps trying to push it in my hand. Seems they got the idea they might not cop before you run out."

"Not yet, Ed. Tell them fools we ain't goin' run out no time soon, so rest easy." Porky wished the words were true as he said them. He knew the dope would last a while because he had ten pieces, but as big as his business was he'd be out of dope in less than two days.

Gee Gee came into the room in time to answer

the phone. "It's Snake on the line, Porky. He wants to know if you're all right."

With a grotesque smile, revealing his yellow teeth, Porky reached for the phone. "Well, well, well. If it ain't the big dope dealer himself. What can I do for you, king Snake?"

On the other end of the line Snake could feel the blood rushing to his head. Instantly the thought ran through his mind: *They got some dope.*

"You all right, Porky?" he asked, unable to control the pleading note in his voice.

All at once Porky began to laugh. The feeling of importance filled his very being. He could almost reach out and touch the vibration of fear in Snake's voice. He knew Snake was afraid of being denied the opportunity to cop from this more influential dealer. For a moment Porky toyed with the idea of just turning him down, but his capricious disposition, mixed with his greed, was too much.

"The only thing I can let you have, Snake," Porky said, his agile mind adding swiftly, "is a piece of cut stuff."

On the other end of the line Snake caught his breath. A piece of stuff! He hadn't hoped for such good luck. He glanced around the room at the addicts watching him. He could almost make his money back off of them. "How much, Porky?"

"Four hundred dollars for one piece," Porky replied, then added, making sure he had his fish caught in the net, "I'm selling ten-dollar packs for twenty dollars right now, Snake, so you shouldn't have no problem gettin' your money back out of it." Porky mentally counted up his initial investment. After spending one thousand for a piece of pure, cutting it four times, which gave him five pieces, selling one of those cut pieces for four hundred, he was left with four pieces of cut dope. At that rate, he would have paid six hundred dollars for four pieces of cut dope. When he broke that down, it would come out to about one hundred and fifty dollars a piece. Not bad at all, he reasoned, as he waited for Snake's reply.

After a short debate with Teddy, Snake hurriedly answered. "We're on our way, Porky. Hold that piece for us." He hung the phone up and spoke to one of the dopefiends in his overcrowded apartment. "If anyone comes to the door, Jake, tell them I went to cop. I'll be back in an hour." He hesitated for a moment. "Don't let nobody else in though, until we get back. Just tell them everything's goin' to be all right."

Teddy spoke up from the door. "You better tell them that it ain't goin' be no more ten-dollar packs. All we goin' have is twenty-dollar packs, or three caps for fifteen dollars."

They left the apartment together. Neither man was sick; they had bought some paregoric earlier and cooked it up. "That bastard is sure sticking it to us, Snake. Four hundred fat ones for some cut stuff. How much you figure we can make out of it?"

Snake remained silent, counting to himself. "The way I got it figured, Teddy, is that we can get at least twenty packs out of a fourth of dope. All right, we goin' get four fourths out of a piece, so that should give us at least eighty packs. Eighty packs at twenty dollars a pack should bring us somewhere near sixteen hundred. I'm not counting what we would use ourselves, but there's plenty room."

They climbed in the late model car Snake had bought since they started dealing. It wasn't brand new, but it was only two years old and still ran smoothly. Snake started the motor up, but before he could back up, a car full of addicts pulled up beside him.

"You all right?" one of the dopefiends yelled out of the back window.

"I'll be back with some scag in less than an hour," Snake replied.

"You sure, Snake? We been hearing that same bullshit for the past two days now. Every-goddamn-body will be right back, but we don't never see nobody coming in the door with it."

"Don't worry," Snake answered. "I ain't just talkin' out the side of my neck. I done already called, and the stuff is there. Only thing about it is that it's goin' cost twenty dollars for a ten-dollar pack, and we ain't givin' up no credit."

A noisy chorus of voices answered him. Most of the addicts were angry over the extravagant price, but their mutterings died down as the thought sank in that Snake really was on his way to pick up some dope.

The driver pulled the car out of the way so Snake could get past. Before he could get away from the curb, a cab pulled up beside him with two women in it, one white and one colored.

"Snake," the colored woman yelled. "You all right, honey?" she asked while wiping her nose with the back of her hand.

"Yeah, Shirley. Everything sweet as it could be." Before he had finished speaking, she was climbing out of the cab. Her partner paid the driver and jumped out on the other side. Snake raised his eyebrows at the other girl.

"She's all right," Shirley said, coming up beside the car. "We work out of the same hotel. She left her man a couple of days ago, so we been staying together."

"Do she use?" Teddy asked from the passenger side of the car.

"Carrie," Shirley said as soon as her girlfriend walked up. "That little man over there wants to know if you use."

Carrie laughed lightly. She was tall and blonde, with a long keen nose and pale blue eyes. As she leaned down, Teddy could tell she used because her eyes were beginning to run and she kept sniffling.

"Fuck all that shit," Snake said and opened the car door. "Come on, we got business to take care of."

Both women climbed into the back of the car. Teddy turned around in the seat and stared at Shirley. She was a tall, light-colored woman with a dazzling smile. She had been on stuff for over a year, but it had not caught up with her yet. She still had a beautiful shape and was able to make quite a bit of money whoring out of the large white hotels downtown. She was one of the few black women Teddy had ever seen with freckles.

"Your friend work downtown with you, Shirley?" he asked as Snake pulled away from the curb.

"Yah, baby, and she's the only cool 'fay down there, too." Shirley lit a cigarette before adding, "Would you believe that a good whore like her ain't got no man either?"

Without turning his head Snake growled. "You two whores ain't nothing but sisters under the skin, Shirley. What you got planned? You choose me and Carrie ends up with Teddy?" Both women laughed.

Now that the fear of not copping was over, both women started to relax. "What's wrong with that, Snake?" Shirley asked.

"Nothing, except I know that you're a bag-chasing bitch, and it looks like your partner might be following in your footsteps," Snake answered coldly. Ever since they started dealing, women had been no problem. Each night they would have to run the female drug addicts out before they went to sleep.

He turned on the block where Porky lived and parked. The street was jammed with cars. Everywhere he looked, he could see a car full of addicts waiting for their buyer to come back.

Teddy cursed. "Damn, you don't have to worry about whether or not Porky got any stuff. Just look at the cars. Man, every dopefiend in the city must be at his house."

"I better hurry up before he changes his mind, too," Snake answered as he climbed out. "You goin' wait until I get back, Teddy?"

"Yah, man. I think I'll keep the women company. You ain't goin' shoot no stuff while you're in there, are you?"

The question went unanswered because Snake was already on his way across the street. When he finally got inside the apartment he almost had to fight his way through the milling crowd. Addicts were everywhere.

Minnie and Terry were still in the apartment. They had finally got waited on. Minnie split the twenty-dollar pack. Terry stared at her small amount. She realized that it would not be enough to take her sickness off if she snorted it.

Minnie read her mind. "You better get you a set of works, honey, if you want to feel that dope."

For a moment a feeling of being utterly lost washed over her. In the back of her mind she knew she was getting ready to go over the last barrier. There was no way around it; she had to get rid of her junk sickness, and the dope she had was not enough. As she stared at it, she wondered if it would be enough even if she shot it.

"Could I use that set of works you had?" she asked the addict sitting next to her.

He removed a neatly wrapped bundle from his coat pocket. "Just be sure you clean them out when you finish using them," he said and held his set of tools out to her.

When Snake passed the couch he stopped for a moment and stared as an addict hit Terry in the arm. As he pressed the dropper, her eyes closed. Snake walked on past. It was just another step down the line for her, he thought. Not surprising, really. Just about any user would eventually start shooting instead of snorting, if he had any veins to go in. In the long run, it was a whole lot cheaper to shoot than to snort. He reached the bedroom door and knocked.

"Who the hell is that now?" a voice yelled from the other side of the door.

Snake tried the door; when it opened under his hand, he walked in. "What's happening, Porky, what's the real deal?" he yelled across the bedroom.

Porky was busy trying to hit his woman in the groin. "What's wrong with you, nigger, don't you believe in waitin' until someone lets you in a door?" he snarled. The day's events had just about worn Porky out. He had never seen the likes of this before. His two dogs stood up and growled as Snake walked across the floor.

"You still got that piece for me, ain't you, Porky?" he asked nervously.

Porky nodded towards Big Ed who was standing in front of a mirror trying to hit in the neck. "He got it. If I had known it was going to be like this, Snake, I'd never have sold that piece to you."

Before Porky could change his mind, Snake pulled out his money and started counting out the four hundred dollars. He walked over to the dresser and laid the money in front of Big Ed. "You think you'll have enough to sell me another piece tomorrow, Porky?"

"Hell no!" Porky exclaimed. "Fuck no! You're gettin' a goddamn break on this fourth now; you think I'll go for the same fucking thing again tomorrow?"

Pulling the needle out of Smokey's groin, Porky cursed. "This goddamn bitch ain't got no veins nowhere. I should make her take her funky ass to the hospital and kick."

"How about tryin' and find a hit for me, Snake?" Smokey asked, her voice rising slightly. Her hand shook as she held the works out toward him. "You might be able to hit that same vein as the last time you hit me. I ain't been back in there since, 'cause I don't let just anybody hit me under the arm." She pulled her dress down and stood up.

For a brief moment Snake wanted to say no, but after looking in her face he knew he couldn't turn her down. He waited until she removed her blouse and raised her arm. As he probed for the vein with his finger, he thought cruelly to himself, at least the bitch changed bras since the last time. After about ten minutes, he finally hit a vein. The dark blood that filled up the dropper told him he had a hit. Before the works had time to clog up, he pushed down slightly on the bulb, and the blood and dope disappeared in the hidden vein under a mass of dark hair.

Before Snake reached the car Porky had received a long-distance call from Chicago. He was now beginning to get some action on all the calls he had made in the past few days. He talked quietly into the receiver for a few moments, shook his head in agreement, then hung up.

He walked slowly towards the door and opened it. "Everybody out," he said. As Big Ed passed him, he whispered, "Get ready, Ed; we'll be leaving for Chicago in the next few minutes."

As soon as the room emptied, he smiled gleefully at his woman. "Get me six thousand dollars together, Smoke; I'm gettin' ready to ride out, and when I get back, we'll bust this panic wide open."

Smokey moved off the bed with more speed than she ordinarily displayed. "Who was that, Porky, Sid?"

"That's right, baby. He said I could get all the P,

pure, I wanted, at six hundred apiece. He thinks he's charging me top dollar for it, but I'll make so much money off it, we'll be nigger rich when I get finished."

Smokey walked over to the corner nearest to the bed, where the dogs slept. She pulled back a floor rug that the dogs lay on most of the day. Next, she removed three boards from the floor, then pulled out a small tin box. Removing a key from around her neck, she opened it. "You still got that three thousand I brought back earlier, Porky, in your pocket, so all you'll need is three grand more."

"Better give me four, girl. You never can tell what might happen when you're in Chicago." He continued to dress as he talked over his shoulder to her. "Count up how much we got left in the box, too. If it's too much, you better get ready to make a trip to the bank."

Smokey sat down on the floor with her back against the wall between the dogs. "That don't leave but two thousand with me, Porky. I ain't counted up what we done made so far today, but it ain't hardly over a grand."

His eyes caught hers briefly as he dropped his pants. "You better hold out a piece of stuff for yourself, in case I should be longer than what I plan." He slipped on the pants to his suit and put on a gold silk shirt. The suit he wore was very expensive, a black silk mohair. After dressing, he stuck a large cigar in his mouth. Porky actually dis-

186

liked smoking them but thought they went with his big-shot appearance.

He stuck two more cigars in his pocket. "I should be back before daylight in the morning, but if I ain't, don't worry. Oh yeah, if anybody wants to buy a piece of stuff, sell it for five hundred. You can call Snake and Teddy up and let them know they can cop another piece, only it will cost them an extra hundred."

Porky walked over to the closet, pushed two of Smokey's minks aside, and pulled out his cashmere overcoat.

Smokey got up off the floor and went to the closet. She pulled out three hat boxes and set them on the floor. In each hat box there was a Knox One Hundred, each one specifically made to order.

Smokey took a sincere interest in seeing that her man was dressed right, and he did the same thing in regards to her. They shared a tacit understanding when it came to clothes. Though neither really cared about dressing, they had just about everything a person could want in their closets.

Porky walked over to the bedroom window and glanced out, trying to gauge the weather. "It might snow while we're on the highway," he said offhandedly, not really speaking to her but voicing his thoughts out loud. It was already starting to get dark, though it was still early in the evening.

Smokey held out Porky's hat to him. He broke the stingy brim down and set the hat ace-deuce across his head. While he was adjusting it in the mirror, Smokey stuck her hand under the pillow and came out with a small .38 derringer pistol. She silently held the gun out to him. He stuck it down in his huge waistline, his enormous stomach completely covering the small pistol.

Big Ed and Dave led the way down the stairs, with Porky following them closely like some monstrous, prehistoric beast.

Outside, the chilling wind tugged at their clothes as they made their way toward the long Cadillac brougham sitting at the curb. Porky climbed in the back, taking up most of the seat, while his gunmen got in the front. He waved at Smokey, who was watching him silently from the window, and the large car leaped away from the curb.

Five hours later, they roared in off the highway. Chicago's lights seemed to wink at them as Big Ed steered the car off the freeway and into the heart of a black ghetto. Porky gave him directions from the backseat until finally they pulled up in front of a motel. Dave jumped out and ran over to check them in.

He came back dangling a key. "How long you figure we goin' be over here, Porky?" he asked as he climbed back in the car.

"That's for me to know, nigger, and for you to find out," Porky replied sharply.

Big Ed drove the car up the driveway of the

motel until he found their unit, then parked in front of the door. They all piled out. Dave removed a small overnight bag from the glove compartment and carried it in. The motel room was similar to motel rooms all over the country. Small, neat, with a dresser and tiny kitchenette.

Porky dropped his coat on the bed and picked up the phone. He gave the unit number of the motel to the person he called and hung up. Twenty minutes later, they heard the sound of a car pulling up beside theirs.

Porky motioned Dave to go into the bathroom, while Big Ed continued to measure out small amounts of milk sugar on the dresser with a ten-dollar spoon. Porky peeped out the window as someone knocked softly. Satisfied that it was the right person, Porky opened the door.

Sid walked in with a small weasel-faced man following him. Sid was short and fat, with a jet-black complexion. He twisted a cigar around in his mouth as his small pig eyes swiftly scanned the room. He noticed the partially opened bathroom door. "Who the fuck you got in there, Porky?" he asked sharply, his hand slipping under his overcoat.

The question caught Porky by surprise. "Just a little precaution to make sure I don't get ripped off while I'm over here," Porky answered as he removed the money from his pocket and laid it on the dresser.

Sid ignored the money. "Get him out here!" he commanded harshly. He stepped back against the wall. His bodyguard leaned against the door, his hand conspicuously bulging from his overcoat.

"Dave, Dave! Get the fuck out here!" Porky yelled, wiping the sweat from his brow with the back of his hand.

The door opened quickly and Dave walked out. His face twitched nervously. He could feel the muscles contract but couldn't control them. Guns and violence were something he had an innate fear of; he knew better than anyone that he was completely out of place trying to act the part of a gunman.

Sid nodded towards his bodyguard. The man moved quickly to the bathroom and kicked open the door. Finding it empty, he turned back and faced the room.

With a cold smile that never touched his eyes, Sid said, "Just checking, Porky. I wouldn't want to walk into no well-planned stickup either." The room was full of hostility. Neither person trusted the other. Sid picked up the money and counted the bills quickly with a sureness that comes only to those used to handling large amounts of money.

Again he nodded. His gunman moved to the window and pulled back the drapes. He removed a small flashlight from his pocket and blinked it twice.

Porky's heart skipped a beat. There was fear inside the room; everyone knew that the first wrong step would fill the small bedroom with violence.

"It's just my woman, Porky, bringing the stuff in," Sid explained quietly. "I don't take no chances with people from out of state. I know you know what I'm talking about."

It didn't need explaining, Porky knew just what he meant. His city was beginning to get a reputation as a city full of informers. He stuck a cigar in his mouth, his stomach swelling with knots of fear.

The knock came almost unexpectedly. Big Ed moved over to the door and glanced out. His hand clutched a .38 automatic. "It better be a god-damn woman," he growled. He relaxed and opened the door, holding the gun down so she wouldn't see it.

A small, light-brown-skinned woman entered. She was dressed expensively. At the sight of Porky, she hesitated for a brief second, shocked by his hugeness. Her three-hundred-pound Sid was dwarfed by comparison. Porky looked to her like an expensively dressed gorilla smoking a cigar.

"Give me that stuff, woman!" Sid ordered. "I got ten pieces, Porky, that you can put a six on."

Porky took the stuff from her outstretched hand and held it out to Big Ed, who pocketed his gun and carried the dope to the dresser. He opened one of the packages and filled up his ten-dollar spoon and sprinkled the dope on top of six piles of milk sugar which he had moved to the center of the dresser top. He sifted the dope and milk through his sifter over eight times until they were thoroughly mixed together. Then he measured out a ten-dollar spoon and dropped it in a cooker. Dave started cooking the dope up for him as he tied up his arm. Quickly he found a vein, filled the dropper up with dope and hit.

Impatiently Porky waited for his judgment. "Well," Porky asked, unable to hold back any longer, "is the shit worth it?"

Big Ed closed his eyes and wet his lips as though he were tasting the dope. "It ain't nothing to write home about, Porky, but it will sell. It's just about as good as that stuff we got now."

Everybody in the room seemed to have been holding his breath waiting for the decision. Sid laughed, relieving some of the tension in the air. "Is that good enough for you, Porky?" he asked as his fingers closed over the money.

Staring at all the loose dope on the dresser, Dave got excited and started to fart loudly. Porky laughed. "That's one way I can always tell dope, Sid," he said in an amiable tone. "Every time that nigger gets around some dope, he starts to fart."

Both men laughed agreeably as they watched Dave rush to the empty cooker and push a small amount of the dope into it and drop water on top of it. Sid picked up the money and started toward the door.

"Anytime you want to get down, Porky, just give me a ring. It's nice doing business with you." His bodyguard peeped out the door first, while Sid gave the envelope full of money to his woman to carry. It was just another precaution he was taking, one Porky was quite familiar with. If anyone got busted, she would be found with the money, and it was much simpler to fight a sales case on your woman than one on yourself. Even if the woman was found guilty and sent to prison, she was easy to replace.

As soon as the door closed behind them, Porky wrapped up the ten pieces of pure he had bought. "Get them works cleaned; we're leaving!" he snapped. "That's yours and Dave's, Ed," he said, pointing towards the small amount of dope they had cut up to test.

He waited until Ed had picked up his dope. "Let's go!" Porky yelled, nervous now that the business had been completed. Dave snatched the works out of his arm, wishing he could have jacked off the works a couple more times. He rinsed out the works quickly. Porky and Big Ed were already at the door.

"Here," Porky said, handing Big Ed all of the dope. "Bring your goddamn ass on now, Dave, or we goin' leave you in this fuckin'-ass motel."

Dave ran out the door behind them. "You want me to turn the key in first, Porky?"

Porky climbed in the back of his brougham.

"Goddamn the key," he snarled. "They can keep the deposit and shove it up their ass for all I care." He settled back in the comfortable cushions of his car. In less then ten minutes they were back on the highway. They hadn't been in Chicago an hour, and now they were on their way back home with a car full of dope.

# 13

The wind rattled her windows and she could feel a draft coming through the broken pane where papers covered the jagged hole. The noise from her single radiator had kept her awake most of the night; the steam hissed constantly and the pipes rattled loudly. When she became fully awake, her first thoughts were fear-ridden. It was not the first time she had awoken with this nagging feeling of dread for the coming day, nor would it be the last.

Terry rolled over and sat up. Her blanket slipped down to the foot of her bed, and as she tossed back the sheet her lovely breasts could be seen through the transparent nightgown. Only there was no one to admire her in her lonely room. Her nose was running as though she had a cold. But it was not from a cold; it was past time for Terry to have her morning fix. She sniffed as she climbed out of the bed and made her way stiff-legged to the dresser. She fumbled around, searching for old used pieces of cotton. After she found five of them, she put them in a cooker and poured water on them. She lit two matches and held them under the cooker until the water got hot. She pulled out her dropper and stuck it in the cooker, drawing up the stuff, hoping and praying that it would be enough to get her sickness off. After shooting the water into her arm, she cursed angrily. It hadn't been enough. She was still sick.

Suddenly there was a loud knock on her door. She could hear Minnie hollering on the other side. "Wake up, Terry; somebody's taking your car away!"

Terry ran to the door, then turned around and ran back and grabbed her coat off the only chair in the room. She put it on and ran out of the room, following Minnie, running barefooted. They got outside just in time to see a tow truck pulling away from the curb. She stopped as the icy snow began to freeze around her bare feet. A sob escaped from her as she watched her car disappear down the street.

"Who do you think it was?" Minnie asked brokenheartedly. It was a deadly blow to her, losing that car. For the past two months she had come to rely upon the transportation. Her stomach had become so large from her pregnancy that it was almost impossible for her to catch a trick. Her only chance of making money had been when Terry took her around to the shopping centers to shoplift.

Both women stared after the car dumbfounded. They stood in the street watching long after it disappeared, as though some freak chance of fate would bring it back. Terry was openly crying now, tears running down her cheeks.

She happened to turn and look up to find Porky's evil face leering out of his window. He had known her car was being repossessed even before she had.

He licked his lips as he watched her from his window. Slowly he stuck his tongue out at her, knowing she understood what he meant. He watched as her head jerked up and fire leaped from her eyes. Some of the old arrogance was still in her, but he knew it wouldn't last long. Just wait until the junkie sickness hit her, then he'd see just how proud she would be.

"What we goin' do, Minnie?" she asked childishly as she retraced her steps back towards the hotel. "I ain't even got nothing to wake up on."

Minnie took one last look down the deserted street. "I ain't either, Terry. I had a little left from last night, but I shot that this morning before I went outside."

They walked side by side into the hotel. "Porky

ain't goin' give us no credit unless you give him some sex, Terry, so asking him for credit is one wasted effort."

The enormity of her problem began to penetrate her consciousness. "Ain't no sense thinkin' about asking Teddy to give us some credit," Terry said, " 'cause since he copped that white girl, he don't even want to talk to me." The mere thought of Teddy aroused her anger. "Anyway, I wouldn't ask that little sonofabitch for nothing if I was dying."

"Well then, what we goin' do?" Minnie asked, repeating her question.

Minnie led the way into her room and they sat on the bed. "Terry, I know how much you dislike the idea, but ain't but two things we can do." She waited for a minute to make sure she had Terry's attention. "We can both try to get committed in a hospital, and that ain't too likely, or we can go up on the street and try and stop a trick."

At the mention of selling her body, Terry's face twisted into a frown. Before she could comment, Minnie rushed on. "We ain't got no other choice, Terry. Either you can wait until you're real sick, girl, and by then it ain't going to make you no difference about turning no tricks, or go and do it now."

Terry's conscience set up a small warning. She could see herself slowly retrogressing. Each week it seemed as though she would end up breaking another principle. Soon all of her little morals would be gone, and then she wondered what would she be—nothing. The thought of trying to kick entered her mind, but just as quickly she rejected it on the grounds that she was too sick today. Maybe tomorrow she'd get up early and try to find a hospital. But today, she would have to have one more do.

Minnie began to sense her surrender and pushed her point home. "It ain't as bad as some people think, Terry. I'll show you how to hold your legs so you won't get female trouble." Minnie waited eagerly for Terry's reply. Everything depended on Terry; Minnie knew she had become too large to make money herself.

There was a hardness in Terry's voice as she answered. "I guess one or two won't kill me." She didn't bother to explain to Minnie that the only man she'd had relations with was Teddy. And that had only been on three different occasions. She knew that her reluctance in sex was not because of her being frigid or anything like that but simply that she had never wanted to have children out of wedlock.

Maybe I've always been too old-fashioned, she reasoned with herself as she got up and started towards the door. "I'm going to get dressed, Minnie. I won't be but a few minutes."

Minnie tried to hide the pleasure she felt. Now everything would be all right, she reasoned. Once

Terry, with her looks, learned how to turn tricks, it wouldn't be hard for her to support both their habits.

With slow deliberation, Terry put on her clothes. She took her time and made up her face so that she looked her best. Next she slipped on a pair of high black boots that matched the black miniskirt she wore under her tan minicoat. Her beautiful legs were displayed to perfection. When she stepped out of the room she looked like anything but a dopefiend.

After Minnie showed her how to hold her legs, they started out the door. "If you should get a trick that wants some head, Terry, it's easier than having him jump up and down on your stomach."

Terry stopped in the hallway and put her hands on her hips. "If you're talking about me putting my mouth down there on some man, you've got another think coming."

Dumbfounded, Minnie stared at her. "Well, I was just mentioning it to you. Some of them want you to go that way."

Terry's nature was becoming harder every day. Her voice was harsh and cold as she stared straight at Minnie. "I hope you don't think you're going to be out there just supervising, 'cause that's the last thing I need. I don't see nothing wrong with your head, it's only your belly that's swollen up big as a house."

With a lightheartedness that she didn't feel, Minnie tried to laugh. "Oh girl, I'm planning to take care of whatever business you can't handle."

It was early in the day when they reached the corner. Terry found out it was harder than she thought to sell one's body. They had been out on the corner for over an hour, but still neither one of them had broke luck. At first Terry had been ashamed to yell at the passing cars with white men in them, but as the morning wore on and her monkey began to act up, she found herself whistling and yelling with more vigor each time.

Finally a car slowed down and turned the corner. Terry ran down the street after it as though she had been doing this all her life. The man behind the steering wheel was white and heavyset, with a large gut. After they talked for a few minutes he agreed to spend twenty dollars with her. She was the most attractive whore he had ever seen on this street. She climbed in the car and directed him back to her hotel. When they entered, the old woman in the caretaker's apartment smiled her toothless smile at her as they went up the stairs.

When they entered her room, Terry stood nervously against the door. She could feel the butterflies acting up in her stomach. She gritted her teeth. "Well, I've come this far," she told herself, "so there's no turning back now."

The john removed twenty dollars from his wallet and held it out to her. "Here you go, girlie," he said in a nasal sounding voice.

She accepted the money from his outstretched hand and put it in her bra. "You want me to take off everything?" she asked in a frightened voice.

The trick seemed surprised. "Uh, yes. Do what you want to do," he replied, sitting on the end of the bed and watching her closely as she began to undress. He caught his breath as she came out of her dress. Those golden brown thighs were the loveliest he had ever had the delightful opportunity of laying his eyes on.

He stared in fascination. "My God!" he uttered hoarsely. Terry stood before him in only her bra and panties. He quickly began to shed his clothing. She stretched out on the bed waiting, trepidation in her heart. The only thing that stopped her from running out of the room was her terror of the horror of drug sickness.

The john climbed on the bed beside her. She closed her eyes as she felt his hands fumbling with her panties. As though in a dream she could feel him tugging them down over her hips, then around her legs, and finally down to her ankles. She opened her legs slightly as she felt him climbing between them.

Suddenly she felt something wet on her stomach. Next it moved down to her thighs, then she felt his hands parting her legs. As she opened them, she could feel his lips moving coarsely towards her vagina. Almost immediately she felt his warm, hot tongue invade her vulva. Her whole body turned a dark red as she blushed, embarrassed by her first experience of oral sex. His darting tongue started a tingling sensation inside her womb as it leaped from one tender spot to another. Against her will, she could feel her legs opening wider. Her hips began to move in jerks. Suddenly, without warning, an orgasm shook her whole body. She jerked and twisted from side to side as her sexual excitement reached a climax.

The john raised himself up quickly and inserted his organ in her. Just as soon as he entered her, she could feel him discharging within her body.

After she had washed up, the trick asked about going again. For a moment Terry debated with herself about putting him out, but the thought of more money won out. After going through the same routine again the john got up and dressed, thirty-five dollars poorer.

Terry waited until he had left the building, with a promise to see her the following week, before she went down to Minnie's room. Minnie was standing in the hall waiting. "Damn, Terry, I thought he was going to stay up there with you forever, honey."

Terry flashed the twenty-dollar bill, already planning on using most of the money for her own habit. "He didn't stay up there that long, did he?"

With a pleased smile Minnie answered, "Not if he was spending that much money. It wasn't as bad as you thought it was, was it?"

"Not really," Terry answered quickly. "Minnie, would you run up to the store and get me some cigarettes and matches? I'll go over to Porky's and cop for us."

Slowly the smile left Minnie's face. "You goin' give me a blow, ain't you, Terry?" she asked in a pleading voice.

"Of course I'm going to give you a toot, honey. I just want you to run to the store for me, and when you get back I'll have you a ten-dollar pack waiting."

They went out the door together. Terry held a dollar bill toward Minnie. "Get some pop, too," she said. Terry watched Minnie waddle up the street. She thought coldly, "Minnie better get her mind together, 'cause I sure ain't about to try and keep up no two habits."

Porky opened the door and let her in. He smiled. "I see you done went into business for yourself, Terry," he said, leering. "I can spend more money with you, girl, than any three peckerwoods you pick up on the street, you keep that in mind."

Terry's eyes caught his in a calculating glance. "I don't feel in the mood for any copulating with dogs, Porky. Your taste runs in a very weird bag, baby. I don't think I'm able to handle it."

"Ain't no dogs involved in what I'm talking about, Terry. Just you and me," he said flatly.

"Let me get a half a fourth from you for twenty-five dollars then. Show me you like me a little," Terry said and pinched him on one of his fat cheeks.

Before he could reply, Smokey spoke up from the large chair she was sitting in. "The little bitch thinks she's playing on you, Porky." She said it loudly so the whole room could hear.

"Take care of your own business, bitch," Porky growled angrily, staring around the room at the addicts as if daring one of them to say something.

Smokey turned her back and continued trying to find a hit in one of her veins. Ever since the panic, she and Porky had gotten closer together. They had amassed a huge sum of money before the dope began to flow back into the city.

"Okay, Terry. I'll let you have a half a fourth for that. One of these days you and me are going to have one hell of a freak party, you can bet on that," Porky said.

Terry waited until Big Ed brought her the dope before finding some paper that had had dope in it before. She shook out a small amount, making sure it was less than what a ten-dollar pack would be, and wrapped it up the same as all of Porky's packs.

"Ain't you gettin' cute." Porky's loud laughter rang out. "I'll just bet that little amount is going to your smart-ass friend."

Her eyes narrowed slightly, but she continued to fold the tiny pack. "It ain't your concern one way or the other," she answered sharply. Terry finished folding it and got up. Big Ed let her out the door. As she passed him, he reached out and rubbed her ass.

"Your mammy should have taught you to keep your hands where they belong," she yelled over her shoulder as she continued down the stairs.

When she got out on the street Minnie was standing in the cold waiting for her. "Did you get that for me, Terry? Did you get it?" she asked in a frightened voice. Ever since Terry had left to cop without her, she had harbored the fear that Terry would return without any dope for her.

Without replying, Terry held out the tiny package to her.

Minnie snatched at the package. It was as though she couldn't really believe it was hers until she held it in her hand. "Thank you, honey. I'll pay you back for this, don't worry."

Shrugging her shoulders Terry led the way into the hotel. "I'll be in my room if you want me, Minnie," she said and ran up the stairs. She cooked up her do and hit in the vein in the back of her hand. Since she had just started shooting, Terry had no trouble finding a vein that would pay off. In time, if she kept using, the veins would become harder and harder to hit.

After shooting up part of her dope and cleaning up her works, Terry stretched out on the bed. She could feel the dope working. She lay back and stared at the ceiling as a warmth invaded her soul. It felt as though she were drifting in a sea of foam. Soon the foam enveloped her in a mist of well-being and her sordid surroundings became an illusion. Her world now became the world of dreams, devoid of fears, pleasing to the senses. As long as the dope she had on the dresser lasted, she would drift through an infinite time, bound-less, with no regard to past or future.

# 14

———

The snow continued to fall, bringing Terry much difficulty in her new profession. She cursed the snow, cursed Minnie, who had become a parasite, cursed Teddy, who had started her using. Again she mentally counted the money in her bra. No matter how many times she counted it, it wouldn't get past the fifteen-dollar mark until she turned another trick. She had enough to go in now and get a fix, but there was always the morning to worry about, and she had had enough of waking up sick.

A redheaded teenager blew his horn at her while pulling over to park. She ran over to the car before any of the other girls on the street could get to him.

She jumped in beside him. "Hi honey, you

looking for a girl?" she asked as she quickly put her hand on his leg and rubbed his thigh.

"Yeah," he gulped, his face turning red. He was young, with long red hair and freckles.

"How much can you spend, honey?" she asked softly, her hand running up higher on his leg.

"Just eight dollars," he managed to say.

"Honey," Terry dragged the word out as though it were a caress. "That ain't enough money to give no girl for making love to you. How you expect her to pay the hotel room and everything out of such a little amount of money?"

He hesitated for just a moment, the feel of her hand on his leg making up his mind. "I got five more dollars, but I need that to buy gas the rest of the week so I can go to school."

She removed her hand from his leg and pretended to reach for the door. "Well, if you think I ain't worth thirteen dollars, I might as well find me somebody who does." Again she reached for the door. "You can always borrow five dollars from one of your friends so you can go to school."

He blushed. "Well, I guess I can." He removed his wallet and gave her the money.

After sticking the money in her bra, she smiled. "This ain't really enough for us to be going to no hotel for, you know. Would you mind if we just did something in the car?"

He was too much out of his league to argue with her. "I don't care. I just don't know where to go."

Her sharp eyes had spotted two large bills in his wallet when he opened it. She quickly made up her mind to play for it. "Just pull around the corner and turn up in the nearest alley," she directed.

Following her directions, he drove until he found a deserted garage and pulled up behind it. He parked and shut off the motor.

"Should we get in the back?" he asked timidly. His hands were shaking as he tried to light a cigarette.

Terry removed the cigarette from his hand and lay up against the door. "Come on, honey, we ain't got all day." She squirmed down on the seat with her back against the door. With slow deliberation she began to pull up her skirt, tantalizing him with her smooth motions.

His breathing became harsh as he stretched out on the seat beside her. She loosened his pants and pushed them down around his hips. With her hand, she guided him into her, while her dexterous fingers removed his wallet. While he was engrossed in the sex act, she fumbled around until she found her coat and stuck the wallet down in it.

As soon as he finished, she jumped up. "I'll wash up outside," she said and leaped out of the car. Once her feet hit the ground she was running. She passed the garage flying and ran through the yard. When she reached the street she kept going straight across until she entered another alley. Her breath was coming in gasps, but she continued running.

Terry reached another street and started walking slowly, watching the traffic coming both ways. "Terry, Terry!" She turned to see Rico, a tall, light-complexioned. dopefiend, calling her from his front porch.

He beckoned for her to cross the street. She looked up and down the street closely before crossing. "What's the deal, Rico?" she yelled as she ran across the street and joined him.

"Hey baby," he said. "I just wanted you to know I got the bag now. If you want to cop, you can give me a little bit of that good business of yours."

Her sharp bitter laugh rang out. "Honey, stuff cost too much money for me to be wasting my bread on some flee," she said flamboyantly, proud of the sting she had just taken off.

"This ain't no flee, Terry. I'll tell you what, if you cop and don't like it, I'll give you your money back," he said before adding, "plus, baby, I got some dollar caps."

Since she wanted to get in off the street anyway, she followed him inside the flat. She stared around in surprise when she entered. The apartment was completely vacant of furniture. The only thing in the whole living room and dining room was an old mattress. The floor was covered with cigarette butts, and around the mattress were empty red caps.

"Goddamn, Rico, I thought I was living hard,

but you win hands down," she stated with honesty. Terry removed the wallet from her coat pocket and counted the money. "The lying son of a bitch," she said under her breath as she removed three twenties from the wallet.

Rico stared at her with interest. He had been watching her, and for a dopefiend she was becoming one hell of a whore. "What you do, baby? Take off a sting?"

She nodded her head in agreement as she stared around the large empty flat. "This could be one hell of a place, baby, if you'd fix it up."

"All it needs is a woman's touch," he said, dropping his hint.

Terry ignored him. She removed a ten-dollar bill from her bra. "Give me ten of them caps, Rico, Remember what you said, now. If it ain't nothing but flee, I get my money back."

"You'll like it," he said, grinning as he pulled out his bag. He had the pills in a bottle, so they would look like ordinary pills. It wouldn't fool anyone on the vice squad, although it might take in some rookies.

Terry took off her coat and sat down on the floor. She began opening up the caps, dropping them into a cooker. "How about getting me some clean water, honey?" she asked in a husky voice.

When Rico returned with the water, she had already dumped all the caps. She took the water from him, stuck her works inside the glass and drew up some water in the dropper. She squirted the water on top of the dope inside the cooker, laid the tools down and got out a book of matches. She held the flame under the cooker until the dope dissolved. Next, she picked up her works and drew some dope up into the dropper.

"You want me to hit you, Terry?" Rico asked politely.

She shook her head as she tied up her arm with a necktie. "Don't need no help," she replied, too busy to look up. Her eyes closed as the needle slipped into her vein.

Rico watched her closely. As soon as the dope took effect he was aware of it. "You like that, don't you?" he asked quietly.

She opened her eyes and stared at him. "It ain't nothing to write home about, but it will do," she replied sharply.

He waited a minute and then blurted out, "Why don't you go on and choose, Terry? If we hook up, ain't no stoppin' us."

Her laughter was harsh and cold. "Hook up! Nigger, you ain't able to manage your own money, so how the fuck you think you goin' be able to manage mine?"

His eyes narrowed in anger. For a moment she thought she had gone too far. He stared at her coldly for a minute. "All right, jazzy-ass bitch, when that monkey on your back gets too heavy for you to carry, remember me, 'cause I'll still be here dealing and waiting for a smart-ass bitch like you to come asking for credit."

"Okay, big man," she said, climbing to her feet. "When you get big, I'll come by and see if your offer is still open."

"Ain't no room in my house for no bag-chasing bitch, Terry," he answered, still angry. "The only bitch I'll accept is one that chooses me while I'm down. I damn sure ain't goin' need no dopefiend whore when I get on my feet, and you can bet big money on that."

Terry walked to the door and looked back. "Well, we can at least still be friends, can't we, Rico?" At the last minute she remembered that the little man with a dope bag today could be the big man with the bag tomorrow. The last thing she wanted to do was ruin something that might be beneficial to her in the near future.

"As long as we understand each other," he answered, following her to the door.

The snow was now falling with such consistency that it was difficult to see farther than ten feet in front of you. Even with the snow falling, Terry kept her eyes open, making sure she didn't run into the arms of the trick she had just beat. The dope she had just shot was all right, but she was on her way to Porky's, where she could buy a quantity of dope at discount prices. Porky had never given up the hope of getting her into his bed, and she meant to keep him that way. When she came to the main street where most of the girls worked, she took her time and looked carefully around before running across.

Porky sat in front of his window looking out. He had deliberately turned his back. Minnie had been there for the past hour begging for some credit. Her whining voice came to him sharply, piercing his ears.

"I done told you what you can do, bitch," he growled over his shoulder. "If you want some free dope, all you got to do is put on a freak show with one of my dogs."

"Oh Porky, I swear before Jesus, I'll pay you your money before this week is out." She dropped down on one knee and tugged at his shirt.

"Jesus hell, bitch! Jesus ain't goin' help you! The only help you're going to get is when you pray to Porky. Don't you understand that, bitch?" he yelled, snatching his shirt loose from her grip.

"Please, Porky, please. I'll pray to you if it will do any good," she begged, still on her knees.

One of Porky's gunmen walked over and pulled her away from him, dragging her roughly across the floor. "You want me to toss this bitch out the door, Porky?" he asked harshly.

"Just a minute!" Porky commanded, looking out the window. "Here comes your guardian angel in disguise, running. She must be done turning a trick, 'cause she's sure in a hurry," Porky said, then added under his breath, "The dirty bitch."

"Is that Terry, is that Terry?" Minnie screamed, breaking away from the man holding her.

When Terry entered, the first thing she saw was Minnie on the floor crying. Her heart went out to her pregnant friend. "What's the matter, honey, won't Porky give you no credit?"

"You can't get none either, bitch," he growled viciously from the window. "I'm tired of you dopefiends thinking I'm something soft."

Minnie screamed, almost hysterically, "The dirty sonofabitch wants me to fuck one of his dogs in front of everybody, before he'll give me any credit."

Porky laughed. "I always knew you'd do it. What's wrong? You just 'shamed to do it in front of everybody?" His diabolical laughter filled the room. "You funky dopefiend bitches kill me. You try to put up your little fronts, but you don't fool me. You'd suck a shaggy bear's dick if you could get a blow out of it." He added for emphasis, "Every one of you is more freakish than a frog with a mustache."

Terry snorted. "Ain't nobody in the world no more freakish than you," she said angrily.

Her girlfriend pulled at her coat sleeve. "Don't make him mad," Minnie pleaded. "You know he just likes to have his fun."

Porky roared. He sat back in his chair and laughed until tears ran down his cheeks. "As quiet as it kept, Terry," he said. "You can perform in the freak show with your friend. I got a dog for each one of you."

"You try holding your breath, Porky, just do

that until you see me put on a freak show for you." Her voice was cold; there was a harshness to it that wasn't there a month ago. She reached in her bra and pulled out her bankroll. "Can I buy some dope here, or has my money become funny?"

His eyes became hard as he stared at her. "Your money is good, Terry; just make sure you always have some, that's all."

She counted out fifty dollars and held it towards Big Ed. He took the money and counted it. "She ain't got but fifty dollars, Porky. Should I let her go for that?"

"Hell no! From now on that bitch there has got to spend top dollar, with her smart ass," Porky shouted at the top of his voice. His outbreak was enough to make Smokey come out of a deep nod and stare around, then drop her head again.

Terry pulled out five more dollars. "Is that enough?" she asked, holding the money out towards Big Ed.

He took the money and folded it. "Yeah, baby. That should handle it." He walked over and shook Smokey. When her head came up, he put the money in her lap. Like a sleepwalker, she got up and walked towards the bedroom, carrying the money in front of her.

"Here, honey," Smokey said as she walked over to Terry and handed her the heroin. The two women stared at each other for a moment. "It's a mean, cold world, Terry." Smokey's voice was low and husky. "So make sure you don't get caught out in a blizzard with nothing on but your bloomers. You might get a hell of a letdown when you find out ain't nobody there to loan you a coat."

"I'm beginning to learn that God blesses the child that has his own," Terry replied over her shoulder as she walked towards the door, closely followed by Minnie.

When she reached the door she stopped and stared directly at Porky. "If you should catch me out in a blizzard without a coat, your best bet is to either pour water on me or watch yours real close, 'cause I just might end up with it."

Her fading footsteps could still be heard as Porky spoke under his breath. "The bitch done become a real snake. King cobra in a female dress."

# 15

---

The courtroom sounded like a king-sized bee-hive as the various voices mingled, most of them speaking just above a whisper because of the strange environment. Many of the individuals sitting in the crowded court had had some experience before with courtrooms, yet because of external influences they were still affected with an unknown dread. They continued to whisper quietly to their friends and relatives, while waiting for the presiding judge to reappear. The morning was almost gone and it had been slow and repetitious. The first people to come before the judge for sentencing had been a long line of drunks, each one using a feeble excuse in an attempt to regain his freedom so he could continue his sordid life of deterioration.

Teddy and Snake had long since given up their

seats on the hard benches to stand in the back of the courtroom, both leaning insolently against the wall. Beside them, other young men leaned or stood posing, all of them neatly dressed, all of them waiting on the same thing. Every now and then a fast-talking lawyer would seek out one of them in the crowd.

"Goddamn judges," Teddy swore angrily. "We been down here waitin' over three hours and the bastards ain't brought the whores out yet."

"That's part of the game the would-be big fellows play," Snake replied. "First they come out and work for a half an hour, then they go sit on their fat asses for two hours."

One of the loungers in the crowd spoke up. "I hear they goin' have a murder trial today, and they ain't going to bring the girls out until after the trial."

"Bullshit!" a man farther down the line said loudly. "If they was going to have a murder trial, it wouldn't be in this courtroom. Judge Sherdalski is holding court this month for all the heavy cases. Picking up prostitutes and drunks ain't nothing but another way for the judges and lawyers to keep their pockets lined with our money."

He continued, now that he saw he had a listening audience. "They done picked up my woman three times this month, and each time it just costs a little more."

Suddenly a policeman came through a side

door followed by a line of well-dressed women. Most of them sported expensive wigs and their clothes were a little too expensive for the average housewife to buy. They came in quickly, followed by another policeman with a policewoman close beside him.

The men against the wall began to point out their various prostitutes, their voices extra-loud to let the people sitting on the hard benches know they were pimps. As the girls marched towards an empty box seat that was sometimes used for juries on serious crimes, their eyes searched the back wall, reassuring themselves that their men wouldn't leave them in the lurch.

Teddy caught Carrie's eye. "There's Carrie and Shirley, Snake," he said, all the time knowing that Snake had seen them already.

Their lawyer came hurrying up. "I got it fixed, boys, so that your girls will be just about the first ones called up." He removed a silk handkerchief from his pocket and wiped his bald head. He was a portly white man in his early sixties. His face was blotched red from too much rich food, while his chin was nothing but folds of fat. His huge belly shook as he pretended to be full of mirth.

"You boys ain't got nothing to worry about; it's all in the bag. The judge is an old friend of mine, so we haven't got any worry on that problem. When the girls come up before him, he'll just give them a fine, then you can be on your way." He rubbed his fat hands together. "Now if you fellows will just get the rest of my money together, I'll get on up there and take care of the business."

"It's worth it if they can get out today," Snake said, holding out a hundred dollar bill. They watched in silence as the lawyer waddled up towards the front of the courtroom and spoke to the girls.

One of the men against the wall spoke up. "Man, you must be crazy. That was a hundred you just gave away. You didn't need no lawyer. The judge is going to find them guilty anyway. All you had to do was wait until he found them guilty and then paid the fine."

Some of the older men against the wall laughed, but the merriment ended as soon as the judge entered. Everyone in the courtroom stood up briefly, waited until the judge took his seat, then returned to his own.

The judge was an elderly, distinguished-looking man with silvery white hair. His eyes were cold and bleak as he surveyed the room. When his glance came to rest on the men standing against the wall in the back of the courtroom, sparks leaped from his pale blue eyes. He turned to stare at the women briefly.

The first case he called was Shirley and Carrie. Their lawyer stood between the girls and pleaded their innocence, but the judge seemed to not even hear him. He asked the women a couple of questions, then fined them two hundred dollars apiece or six months in jail.

Teddy cursed quietly. "Goddamn, man, them whores will be all week trying to make that money back."

"I ain't worried about them making it back, Teddy. What hurts is that it's part of our cop money." Snake's voice was low. "That don't leave us but three hundred to get over with." He continued, "Much dope as you and them bitches shot, we goin' have a hard time gettin' our bankrolls together again."

Their lawyer joined them. "You boys know where to go to pay the ladies' fines, don't you?"

Snake pulled out his money. "For the price we paid you, I don't see why you don't take care of that for us." He held the money out towards the lawyer.

The lawyer hesitated for just a second. "Well, I don't usually do this, but for you guys, I'll take care of it." He accepted the money from Snake. "I won't be but a few moments, you can wait out in the corridor if you want."

They followed slowly behind the lawyer as he hurried out of the courtroom, aware of the sneering looks cast after them as they passed. Both men walked a little faster to get away from the leers.

"I feel like a goddamn fool, giving that fat sonofabitch our money that way," Snake stated as they entered the hall. "Well," he continued, assuming an attitude of indifference, "you ain't goin' go through life playing on everybody. You get some, while others get you."

"It wasn't nothing but a bill," Teddy stated, trying to pretend it really was nothing.

"Here comes one of them now!" Snake yelled, staring over Teddy's shoulder.

Teddy turned and stared at Shirley as she came running up. "Where the hell is your partner at?" he asked, his voice gruff, full of anger.

She flung her arms around Snake's neck and kissed him. "You don't know how glad I was to see you out there in the courtroom today," she said, hugging him tightly.

"I got bad news for you, Teddy," she stated while wiping her nose with the back of her hand. "Damn, I'm getting boogy. I hope you saved me a do, Snake, 'cause I'm sure gettin' sick."

"What kind of bad news?" Teddy asked sharply.

"Carrie won't be gettin' out today," she answered flatly. "Seems as if her probation officer put a hold on her."

"Put a hold on her!" Teddy screamed. "What about my two hundred dollars?" He was so angry he began to shake.

"Well honey," Shirley said softly, trying to pacify him, "it wasn't her fault. If you hadn't paid the fine, she would have had to serve six months first, then her probation officer would have put a hold on her before she got out and brought her back to court for violating her paper. This way, the most time she can get is the ninety days she got left on her paper."

"Let's get the fuck out of here," Snake said as Teddy continued to grumble. "It ain't goin' help none, us just standing around hoping we might be able to get her out."

"That's right!" Shirley agreed quickly. "She said she'd call you, Teddy, as soon as she found out what they was going to do to her, so we might as well get home so you can catch your call."

They walked out of the court building, with Teddy following slowly behind them. It was a clear day, but the wind was blowing off the river, causing everyone to shake from the chill.

"I sure am glad to get outside. Damn, I almost forgot how nice it was to be out," Shirley stated, pulling her coat up around her neck.

"Nice, hell! I don't see a motherfuckin' thing nice about it," Teddy growled as he caught up with them.

Snake grinned to himself and kept on walking. He was used to hearing his partner bitch about something or other. "Since you ain't got Carrie no more, Teddy," Snake said, "you might as well try and cop Terry back. They tell me she done become one hell of a whore."

"I don't need no whore," Teddy replied arrogantly. "That goddamn Carrie done shot up more dope than she'll ever be able to pay for if I kept her a year."

Shirley stuck her arm through Snake's. "Come on, honey, let's hurry, please? My nose is running, plus I'm starting to get flashes."

They finally reached the parking lot where they had left the car. After Snake paid the parking lot attendant, they all piled in, huddled together for warmth.

Shirley's teeth began to rattle. "Damn, I don't know why I keep on using. I ain't got no blood left in my veins. It ain't no sense in nobody gettin' this cold just walking a few feet."

"Man, cut that damn cold-ass heater off," Teddy yelled when a blast of cold air hit him.

"I suppose you're gettin' sick, too?" Snake asked sarcastically, as he drove out of the parking lot.

The drive back across town to their apartment was swift. Traffic was at a minimum; it was still early in the day. Snake parked and the three of them hurried towards the apartment, all driven by the same desire. As soon as Teddy put his key in the lock and pushed open the door, Snake and Shirley rushed past him. Everybody made a beeline to where they had stashed their personal works.

"This is the last of the bag, Teddy," Snake stated as he came back from the bedroom carrying a small amount of dope on an album cover.

"How much you think we got there?" Teddy asked curiously. "It don't look like it's enough for all three of us."

"Shit!" Shirley exclaimed. "Both of you done already had a fix. You should at least give me that so I can get myself together."

Teddy laughed harshly. "You'll never get yourself together if you're depending on shootin' my stuff up. Maybe your man might feel like he don't need no stuff, but I sure need mine."

Without bothering to look up, Snake continued to split up the small amount of dope. He made three small piles. "Here's yours, Shirley," he said, pushing a pile of dope toward her. "And that one there is yours Teddy." He pointed at the pile of heroin left on the album, as he pushed his own share into a cooker.

"How come when you split the dope up, Snake, you don't let me pick the pile I want?" Teddy asked indignantly.

Without seeming to hear Teddy's complaint, Snake continued to cook up his dope.

Shirley quickly snorted up part of her dope. "You are beyond a doubt the most crying little bastard I've ever seen, Teddy," she said between snorts. "If you ain't bitchin' about one thing, it's something else." Her voice had become lower and she dragged her words out now. The heroin was quickly taking effect.

"Take care of your own business, bitch," Teddy answered, holding a tie between his teeth as he felt for a vein. "Why don't you check your whore, Snake? The bitch ain't got no business in my conversation."

Snake sat back in his chair and jacked the works off in his arm. He would let the dropper fill up with blood, then run it back into his vein. "That shit both of yah talking about ain't nothing. Give me some of that dope you got on that paper, Shirley?" he asked.

She bent down and snorted up the rest of the dope. "I ain't got none left."

"Greedy-ass bitch. That's all you is, Shirley," Teddy stated emphatically. 'That's all you and your girlfriend is, is two walking vipers. Two dopefiend-ass bitches—greedy bitches, at that."

"Honey, you goin' let him talk to me like that?" she asked Snake. Her head dropped down on her chest as she nodded.

Before Snake could answer, someone knocked on the door. "Make yourself needed, baby," Teddy said. "Try answering the door."

Shirley got up and walked toward the door, moving with a swaying motion. She was tall, with graceful legs, long-limbed. The minidress she wore revealed her large, well-formed thighs. She opened the door without bothering to look.

Four men rushed through the door. Teddy looked up from his cooker and his heart lurched with fear. He knew only one of the men; the three that he didn't know spread out around the room.

Snake must have felt a similar fear. He stood up and shouted, "What the fuck is going on here?" He stared around the room at the four men.

One of them pushed Shirley back towards the

middle of the room, while another opened the bedroom door and stared inside. Three of the men displayed pistols. Shirley started to cry loudly.

It had never occurred to Teddy that they might get stuck up. He had relied on Snake's reputation for being bad. Now, as he looked from one face to the other, he could feel his bowels about to move. His stomach shook as if he had a vibrator machine around his waist.

Snake's handsome face was drawn tight with anger. "Just what the fuck do yah think you're doing?" he asked harshly.

One of the gunmen, his pistol already half cocked, stepped forward and swung the gun against Snake's head. Immediately a loud shot filled the room. The gunman jumped back surprised, as Snake fell to the floor. He stood staring down at Snake, shaking, his face filled with fear. Two of his partners knelt beside the body.

"My God!" one of the men exclaimed. "You done killed him!"

All of the men became excited now, fear showing on all of their faces. "You!" one of them said pointing his gun straight at Teddy. "Put all of the money and dope on the table. Don't get smart or you'll end up on the floor with Snake."

Teddy hurriedly dumped all of the money out of his pocket on the table. "We ain't got no stuff, man. We was just gettin' ready to make up."

The same man who had spoken to him hit him

upside the head with the barrel of his gun. "Nigger, we ain't got no time for lying. I'm goin' ask you one more time, where is that dope?"

Teddy, sprawled out on the floor, climbed to his knees. Blood ran down the side of his face from the blow, and tears of fear mingled with the blood. He blubbered as he tried to speak. He pointed his finger at Shirley. "Ask her if you think I'm lying. She knows. We just split the last stuff in the house and shot it up."

The gunman kicked him viciously in the face. "I ain't jokin' with you, nigger. I want that dope!"

Shirley hastily fell to her knees. She realized that, if they killed Teddy, they would kill her so that there would be no witnesses. "Please, mister, please. He's telling the truth. Snake got the rest of the cop money in his pocket. They just got me out of jail, and we was on our way to cop after doing up."

The gunmen stared at each other uneasily as one of them went through Snake's pocket. "Here's the rest of the money," the searcher said.

"Who you cop from?" one of them growled. "Maybe we can go take him off."

"Porky!" Teddy answered quickly. "We cop from Porky over on Darwin Street."

Two of the men cursed. "We can forget about that, then," one of them said as he backed toward the door.

The one who had done the shooting regained

his courage. "What we goin' do about them? We just can't walk off and leave them."

"You ain't about to get me mixed up in no mass killin'," another one replied as he backed toward the door. The rest of them followed suit, and soon no one was left but Shirley and Teddy.

They stared at the body in terror. "What we goin' do?" Shirley asked in a trembling voice.

"We got to get the hell out of here before they come back," Teddy stammered. "Then we got to notify the police."

They left the apartment together, clinging to each other for courage. After calling the police, they sat out in the car and waited for their arrival. The cut on the side of Teddy's head turned out to be only slight, but his lips were puffed out from the force of the kick.

After the police arrived they sent Teddy to the hospital to get some stitches in his lip and took Shirley to the station to get a full report.

Later in the evening they got together again. Teddy still had Snake's car, so he dropped Shirley off at work. The excitement of the day was over; now they both had to take care of their immediate problem. It was time for them to get up some money. They both needed a fix.

# 16

The night had passed slowly for Teddy since Snake's death, not because of any deep concern he had for Snake but because of Snake's woman. Shirley had promised to meet him after work in the morning so they could go and cop together. He had watched closely for her, since he hadn't made any money. Now with daylight shining through the restaurant window, he forced himself to accept the fact that she wasn't coming. At least, he reasoned with himself, he had gained something from the ordeal. He had Snake's car, and he wasn't about to give it up to none of Snake's kin.

He stared at the waitress angrily until she turned her head. His nose had started to run, and he didn't want to hear no shit. He had been sitting in the restaurant since midnight; it was now going on eight o'clock in the morning. The day-shift waitress came on duty, and the two women talked in a hushed tone, every now and then glancing up to see if he was watching.

Someone came in the door. He looked up hopefully. It was just another one of the girls who had been working the streets all night, coming in for her breakfast.

"Hi, Teddy," she said, sitting down beside him. "Didn't you say earlier you was looking for Shirley?" She went on before he could answer: "I saw her get in Pee Wee's Cadillac. From the way they'd been talking, I think they went to the west side to cop."

Teddy felt his stomach sink. "How about loaning me five dollars, Bee. I'll give it back to you as soon as I get my bag together."

"No bet, baby," she said, getting up. "If my man heard about me loaning you some money, he'd kill me." She walked over to the jukebox and played some records, then sat down at a table by herself.

A sigh of despair escaped from Teddy. He knew now he was right back where he started from—only this time he had transportation. He got up and walked slowly toward the door. He had already gotten a blow from Porky after telling him the news, so he knew his credit wasn't any good. He felt in his pocket. It hadn't grown any money since the last time he reached in there. He still had about fifty cents worth of change. He decided to put that in the gas tank.

He drove up and down the street slowly, looking for Terry. If he could find her, he thought, he'd take whatever money she had made. Unable to find her, he pulled up in a gas station and spent his last fifty cents. While he was there, he opened the trunk and noticed the spare. He ended up pawning the spare tire and jack for five dollars. He rushed over to Porky's house and spent it. It just barely knocked the chills off, so he was back where he started, minus one tire and jack.

His mind started working feverishly. Today was check day. If he could cut off the mailman, he could get his sister's check and cash it at the neighborhood grocery store. As he jumped in the car and raced toward his old neighborhood he promised himself that, as soon as he turned the dope bag over, he would return his sister's money. If I move fast, he thought, I'll have her money back no later than tonight.

It was still early when he parked a few doors away from his mother's house. He cut the motor off and sat watching the street. After about an hour, he saw the mailman turn into his block. He started the car and drove slowly toward the man.

"Hi there," he yelled out the window, "you got a minute?"

The mailman walked slowly toward the car, a handful of letters gripped tightly in his left hand.

"Hi, Teddy, what you doing up so early? I always thought you was a late sleeper."

Teddy grinned. "I got to take Bessy to do her shopping, Al," he answered, using the mailman's first name. "She asked me to pick up her check from you, so that we could be on our way." Before the mailman could reply, he continued, "She's getting dressed and figured, if I could get the check from you and cash it, we could save some time."

For a moment the mailman was undecided. "I don't like to give out other people's checks, Teddy, but since she's your sister, I guess it's all right this time."

His words were like a stimulant for Teddy. He couldn't believe his good luck. He held his breath while the mailman looked through the mail. Finally he found a long envelope and held it out toward Teddy.

Bessy had grown tired of waiting for the mailman to show up with her check. She grabbed her coat and stepped out on the porch. "I'll be back shortly, Momma," she yelled at her mother as she went out the door. "I just want to see if the mailman's coming." She stepped out on the sidewalk and stopped. Damn if that don't look like Teddy, she thought as she put her hand up, shading her eyes from the glare of the sun. She saw the mailman hand him something, and her heart leaped. It couldn't be, she told herself, as she started running in that direction. She watched Teddy as he climbed back in the car and drove off. Tears ran down her cheeks as she tried to run faster.

Before she reached the mailman, she started yelling. "He didn't get my check, did he? You didn't give him my check, did you?" Her voice sounded shrill in the still morning air. The mailman stopped and stared stupidly. He had heard her, yet the words didn't seem to make any sense.

She finally reached him. She clutched at his arm. "He didn't get my check, did he?" she asked breathlessly. The wind blew her hair in her face, covering some of the tears running down her cheeks.

The mailman nodded his head up and down, too shocked to speak, wondering what he had gotten himself into. Already he was thinking what he could say to his supervisor to explain this mess.

Suddenly a police car turned the corner and came slowly down the street. Bessy ran out into the street and blocked its path. Before it could stop she ran around the car and began talking.

"Just a little slower, ma'am," the driver said. His partner opened the door for her to get in.

The mailman came over and explained what had happened, then pointed out the direction Teddy had taken.

"I don't know what we can do, other than make out a report, miss. He's probably long gone by now," the driver said in a bored voice.

"If you hurry we can stop him," she blurted.

"He's got to cash it, and I don't think he knows but one store to cash it at."

"You know where that's at?" the driver asked quickly, the excitement of an arrest instantly replacing any feelings of boredom.

He turned the car around as she gave directions. In a matter of minutes they were parking behind Teddy's car. He was leaning over the counter, writing on the back of the check, when Bessy and the two policemen walked in.

At their approach he wheeled around. Fear instantly flashed across his face. He could feel his stomach lurching and his knees began to tremble. As his sister snatched the check from him he turned his face away so she wouldn't see his shame.

"How could you, Teddy? How could you?" she asked angrily. "You know damn well we need this money to feed the family with. Whether it's mine or not, you know Momma needs part of it for the rent."

As they led him away, the driver spoke to her. "You'll have to come downtown to the station with us, miss, and file a formal complaint. Since it's your brother, you better talk to the sergeant."

In the back seat of the police car, on the way to the station, Teddy pleaded, "Bessy, I was goin' bring you your money back tonight, really, baby. Don't do this to me. I'm your brother, honey. I know you don't mean to do this to me, girl.

You're just mad right now, but if you stop and think about it, you'll change your mind."

She shook her head stubbornly. "I don't care what you say, Teddy, I ain't going to change my mind. I'm doing it for you, man. If you continue shootin' that dope, you going to end up dead."

At the mention of drugs both policemen became alert, but neither spoke, fearing she might change her mind. At the station, they quickly fingerprinted Teddy, while Bessy filed her complaint. She took time out to call her mother and tell her what had happened. After she hung up the phone there were tears in her eyes, but she didn't change her mind.

Teddy watched Bessy leave through the front door. Fear was a large ball in his throat. After leaving all of his personal belongings with the desk sergeant, he followed the turnkey up the stairs. The turnkey stopped in front of a large steel door with a small barred window across it. He opened it with his key and shoved Teddy inside.

Once inside, Teddy stopped and stared around. It was a large room with two iron benches in it. Stretched out on the benches in various positions were four men. All were slovenly in their attire, and their hair was disheveled from trying to sleep on the iron benches and floor. In one corner of the large cell a toilet gave off a vile odor of stale piss.

One of the men got up from the bench and

stretched out on the floor. "You can lay there, man," he said. "The goddamn floor is softer than them goddamn benches."

Teddy took off his overcoat and put it under his head. He stretched out on the bench, with one cold, chilling thought racing through his mind: how can I get out before I get sick?

The rest of the day passed slowly for the five men. Every now and then one of them would get up and pace up and down. Just as quickly he would get tired and sit back down on the hard bench. They had each revealed to Teddy what they were in jail for; now with the coming of night, there was not too much more to say. Each man stared out into the empty space, alone with his fears and private thoughts.

When the midnight crew of turnkeys came on duty, Teddy got up and pressed his face to the bars. "Turnkey! Turnkey!" he yelled over and over.

"What you want back there?" one of the guards yelled back. The young guard walked up and stared through the bars at Teddy. "What you want, boy?" he asked in a harsh voice.

"I tried to tell the other turnkeys, man, I'm a dopefiend. I got to have some kind of medicine. How about sending me over to the hospital?"

The guard's loud, brutal laughter filled the cell. "Well, what do you know about that! We got another dopefiend. You should have thought about that, boy, before you got put in here. The only thing you'll get from us is a kick in the ass if you keep yelling. You might as well make up your mind to kick cold turkey, 'cause we ain't got nothing for you. You understand that, boy? Nothing!"

Teddy listened to the sound of his footsteps as he walked away. The other men inside the cell watched Teddy silently, feeling sorry for him, yet too aware of the facts of life to intrude on his privacy, knowing there was nothing they could do for him. It was his problem; they had witnessed many addicts come and go, all of them fighting their problem in different ways, some silently, others climbing the walls. If he got too sick, the police would come in and take him out and toss him in a cell by himself, probably further down the rock, where they wouldn't be disturbed by his outcries.

As the night dwindled on, it became a nightmare for Teddy. He was past the stage of just being bothered by his nose running. Hot and cold flashes shot through him. He climbed off the bench and lay on the floor. His skin began to feel as though insects were crawling under it. He twisted and turned on the hard concrete. He pulled his legs up tight and tried to sleep in a ball. Soon that position became unbearable and he moaned and cried out loud, shattering the silence of the night.

Every now and then one of the other men would mutter encouragement. "Fight it, boy, you'll be all right. Just don't give in. You're bigger than any old monkey."

When daylight came, his clothes were soaking wet and his hair was stringy. His face was filled with shock. He had looked into the pits of hell. The thought of at least two more days of this terrified him beyond all reason. His only thoughts were of dope. He had gotten up and searched his pockets frantically after dreaming during a catnap that he had some dope in his pocket.

"You all right, Teddy?" one of the men asked, his voice expressing real concern. "You might be able to get some kind of aspirin from the crew coming on now."

Teddy climbed to his feet and stumbled over to the commode. He vomited until nothing more would come up. Green slime clung to his chin as he continued to dry-heave.

It was later in the day when a turnkey came and called his name. He staggered to his feet and stepped over the food trays as the officer opened the door.

"You got a visit, son," the elderly turnkey said, compassion in his voice. He had been working on this same floor for over ten years and he had seen the addicts come and go. He had come to realize that when a real dopefiend came in off the streets, it was a pitiful sight.

He led Teddy down the corridor, opening and locking doors behind them. As they progressed through the jail, Teddy could hear the voices of faceless men yelling back and forth between the different cells.

The turnkey stopped in front of a small cell with bars, covered with a thin screen, the wires so intricately woven together that a cigarette couldn't be shoved through the tiny holes.

The officer closed the door behind Teddy and stood outside. From a distance Teddy could hear his mother's voice.

Suddenly she was standing before him, his sister beside her, staring at her son in horror. There was a small patch on the side of his head from where he'd been hit with the pistol; at one time it had been white, but since sleeping on the filthy floor, it was black. His bottom lip was stitched up, and his hair full of debris.

He clutched the bars and sank to his knees. "Momma, please Momma, help me," he cried. Tears ran down his cheeks and mingled with the dirt.

Her hands flew to her heart, and her dark face twisted with despair and agony. "Son, son, son." Her voice was feeble with anguish. "What you trying to do to me? I can feel it in my soul, Teddy. You killin' me, child." There was naked despair in her eyes as she tried to reach out and take her son in her arms.

"Please, Bessy, please," she cried from her knees. "We can't leave my son in here." She stared up at her daughter, tears of pain running down her face.

Bessy pulled at her mother's arms. "Momma, Momma. Get up, please. He goin' be all right. It won't kill him." She tried to pull her mother to her feet.

Her mother shook her head stubbornly. "Dear God, Jesus. I'd rather see him dead than in here like this. I can't stand it, Jesus, I just can't stand it." Her voice shook with her grief.

She climbed off her knees, a large woman who knew nothing but how to get in a kitchen and make the pots ring. Her sole happiness lay in seeing her children happy. A woman who had spent a lifetime raising her children, working from sunup till sundown, never spending her small amount of money on herself, always on her children.

She staggered toward the turnkey. "Officer, officer. Please sir, let my boy go." She reached out for his arm. "He won't do nothing no more, just please let me take him home this time." She would have fallen to her knees in front of him, but he held her arms.

He stared past her shoulder at Teddy. He had to admit it was a sorrowful sight. The boy looked like someone had beaten the hell out of him. "I can't do nothin', lady. It's up to the detectives. You'll have to talk to them."

Bessy stared at her brother clinging to the bars. "I swear to God, Teddy, you're the sorriest excuse for a man I've ever seen." She walked over and put her arms around her mother's shoulders. "Momma, Momma, don't carry on like that. He just ain't worth it."

Her mother turned and stared at her. There

was anger in the tear-filled eyes. "Don't tell me what my child ain't worth, Bessy, you hear? Just don't do that. I had him, just like I had you. You two is all I got in this world, next to your children, so don't tell me he ain't no good."

"What you want me to do, Momma?" she asked in a subdued voice.

"You got him in here, Bessy, now you get him out." She walked over to the bars. "I don't care what you done did, boy, you're mine, and I'm going to do all I can to help you."

Teddy got up off his knees. He was feeling better already. Just the thought of getting out was like a burst of sunshine on a cloudy day.

Bessy walked up to the bars. "I ain't said nothing about gettin' you out, Teddy," she said without conviction. "Momma, he needs to be here for a while," she said, trying to reach her mother, hoping to make her understand. "Momma, he's a dope addict. It ain't no way for him to help hisself unless he stays in here and kicks that habit."

Her mother began to plead. "Bessy, I'm asking you, child, to get your brother out of here." Her voice became firmer. "If you won't do what I ask you, Bessy, I'm going out of here and go to the bank and get that money I been saving and get him a lawyer to get him out. It's up to you."

"You can't do that, Momma. You been saving that money for two years so you could get you another stove," Bessie said, still trying to use reason.

"Stove don't mean nothin' to me, child. I want

my boy out of there, if it takes the last penny I got in this world."

Bessy shrugged her shoulders and turned to the turnkey. "I guess I better see the detectives. Could you show me where they're at?"

"You'll have to wait until after I lock him back up, then I'll come back and show you the way," he answered. He led the women toward the elevator, then returned and took Teddy back to his cell.

Teddy paced back and forth in the large cell. The monkey seemed to sense that relief was coming. His legs continued to ache while flashes of chills raked his body, but he managed to suppress most of the pain. His mind was fever-ridden; all he could think of was where to get a fix. He tried to sell his shoes to one of the inmates, but the man only laughed.

"You goin' need them, boy; it's snowing outside," one of the other prisoners said.

Each time he heard the turnkey coming down the hall, rattling keys, he rushed to the door and stood there shaking. After what seemed like an eternity, he heard someone unlocking the door.

The guard called his name. "I'll be seeing you guys," he yelled as the guard told him to bring all his belongings. The prisoners watched him leave, torn between wishing it was one of them leaving and being glad to see him go.

One of the men stood with his face pressed against the bars until Teddy was out of sight.

"Well, there he goes," he said. "I wonder how long it will be before he's back again."

The turnkey pushed all of Teddy's belongings across the desk to him. "Well, your sister dropped the charges, so you're free to go. Your mother is waiting downstairs for you. You can take the elevator down if you want to."

Teddy glanced at the stairway. "Don't the stairs lead down there?"

"No," the guard answered shortly. 'They lead to a side entrance, as you probably already know." He watched coldly as Teddy headed for the stairway. He slowly picked up the phone. I might as well save that poor woman a long wait, he reasoned.

The desk sergeant cursed under his breath as he hung up the phone. It was to a bewildered, broken-hearted old woman that he told the news.

# 17

---

The snow started to fall in a steady pattern. Minnie stamped her feet in the doorway in an attempt to start some circulation. She rubbed her cheeks roughly, trying to bring back some warmth. When these attempts failed, she left the doorway and stepped out from the shelter into the chilling wind. She stared at the traffic passing slowly by. Idly she glanced across the street at the East Side Cleaners' clock in the window. It was ten minutes to twelve. Damn, she cursed under her breath, here it was nearly noon, and she still hadn't caught a trick. As she wrapped her arms around the thin winter coat she wore, she began counting up the hours she had been working without breaking luck. Since ten o'clock last night, she remembered angrily. Over fourteen hours of walking back and forth on this corner without any luck.

She stopped and leaned up against Stevens' pawnshop window. She could feel the baby kicking inside of her, but it didn't bring her any joy. She cursed the snow, the cold, and the baby.

Her junkie sickness had been coming down on her gradually at first, but now the slumbering monster was awakening, taking complete control of her consciousness. She stared through the window at the radios, wondering if she could break the window and grab one and run. She shook her head and walked on down the street. It was becoming apparent that she would have to get some money from somewhere before she did something desperate. For a moment she toyed with the idea of going back to the hotel and waking up Terry again but quickly gave up the idea. Terry had cursed at her through the door earlier that morning when she had awakened her. It had been a slow night for Terry, too; after making enough money for her fix, she had gone in, getting away from the freezing cold. Minnie stopped in front of Ned's Supermarket and stared through the window. She watched the old white couple behind the counter, as the wife waited on two children. She gave up the idea of going in because there was nothing out on the counters worth stealing.

A sharp pain shot up from her stomach, causing her to bend over. She waited until it had passed, trying to make her mind stronger than the pain.

From the dilapidated doorways, other prosti-
tutes watched Minnie from hooded eyes. Some of them had the same problem: their monkey was hungry this morning, too. Others had a problem, but it wasn't a habit. It was the headache of trying to satisfy a money-hungry pimp. A pimp could be cruel, Minnie thought, but the most vicious pimp could never arouse the fear and pain an expensive dope habit brought on.

A woman passed leading two little children. She stared at Minnie angrily, as though Minnie had personally done something to her, and pulled her little girls out of Minnie's reach. Both children were dressed neatly in matching snowsuits.

Minnie stared after the children. They brought back memories of her childhood. Only there were no cute snowsuits that she could recall. It had always been cold, as she remembered it. Even then, she wore a thin fall coat she had to make use of in the coldest of weather. Snow boots had been a dream of hers for years when she was a child. She hadn't owned a pair until after her thirteenth birthday, and then only because she had been able to steal them from the girls' lockers at school.

She watched a drunk stagger down the street toward her. Before she could reach him, two other girls bore down on him from out of a darkened doorway. She ran up to the crowd, ignoring the angry stares the other two women cast at her.

The two women were holding the drunk up, each one holding an arm. Minnie walked straight up to him. As the wind whipped his coat back, she put her arms around his waist, rubbing her huge belly against the Negro trick's stomach. He tried to focus his fire-red, beady eyes on her, but before he could even see who was hugging him, her dexterous fingers went to work. She plucked his wallet out before the other girls became aware of what she was doing. They didn't know what was happening until she released him and took off down the street. Their shouts of anger followed her as she tried to run, her huge belly bouncing up and down.

The colored drunk turned around as the women released him and stared after her. He could have still caught her, but he was the only one on the street who didn't realize what had happened. She had dipped so neatly that he hadn't felt a thing.

Minnie turned the corner and kept on running. Her breathing became hard, and she had to swallow her spit. She opened and closed her mouth as though she were a fish out of water. Her hand clutched at her side, but she continued to run. When she reached the hotel she glanced back over her shoulder before turning in. She ran up the steps and stopped inside the doorway.

When she saw the caretaker staring out of her door at her, she went on up the stairs toward

Terry's room. She wasn't in any mood to be bothered about back rent. She prayed that the wallet held enough money so she wouldn't have to go back out in the streets for at least two days. Maybe, even enough money so she could pay up on her rent. Her fingers trembled as she began to open the wallet. She peered inside, slowly.

Suddenly her fingers started to search, wildly. She stopped and stared, then slowly removed two dollars from it. It felt as if the world was coming to an end. Disappointment ate at her. Her eyes filled with tears. She began to weep, slowly at first, then louder and with complete despair. Frantically she snatched the rest of the papers out of the wallet and tossed them on the floor.

Using her foot, she scattered them over the hallway, then stumbled down the hall to Terry's room. She pounded on the door, weeping and crying out, "Terry, Terry, open the door, Terry."

Inside the room, Terry lay on her back, staring at the ceiling. She listened to Minnie's pounding; it seemed to be coming from a long way away. Her eyes scanned the dresser first, making sure her dope was out of sight, before climbing out of the bed and making her way to the door. Her long black hair fell down across her shoulders, and she took her hand and tossed it out of her face. She was still very attractive, yet her eyes were beginning to show the strain of constant using.

"What you want, girl? A person ain't able to get no sleep in this goddamn hotel for your ass. Don't you never get tired of beating on my fuckin' door?" Her words were hard, but her voice was low and without malice as she opened the door.

"I just beat a trick for his wallet, Terry, and wasn't nothing in it but two dollars," Minnie managed to say, fighting to regain her breath. Her words came out in a rush, but they were so mixed up with her sobs that for a moment Terry couldn't understand her. Minnie leaned her back against the door, still trying to regain her breath.

"Is that all you woke me up for?" Terry asked, unable to hide her rising anger. "You could have at least waited until I got up. You know damn well I worked all night, and I just come in a few hours ago." Her voice was sharp from the lack of sleep.

Minnie fumbled in her pockets until she found the two dollars she had stolen. "He didn't have but two dollars in his wallet, Terry, so I come up here. I thought if he'd had a fat wallet, I'd buy us both a blow this morning." She waited, staring at Terry's face. "That's the real reason I came, honey. I thought I had made a big sting, but I didn't open the wallet until I got outside your place, so after I found out there wasn't no money in it, I come in anyway."

Terry looked up quickly. She knew what this was leading up to. "Well, I could have used a toot this morning, because I sure didn't make any money last night." She looked away, not wanting to see the disappointment that spread over Minnie's face. She tried to make her heart cold. There was really nothing she could do for Minnie this morning. Her money was short.

Minnie could feel her stomach lurching. There was despair in her voice as she asked, "I don't need but three dollars more, Terry. Then I could get a blow and get my sickness off."

"Ain't nothing I can do about it," Terry stated, her face assuming the expression of a ruthless dopefiend, lips turning downward in a cruel, un-yielding line. "I ain't got but ten dollars left, baby, and I need that for when I get up."

There was desperation in Minnie's eyes as she walked over to the bed and clutched at Terry's arm. "Why don't you loan me half of that, Terry? I'll make it back before you get up."

Terry shook her arm free and drew back. "No good!" she yelled and shook her head. "I ain't buying that shit. When I wake up I'm going to be sick, and five dollars ain't goin' get my sickness off. You been out workin' since last night, girl, and you ain't made but two dollars. How you think you goin' make any money in the next two hours, if you didn't make any all night and morn-ing?"

Minnie stared down at her girlfriend, too sick to argue. For a full minute she thought about the knife in her coat pocket. It wouldn't be hard to pull it out and make Terry give up the money. She was tempted to try but rejected the idea. Ten dol-lars wouldn't get but one fix, and then she would have blown Terry's friendship. In that light, she decided to pass it up. Sometimes when Terry took off a good trick, she would find her and give her a blow.

With that in mind, she turned and staggered from the room. Terry watched her go with mixed feelings. As soon as the door closed, Terry ran over and locked it. She then walked to the dresser and removed a small package from a drawer. She opened up the small pack of dope; there was just enough left in the package to make up two more hits. Her conscience disturbed her for a moment; she could have given Minnie a blow and still have enough to wake up on. She also had ten dollars worth of cash left, but she always kept ten dollars for don't-go money.

Terry took her time fixing up. The thought ran through her mind, just before sticking the needle in, that she could still run out and catch her friend. She pumped the dope into her vein. The drug hit immediately. She lay back on the bed and went into a deep nod, the spike still dangling from her arm.

Minnie made her way out of the hotel and headed straight for Porky's. She made herself believe that Porky would feel sorry for her and give her some credit.

Big Ed let her in the apartment. "Goddamn, that stomach of yours is sticking out a fuckin' mile," he said as she came in the door.

"I'll bet that box is hot as an oven," Porky said

from his large chair. He crossed his huge legs and the blood-red bathrobe he wore slipped open.

Minnie made her way over to Porky. "I ain't got but two dollars," she said and held the money out to him.

Porky moved forward and ran his hand under her dress. "Girl, how you can stand working out there in all that cold weather without any pants on is beyond me," he said, still feeling under her dress.

She opened her legs wider, and stood wide-legged. "I'm sorry, Porky, you goin' help me?" There was much more than just begging in her voice; there was the sound of total despair.

He removed his hand from under her dress and stared into her face. It was all there for him to see.

"Will you listen to that, Ed!" he exclaimed loudly. "If I remember correctly, this was one of those smart-ass bitches that talked plenty shit a few months ago."

"That wasn't none of me," she answered quickly, then tried to shift the blame. "You know that's Terry who always talks smart to you, Porky. Not me."

"All you dopefiends are the same," Porky stated brutally. "You ain't got no respect for nobody. Terry been taking care of your habit most of this winter, yet here you are ready to sell her out for a fix." A small gleam came into his eyes as he stared up at her. He stood up. "Come on!" he ordered and walked towards the bedroom, never looking back to see if she would follow or not. He knew she was coming. Her sickness had her in such a way that anything went, no matter what, if she could get a fix out of it.

Minnie followed him into the room and closed the door after Smokey walked past.

"Take your clothes off," Porky demanded. He watched her closely as she undressed.

Minnie had reached the point where she no longer thought, only reacted. She moved now as though she were a robot. She removed her clothes quickly and stood before him naked.

Porky led her to the bed and pushed her over. He spread her legs wide, then using his fingers he toyed with her for a while. First he experimented to see how many of his fingers he could stick up her at one time. Growing tired of this, he tried inserting his huge fist. Next he got up and released one of his large German police dogs. He brought the dog back to the bed and lifted him up between her legs.

Suddenly Minnie realized what was about to happen to her. She twisted her head into the pillow. Scalding tears ran down her cheeks as she felt the dog's paws against her stomach. Animal sounds came to her and she shut her eyes tightly, not wanting to know whether they came from Porky or the dog. She could feel Porky twisting her hair and, without opening her eyes, she opened her mouth to accept the rigid penis he was sticking in her face.

Later, Porky shoved her out of the bed. "Go in there and wash up," he commanded.

She got up and obeyed, moving as if in a dream. When she returned from the bathroom, he tossed two small ten-dollar packs at her. "Take it across to your place and do it," he ordered. "I don't want to see your freakish ass for a while."

She staggered back through the living room in a daze. Big Ed stared at her curiously as he let her out the door. It was not the first time he had seen a woman come out of Porky's room looking as though she had peeped into the bottomless pit of hell. Some like Minnie looked as though Porky had taken away their very souls, leaving only shell.

Minnie made her way across the street and into her room, not really knowing how she got there. The dope was still clutched tightly in her hand. She stared at it curiously for a second, then got up and dumped it all in a cooker. As she worked, without thought, her mind drifted back through the past. Life had always been difficult. Since her early childhood, things had always worked out harshly for her. She thought about the coming problem of raising a child. Tears ran down her cheeks as she saw what kind of life she would have to offer her baby.

She struck two matches and lit up the bottom of the cooker. She had done this so many times that she could do it with her eyes closed. Her mind continued to drift as she cooked up the dope. The thought of her child coming into the world as a dopefiend saddened her. If she had only committed herself, things would have been different. Suddenly the lighted matches burned her fingers. The pain made her release the matches and the cooker. Dope spattered all over as the cooker took a bounce when it hit the varnished floor. She stared down at the spreading puddle of heroin. It had all been for nothing, she thought. Her mind began to play tricks on her. What had been for nothing? For a moment she couldn't remember anything. Then she remembered one of her drunken mother's boyfriends getting into bed with her one morning when she was a child. The pain, her mother's anger, directed more at her than at the man. Later that morning she had prayed to die while lying in her bed. When she awoke she had been hurt and angry that her prayer hadn't been answered.

Without hesitation, she began to pull the dresser into the middle of the floor. When she got it in place, she got the only chair in the room and climbed up on it and cut down her clothing line. Now she moved with calm deliberation, She was doing something she had thought about on many occasions. How many times had she lain in this very room, sick, knowing there was a way around her problem. The idea of not waking up sick any more brought a slight smile to her lips. She undressed slowly, removing all her clothing. She hesitated briefly, wondering if she should wash, but the thought flashed through her mind that no amount of water would ever get her clean again. Then she remembered the dog and Porky. Tears started flowing down her wrinkled brown cheeks.

She reached up toward the ceiling and grabbed the chain the light bulb hung from. She removed the light bulb and placed her clothesline around the chain. She twisted the rope together so that it wouldn't bust from her weight. She tied a sliding knot in the rope and put it around her neck.

When she thought everything was ready, she stepped off the chair. Her legs kicked viciously, reaching out for some support, but she had kicked over the chair. The shadow on the wall revealed a grotesque dance of despair, an ending of horror, the beginning of peace.

# 18

While Porky dressed slowly, preparing to keep a monthly appointment with the vice detectives to pay them their blood money in order to keep on dealing poison, Teddy ran though alleys from the cab driver he had just stuck up. The knife he had used was still clutched in his hand as he ran out from between two houses and made for Snake's car.

He climbed behind the steering wheel, cursing loudly. Six funky-ass dollars, he thought angrily. I risked my life for six stinking-ass dollars. He started the car up. One of them would have to go for gas, he reasoned, staring down at the gas gauge.

When he reached Porky's, he had to stand in line with two other addicts who were trying to get credit. Bear, a short, dark Negro with a long scar across his face, cursed. "I spend close to a hundred dollars a day with you bastards, Ed," he yelled angrily. "I ain't but three dollars short, man, I know you can stand that."

Big Ed shook his head. "Porky's in the bedroom, Bear. I just went and asked him about it, man, and he said he ain't giving no credit up today."

Lennie, Bear's hustling partner, spoke up. "We didn't have no car this morning, Ed; that's why we was short. Now, Teddy here got some transportation, so we'll have some cash in about an hour. All we want is some stuff to hold us until we come back from hustling."

Again, Big Ed shook his head. "Ain't nothing I can do about it. I ain't going into my own pocket to help you junkies out."

Bear glanced around the room angrily. He stared at Gee Gee, who was cradling a shot gun across his knees. "Nigger, don't point that gun in my direction," he stated, his eyes flashing fire. "You punks get these funky-ass jobs of being doormen and let it go to your goddamn heads," he yelled in Big Ed's face.

"That's enough of that shit," Porky yelled as he came out of the bedroom. "You ain't turning my place into no goddamn arena, Bear. The man told you ain't no dope unless you got the money, so make the best of that."

Lennie stepped up; he was tall, thin, with long hair that at one time had been a process. He pulled on Bear's arm. He knew there was no win for them there. Also, he didn't want to be denied entry into Porky's house. It was not fear that made them back up, only a desire not to be refused entry into the best dope house in the city. "We don't want no trouble, Porky. It's just that we was on our way to hustle and we ain't had our morning do yet." He hesitated, then added, "We thought, you know, 'cause we spend so much money with you, we could get a small favor this morning. You know, between us, we spend at least a hundred dollars a day with you."

"The only favor I can do for you is to sell you a ten-dollar pack today," Porky replied coldly. "Every dopefiend that comes through my door spends money with me, but I sure give him what he wants to buy. I'd say if you ain't got enough money, you best pool what you got together and let that hold you."

"I ain't got but five dollars," Teddy said quickly. He wiped his nose on the back of his hand.

Bear went into his own pocket, still grumbling. He pulled out a five-dollar bill and gave it to his partner. All three of the men stared angrily at Porky. It was just a matter of allowing them some time; Porky knew that they could be out in the streets stealing. If they didn't go to jail, he'd get his money, because something would be stolen and sold.

Smokey came out of a nod, and her arm brushed a glass of water off the armrest of the couch. The glass hit and cracked, sending bloody water and glass all over the filthy floor. Her eyes searched the room. "Irene," she called, as she noticed the young, chubby girl sitting at the kitchen table nodding. "Bring a broom out of the kitchen, honey, and clean some of this mess up."

Irene glanced up from her nod, saw who was speaking, and got up to get the broom. As she passed, Teddy grabbed her arm.

"Hey, baby, let me get three or four dollars from you until we get back?" he asked.

She jerked her arm loose, then snarled over her shoulder, "Why don't you ask that white bitch you supposed to have for some money?"

"Fuck that bitch," Lennie said, as he turned toward Porky. "We got sixteen dollars altogether. I'll take the responsibility for the other four dollars, and I'll bring it back as soon as we score."

"Smokey!" Porky yelled. "Make up three five-dollar packs for these people." He turned and grinned at her. "That way they won't be in my debt."

Bear cursed, Teddy groaned, realizing a five-dollar pack might not be enough to get their sickness off. Lennie was too old and experienced to let his feelings show. But in his heart there was a burning rage. He hated Porky with a passion. The years had been bitter for him; he could remember when people like Porky used to bend over backwards to be his friend. Yes, before he started using, it had been a different story. Promising young pimp, with a stable of four whores and a Cadillac.

Smokey made her way into the bedroom without comment. She wondered idly what kind of fun Porky got out of playing with his customers. She knew they were worth the four dollars, because all three of them were thieves. As she started to go past the bed, one of the dogs tried to stick his nose under her housecoat. She ignored him and continued on to the closet. The dog followed, smelling at her feverishly.

She opened the closet door and spun around on the dog. He stopped suddenly, but he was too late. Her hand came out of the closet with a short black whip. The dog tried to escape, but she brought the whip down on his face before he could turn away.

"You black sonofabitch," she cursed. "I may have trained you, but I'll break you too, you bastard." She swung the whip again, catching him across the back. The other dog froze to the floor, not moving, trying to appear a groveling lapdog.

Smokey tossed the whip on the bed and got some dope out of one of the coat pockets. She walked over to the bed and began to make up the packages. When she glanced up at the dogs, both of them were staring at her. She reached for the whip, and both of them started to cringe.

"Just as long as you bastards know your place," she mumbled, but as she said it, she realized that the dogs were becoming a problem. They were both too big to be so freakish; she made up her mind that in the near future she'd have to poison one of them. The other could go a little later. If Porky just had to have a freakish dog, she'd get him a small poodle and train it.

Smokey brought out the tiny bags and held them out to the men. They accepted them because there was nothing else they could do. Porky went back into the bedroom and continued dressing.

A little later, Big Ed came into the bedroom. "Dave's got the car out front, Porky," he said.

"Here, daddy," Smokey said, holding out his cashmere overcoat. Porky slipped on the expensive coat and stood in the middle of the room, undecided.

"I hate to leave them niggers here, Ed," he said, thinking out loud. "Bear might try and get mean when he finds out ain't nobody here but Gee Gee and Smokey." He glanced at his watch. "We still got fifteen minutes. We'll wait until they leave or put them out before we go."

When they went into the living room, Lennie was having trouble hitting in the neck, but Bear finally caught the vein for him. After shooting the dope, they got up to leave. Porky and Big Ed followed them out of the apartment and down the steps. The men didn't bother to speak to each other as each group went its way out on the street. Bear and Lennie piled into Teddy's car.

He started the motor and watched Porky and

Big Ed climb into the Cadillac. "I wonder where he's going?" Teddy asked quietly. "You think he's going to cop, now?"

The question went unanswered as the men wondered to themselves if that was what Porky was on his way to do.

"Why don't you follow him for a few minutes?" Bear asked on the spur of the moment.

The big Caddie leaped away from the curb. The men in it were not aware of the smaller car that pulled out more slowly in their wake.

They hadn't gone more than four blocks when Porky ordered his driver, Dave, to pull up to the curb and park. "I won't be but a few minutes," he said, as he lifted his huge weight out of the car.

Big Ed and Dave remained quiet as he got out. They knew he was going to make the payoff. He did it every month. The only thing that varied was the place where they dropped him off. He never went to the same spot twice. They watched Porky as he waddled down the street, too occupied to notice the car with Teddy driving go slowly past.

When they saw Porky get out of the car by himself, Bear shouted with joy. "He's going to cop," he yelled. "Man, he's really on his way to cop." He turned to Lennie. "Let's take the fat sonofabitch off, now!"

This was something Teddy hadn't figured on. Robbing Porky had never entered his mind, really. He sat shaking with fear, hoping that Lennie would refuse.

"What you think, Teddy?" Lennie asked. "Should we wait until after the fat bastard cops, or should we rip him off now, while he's got the cash on him?"

The question was a two-bladed one. Either way was trouble. "I don't know," Teddy answered truthfully.

"Well, I know!" Bear answered quickly. "Catch up with him," he ordered in a voice that would tolerate no refusal.

Teddy turned the corner behind Porky. Bear watched Big Ed and Dave closely as they turned. "I don't think they even seen us. All they were watching was Porky's fat ass," he said. "Park behind that car up there," he ordered, pointing out a car in front of Porky. "Duck, Lennie," he yelled as they went past the fat man.

Teddy pulled into the curb, moving at the commands of the other man, unable to make his own decisions. Porky noticed Teddy at the steering wheel as the car went past. It only annoyed him that Teddy had seen him walking; his mind didn't give off any warning. He continued on his way, hoping to get far enough away so that Teddy wouldn't see whose car he got into. As he started past the car, the door opened and Bear jumped out.

In that instant Porky realized his mistake. His heart leaped, and fear choked his mouth and throat. It was the same fear that used to fill his soul when he was a child and the neighborhood kids ganged up on him—the terrible fear of not being able to move, of being rooted in cold terror.

Bear snatched him around and pushed him over onto the car. The knife he held was inches away from Porky's face.

"What's the matter with you guys? What you want from me?" Porky managed to ask.

Lennie was already fumbling with his pants pocket. "Where's the rest of your money, Porky?" he asked, as he pulled a large bankroll from Porky's pocket. "We ain't got time for no games, Porky!"

Porky could feel his legs giving out from under him. He wondered if he could stand without their aid. In his heart he knew he was a coward. His huge size meant nothing. Any amount of exertion was enough to cause him pain and loss of breath. Even now, he could feel his breathing becoming shallow. It was pure terror that leaped from his eyes. He glanced up and down the street, praying to catch sight of the detectives.

Bear swung his fist into Porky's stomach. A hard, short blow. Porky grunted as though some-one had let out all his wind. "The rest of the money, Porky," Bear growled angrily. "We want that money you was going to use to cop with."

Hastily, Porky fumbled under his coat and drew out the envelope containing the detectives' one thousand dollars. He shoved the money at them. "That's it!" he cried. "Take it! But please, just leave me alone!"

Lennie grabbed the envelope and glanced in it. He could see the hundred dollar bills. "This is it!" he yelled excitedly. "We got it!" Lennie jumped back into the car. "Come on, Bear, we got it."

Bear didn't bother to answer. His fists began to move viciously. His punches rained down on Porky until the fat man fell down on his knees. Then Bear kicked him viciously against the head. As Porky fell at his feet, Bear took his knife and bent down and stabbed him twice in the fat of his shoulder.

As he watched, Teddy saw the knife plunge down. "Don't kill him!" he screamed in panic. Quickly, he started the motor of the car.

"Oh my God," Porky screamed, then started to shriek at the top of his voice. He sounded like a woman as his voice became shrill. Not wanting to be left behind, Bear leaped inside the car, just as Teddy started to pull away from the curb.

Before the car had disappeared around the corner, Porky staggered to his feet. A black, unmarked police car pulled up in front of him. The two detectives sitting inside the car stared at Porky for a moment, then one of them jumped out.

He grabbed Porky around the waist and tried to hold him up. "Looks like somebody done worked old Porky over," he yelled back to his partner.

Porky stared at the police officers. His voice wouldn't come back to him for a minute. It wasn't the pain, really, it was the shock. He was scared almost out of his mind. He glanced up and down the street, afraid the men would come back.

"I'm going to need some help," the detective called, as he staggered under the load of Porky.

The other officer got out of the car. "Has he still got our money on him?" he asked as he came around the police car.

"I don't know!" the first white officer replied, as he expertly ran his hands through Porky's pockets.

Porky shook his head. He managed to find his voice. "They took all my money. Every penny of it." He felt the blood running down his back and almost fainted. "I'm bleeding to death!" he screamed in the officer's face.

Between them, they managed to get Porky in the car and rush him to the nearest hospital. One of them called Smokey and informed her of what had happened.

Smokey locked up the shooting gallery and rushed toward the hospital, carrying a fresh thousand dollars for the detectives. They met her in the lobby. After she paid them, they left the building, already assured by the doctors that Porky would be all right.

Smokey waited for two hours until Porky was ready to leave, his left arm in a sling. They caught a cab in silence, both of them deep in thought. Porky directed the cab around to where he had left his Cadillac. Dave and Big Ed were still sitting where he had left them. Their faces showed their surprise as they watched Porky climb out of the cab with his arm in a sling. The sight of Smokey beside him was an extra jolt. They both wondered who was at the house taking care of the dope traffic. It was almost unheard of, both Smokey and Porky being out of the house at the same time.

As they rode back toward the shooting gallery Porky explained what had happened. When he got out of the car in front of his flat, he pulled Big Ed aside. "There's three thousand dollars on every one of them motherfuckers' heads, Ed. I want you to take care of this personally. When you get them, bring them here." He held out the key to the downstairs flat. "This will get you in the back door." He removed another key from his key ring. "This is the one to the car. You take Gee Gee with you." They walked toward the house.

When they got inside, Smokey was already on the phone in the bedroom. Gee Gee followed Big Ed into the bedroom and sat on the floor. They listened as she called one dope dealer after another. Each one she promised the same thing. A piece of pure dope if the dealer could help them put their hands on either Teddy, Bear, or Lennie.

"How long you think it will take?" Gee Gee asked as Porky gave him a small amount of dope to use.

Porky shrugged. "I don't care if it takes a lifetime, just as long as one day I see them punks downstairs tied up."

After hanging up the phone, Smokey stretched out on the bed so that Big Ed could hit her in the neck. Before he was finished, the phone rang.

Porky answered the phone, and a smile broke across his face. When he hung up, he walked to the dresser and removed a package. "Bear and Lennie are over to Count's house on the west side." He tossed the package of dope on the bed. "You know where Count's dope house is at?" he asked.

Big Ed shook his head. "I do," Gee Gee stated, picking the dope up off the bed. "What do we do when we get them?" he asked coldly.

"Don't let that worry you, Gee Gee," Porky replied. "Ed knows what to do."

Ed grinned. He ran the dope into Smokey's neck. The sight of the abscess on her neck disturbed him for a moment. "You better do something about this abscess, Smokey. It's gettin' pus in it." He removed the long needle from her neck vein. "What about the money they might have on them?" he asked, well aware of Porky's disregard for money.

"It's yours too," Porky answered. "Just make sure they're alive and kicking when I come downstairs. You can tell Gee Gee about the six thousand dollars y'all goin' have to split between you if you take care of this right." He watched the greed jump up in the men's eyes.

"What about Teddy?" Smokey asked as they watched Big Ed and Gee Gee depart, both men wearing shoulder holsters with .38 police specials riding gently under their arms.

"Teddy! Teddy won't be no problem." Porky laughed for the first time that day. "Teddy won't be no problem at all."

# 19

___

The evening shadows were beginning to invade her room as she rolled over and sat up. For a minute her thoughts were disturbed by a small nagging voice, reprimanding her for her ill treatment of her only friend. She walked over to the dresser and looked at the small amount of dope lying there. She took the back of a matchbook cover and split the dope into two piles. She raked the larger one into her cooker and put water on top of it. She held two matches under it until the white powder dissolved, then drew it up with her dropper. She had a little trouble finding a vein, but at last she hit. She shot the dope in quickly and jacked the works off a few times before pulling out of her vein.

As she dressed, she caught herself glancing at the other pile of heroin, but she fought the desire.

Before she could give in to it, she folded the dope inside some tinfoil and left her room.

Terry knocked on Minnie's door, lightly at first, then harder. When there was still no answer, she tried the doorknob. It opened slowly under her pressure. She stepped into the room. At first, the only thing she noticed was the dresser; then her eyes traveled upwards and the slowly swinging apparition came into view. She opened her mouth in horror. The sight in front of her froze her in her tracks. She stared in terror at the body gently swinging back and forth.

The sight of Minnie hanging there was shocking enough, but when her eyes turned downward, away from the sight of her friend's contorted face, they fell on what looked to be a child's head protruding from between Minnie's naked legs. The head of the baby was covered with afterbirth, while only part of its body showed. The rest was still hung up somewhere inside the dead woman's body.

Terry's first scream shattered the stillness of the small hotel; her second and third followed in a sequence of sound uninterrupted by the arrival of some of the hotel residents. One of the men reached for her in an attempt to quiet her down. She jerked away from him, then her foot slipped and she fell on the floor, her hands sliding through the waste that had escaped from Minnie's body.

She raised her hands and stared at the excrement on them; the feces only increased her horror. She screamed again and again. The men managed to get her out of the room and into the hallway. Once outside, two women tried to help her. She held her hands behind her back, afraid to look at them. When one of the women wiped the feces from her hands, she began to scream again.

The police arrived and called an ambulance. They had to strap Terry to a stretcher before they could get her out of the building. One of them held her down, while another gave her a shot. Her screams still rang from the walls as they took her from the hotel.

People stood around in small clusters and discussed the suicide. It had helped to remove the dullness from their lives; it was something to talk about the rest of the winter. When they mentioned Terry, they shook their heads, not really knowing what would be the outcome in her case. The only thing they could agree on was the fact that none of them had ever heard a woman scream like that before.

Porky sat at his window looking out. His house was empty for one of the few times of its existence. Since Ed and Gee Gee left, he had kept the doors closed, refusing to allow even his best customers in. Smokey sat on the couch nodding. Earlier in the evening he had watched as they carried Minnie's body out of the hotel. His eyes had widened in surprise as Terry came out of the hotel strapped to a cot. Smokey had roused herself enough to go across the street and find out what had happened.

Now, with only the streetlights revealing the shabbiness of the neighborhood, Porky waited and watched. This was his street, he thought. Everything that happened on his block had a way of coming back to him.

Now, as he watched, a car pulled up with a young white man driving. He wondered curiously who the woman could be turning the trick with the whitey. He grinned when the "woman" jumped out of the car. It was tall Donna Jean, a sissy, who worked in drag. The women's clothes she wore were always the most expensive she could find. She stood waiting for the trick to come around the car, her hands on her broad hips, standing invitingly with her legs wide. She had a long face that was quite feminine except for the huge nose.

The couple walked up the pathway leading to the hotel, arm in arm. Porky smiled knowingly. He had wished many times in the past that Donna Jean would become an addict, but the queer was too wrapped up in buying women's clothes to waste money on dope. He would have liked to see if his dog would be interested in Donna Jean. That would be a sight, he imagined, a sissy and one of his dogs, or both, indulging in an orgy.

Without warning, his vivid mental pictures were interrupted by the hotel door flying open. The white trick came running out of the hotel with his coat on his arm. He stopped at the back of his car and managed to get his key in the lock of the trunk. Donna Jean came running out of the hotel, coatless. She made a straight beeline toward the trick. The trick got the trunk open and turned around to meet Donna's charge with a tire iron. The sissy let out a loud scream, twisted around in midair, and ran toward the alley, with the trick in hot pursuit.

Porky opened the window, ignoring the blast of cold air that entered, so he could see better. He followed the running pair until they were out of sight.

"Close the damn window, Porky," Smokey said irritably. "It ain't summer out there yet."

Before he could comply, the couple came running back around the house they had run behind. The sissy was brandishing a large two-by-four and screaming at the top of his voice. His skirt was pulled up above his hips, displaying the jockstrap he wore. The trick managed to make it to his car, but the sissy was so close he couldn't stop to get in. Around and around the car they went. Porky started to laugh so hard that huge tears ran down his cheeks. Smokey got up from the couch and came over to the window.

"Somebody ought to kill that goddamn sissy," she muttered. "All they do is draw heat." As if to prove her correct, a police car came roaring up the street. The sissy saw the police car before the trick did. He stopped chasing the john and ran back into the hotel. When the car stopped, one of the policemen jumped out and ran after him.

Porky closed the window. "He'll never catch that punk," he said loudly. "Them goddamn sissies can run faster than the average man."

Smokey had already lost interest and returned to her couch. "How about giving me another blow, daddy," she asked softly. "All this waiting has got me on edge. I need a taste to smooth my nerves."

He snorted. "If I listen to you, bitch, every time you go take a piss you get on edge. In fact, every time you fart, you need a blow to smooth down your nerves."

Regardless of his words, Porky walked into the bedroom and returned, tossing her half a quarter package of dope to shoot. "Don't ask me to hit you, Smokey!" he stated, leaving no doubt in her mind that he meant what he said.

Some dopefiends parked in front of the house. Porky opened the door and yelled down the stairs as they entered, "Ain't nothing happening. Try tomorrow; I'll be together by then." He shut the door and barred it, not bothering to wait for their reply. He watched from the window as they climbed back in the car. Another hour went by. Smokey finally got a hit in her neck. She held a mirror up and hit in it. Only an experienced drug addict can go in the jugular vein without the help of another addict.

There was a sharp knock on the door. "It's me:

Ed," came the quiet reply when Porky asked who it was. He opened the door slightly, leaving it on the chain while he peeped out. The hallway was too dark for him to see through the peepholes he had in the door.

Porky opened the door quickly. "Did you take care of that?" he asked sharply, his voice quivering with eagerness.

"Downstairs," Ed answered slowly. The thought of the money he would make out of this was burning his brain. He had never had so much money before in his life. "Dave ain't here, is he?" he asked as they went down the stairs.

"Sent him to the movies," Porky answered flatly. "The less people know about this, the better off we is."

They had to go outside and around to the back door to get into the flat downstairs. Porky could see the outlines of his car sitting in the garage. "Didn't nobody see you puttin' them in the car, did they?" he asked cautiously.

Big Ed shook his head, a motion Porky couldn't see in the dark. "Nope, we parked on a side street, and it was empty when we come out. This cold weather keeps most people inside anyway."

They entered the house through the back door, which led directly to the kitchen. Porky locked the door behind them, then followed Ed into the dining room. The house was void of any furnishings. Bear and Lennie were sitting against the wall, their hands tied tightly behind their backs.

"Well, well, well," Porky said and kicked Bear in the stomach. "It's a shame I can't mark you two up. I'd sure love being able to work yah over." He flashed a cold, deadly smile. "Get some water, Gee Gee. Ain't no sense taking longer than we have to." He removed a package of dope from his pocket. "You boys is real lucky, I'm going to give you a dopefiend's dream."

Bear's eyes glittered with unconcealed hatred. He stared at the sling on Porky's arm. "I should have killed you," he stated with arrogance. "If it hadn't been for them tremblers I was with, I'd fixed your fat ass good."

"Goddamn you!" Porky cursed. He could feel his knees beginning to shake with the same fear he had felt earlier. "Get him ready!" he ordered, not wanting anyone to see the fear he felt.

Big Ed snatched Bear away from the wall. When he tried to struggle, Ed hit him viciously against the head. He pinned the struggling man to the floor with his knee, then rolled up his sleeve. Porky slowly cooked the pure heroin.

"You don't even need to cook that stuff, Porky," Gee Gee said over his shoulder as he watched the heroin start to dissolve once the water hit it. "Damn, I wonder what it feels like to shoot some stuff that good?"

Lennie started to beg. "Please, yah. Yah can't do this to us. We done gave back the money, all except what Teddy got." He tried another approach. "Porky," he cried, "I'll tell you where Teddy's at, man. I'll show you what motel he checked in. I'll even take you there and help you get him, Porky. Porky, you hear, man?''

Porky stared into Bear's face as he stuck the needle in his arm. Even with being tied, it still took Ed and Gee Gee to hold Bear down. He looked up into Porky's face and spit. "You dirty no-good fat black sonofabitch," he said as Porky began to slowly shoot the dope into his vein. It happened instantly. Porky hadn't shot out all of the dope before Bear's head dropped.

Porky cleaned the works slowly, watching Lennie out of the corner of his eye. He enjoyed listening to Lennie beg. With Bear, there hadn't been any enjoyment; he had wanted to get it over with before anyone could see his fear.

He stared at Lennie coldly, beginning to feel his penis rise. "If you was a little younger, Lennie, I might take the time out and stick something in you."

Both of his gunmen looked at him curiously. Ed was used to Porky's freakishness, but this was a little too much. If it had been a woman, he could have understood it, but raping another man while not in prison was beyond his understanding.

Porky drew the rest of the heroin up in the dropper. The terror he saw in Lennie's eyes was intoxicating; the mere thought of Lennie lying there, completely at his mercy, was better than any drug on the market. Porky felt his breath becoming harsh. "If it wasn't for this arm being fucked up, I would take the time to dally with you," he said and bent down and felt for a vein.

"Please, Porky, please. Do anything you want, but don't kill me," Lennie screamed. He felt the needle slip into his arm and he screamed louder.

Porky pulled the needle out. "What motel is Teddy at?" he asked harshly. "You ain't got but one chance to save yourself, so you better be telling the real."

Lennie was beyond any reasoning. He didn't stop to think. "He checked in the Blue Gardens on seven mile. It's just left of the freeway. Turn me loose, Porky, I'll take you out there."

Porky's laugh was brutal. He leaned back over and probed for the vein. Lennie's scream was one of sheer horror as the needle sank in. It was over in less than a few seconds.

"Take the bodies somewhere on the west side and drop them off. Then go get Teddy boy," Porky ordered. "He ain't even worth bringing back across town." He pulled the rest of the pure dope out. "This should be more than enough to finish it with. Bring what's left back."

Both men started dragging the bodies towards the door. "Hey," Big Ed yelled. "We don't even know the room number?"

"Goddamn it!" Porky walked up and down the room cursing. He stopped pacing. "I got it. Leave the dope here, you won't need it. Sometime tomorrow he's got to come out and check in again, so all you'll have to do is wait. When he peeps his funky head out the door, use them pistols."

Both men nodded their heads in understanding. Gee Gee grinned. He had never shot a man before, and he looked forward to it. Porky watched them silently as they carried the bodies out of the room. Though neither man knew it, sometime in the near future each one of them was going to have his own little overdose. It was a matter of simple survival, he thought coldly. Two witnesses minus two would leave none.

Teddy pulled back the blinds and glanced out cautiously. Again he wished for the thousandth time that he hadn't let Bear and Lennie know what motel he was checking into. At least he had had enough sense to change rooms, he thought. He turned and glanced at the fourth of dope lying on the dresser. He wouldn't have to go out for a while at least; maybe by then, everything would have quieted down. He stared at the dope and a new idea popped into his head. Instead of checking into this same room, he'd just change motels. That way, he reasoned, no one would have the slightest idea of his whereabouts. Some place out on the highway. It would be nice if he had Terry with him; he could start all over with her. For a brief second he allowed his mind to linger on the idea of picking her up, but he rejected it as being too dangerous. She lived too close to Porky. Now that his mind was made up, he started to move fast. He picked up the dope and put it in his pocket. He took a slow look around the room to make sure he wasn't leaving anything. He chuckled to himself; they had sure put it over on Porky. He could picture the fat man sitting around in his apartment cursing about it.

Gee Gee turned from the window, complaining. "Damn, Eddie, one of us should at least go back across town and get enough stuff to last us. Ain't no sense in us sitting here looking out this goddamn window, and we both sick."

Big Ed walked over and glanced out. They had taken a room on the ground floor, right next to the alley. There was a passageway for cars to drive through. You could come in either the front way or from the alley. It was really a beautiful setup for what they had in mind. Their Cadillac was parked down the alley, near the exit.

"We ain't got the time," Ed stated. "He goin' have to make a move pretty soon. It's damn near checkout time now." He removed his pistol and checked it again. Big Ed was fulfilling one of his wildest daydreams. He had always imagined himself as a professional hit man in his fantasies, and now they were coming true.

Suddenly he tensed. "There's our little pigeon now," he said, his voice full of excitement. He stepped toward the door. His heart was pounding like a giant sledgehammer.

Teddy closed the door behind him. It was a lovely day, he thought. Soon spring would be here. It would be an end to all the cold weather he disliked so much. Suddenly his blood seemed to freeze. From the corner of his eyes he could see Big Ed and Gee Gee coming toward him. It couldn't be, his mind screamed loudly. How could they have found him this quick. Run, something screamed inside him, run!

Before he could react, something slammed into him, spinning him around. Pain exploded in his back as he clawed at the wall for support. His strength seemed to flow from him as he sank slowly toward the ground. The rapid explosion of sound was lost on him, as a blanket of nothing-ness enveloped him.

# 20

___

The shrubbery on both sides of the path leading to the immaculate buildings in the distance gave one a feeling of serenity and peace.

Mr. Wilson held his wife's arm as they walked slowly up the pathway. The past few months had been a complete shock to both of them. Spring had come and gone; now summer was in its brightest bloom, and there was still no change in Terry. It had all been a nightmare, ever since that call late one night, informing them that their daughter was being held in a hospital. The hospital had turned out to be one for mental patients. The shock hadn't come until they had been able to see their daughter, then it had become a nightmare. Even in their wildest thoughts, they had never imagined something like this ever happening to them.

The desk nurse watched them as they came up the corridor. It was pitiful, she thought. Such a lovely young girl. Most of the nurses in the hospital talked about Terry. She was such a lovely thing. The nurse wished she had been gifted with such a shape and face. It wouldn't be going to waste in a nut house, she thought.

They didn't even bother to stop at the desk. They knew the procedure too well. They got in the elevator and spoke politely to the operator. She gave them a hopeful smile as they got out on their floor. They stopped at the desk and spoke to the middle-aged, brown-skinned nurse. She smiled politely at them and got up.

She led them down the hallway, and the room they stopped at was no different from the ones they had passed. They all had one thing in common: each was doorless. There were two beds in the room, one of them vacant, the other occupied by a young girl who was looking out of the window. Her hair was neatly combed back, and when she turned and smiled at them, there was something childish about her that a person couldn't help but love.

Her mother rushed to her and embraced her. "Oh, Terry, you're looking so lovely today," she said as she crushed her to her bosom.

The elderly man standing in the doorway blinked, trying desperately to hold back the tears that welled up in the corners of his eyes.

Check Out Receipt

BPL- Egleston Square Branch Library
617-445-4340
http://www.bpl.org/branches/egleston.htm

Wednesday, April 7, 2021 2:31:28 PM

Item: 39999068251592
Title: Dopefiend
Material: Book
Due: 04/28/2021

Total items: 1

Thank You!

The nurse noticed and glanced away. "I'll leave you now. Terry never gives us any trouble, so you'll be all right. The doctor said you can take her out for a walk if you want to," she added before she left.

"Would you like that?" her mother asked, turning her daughter loose. "It's such a lovely day out."

"Would you like that, daddy?" Terry asked in a childlike voice. She jumped out of bed and ran over to her father. Her every action was that of a child of ten years old. Terry's mind had blanked out all the horrors of her brief adulthood. She had returned mentally to the time that had been most beautiful for her. There was no worry, no responsibilities, only the joy of living. Now in her small world, she had only one fear, and the nurses tried to make sure she never came in contact with it. The sight of a needle would set her off, and for days she would live in a world of absolute terror, afraid to leave her room, plagued by nightmarish dreams.

Her father took her arms and held them out, fighting back the tears, not wanting his daughter or wife to see him crying. "Of course, child. That would be wonderful, just you, me, and Momma, walking in the sunlight." He fought it, but he just couldn't control himself. He pulled her to him. "Oh God, God," he cried. "Why did it have to happen? Why? Why? Why?"

She stared up into his face childishly. "What's wrong, Daddy, what's wrong? Momma, what's wrong with Daddy?"

Mrs. Wilson went to the door and beckoned for the nurse. When she came into the room she immediately saw what was wrong. She led Mr. Wilson from the room. He leaned against the wall and wept silently. His body shook from the dry sobs that escaped from his tightly clenched teeth.

Finally he managed to get himself under control. "Thank you," he said quietly. "I'll be all right now."

"You better be!" the nurse said, pretending to be stern. "You know that doesn't help our little girl in there, don't you?"

He nodded his head. "I know, I know. Sometimes it hurts to see her like that. If you could have only seen her before this happened. She used to be such a lovely young girl."

The nurse agreed. "Yes, it's easy to see that she was a beautiful young lady. Even in here. She's always so polite. Why, everyone on the floor just loves her. Now you march back in there and take her for a walk, and no more mess out of you."

The rest of the afternoon was pleasantly spent, walking around the grounds of the hospital. Sometimes they would wait patiently while Terry stopped and stared happily at the beautiful flowers that surrounded the paths leading to and from the main building.

On the way back to the hospital, they stopped

as Terry's doctor came down the steps of the building. He spoke politely to everyone, being overly kind toward Terry.

She smiled at him. "Hi, Doctor Parrish. Have you seen the pretty flowers yet?"

He was a youthful looking doctor, with blond hair and sky-blue eyes. "Yes, Terry, I've had the pleasure of seeing them earlier." He started to walk past, but Mr. Wilson stopped him.

"Could I walk along with you for a moment, Doctor?" he asked, deep concern showing in his eyes.

"Of course, come along," he replied, and the two men walked off together as Terry and her mother continued up the stairs.

"We've been wondering, Doctor. . . . Terry's been here for over three months now, and we wonder if she will ever get well." Mr. Wilson continued, not wanting to be misunderstood, "We realize you people are doing everything possible, but it's just that we don't fully understand what's the matter with her."

Dr. Parrish hesitated; he had always found it difficult to explain what was wrong with his patients to their kin. "Well, Mr. Wilson," he began, "Terry was admitted to our clinic for observation after the state found her to be mentally incompetent. Now, since then, the staff here has gathered a clinical picture of Terry's problem, which is by no means complete. As of this date, we believe Terry is suffering from what is known as chronic frustration anxiety due to the traumatic experience of finding her friend dead. Through our conversations with Terry, she apparently feels she's at fault, which leaves her with a feeling of deep emotional guilt."

"She's not the cause of that other girl's death!" her father stated flatly, then asked, "Is this the reason why she acts so childish . . . ? Isn't this unusual for a grown woman to act this way?"

"It's only unusual in the sense that you don't see it every day, Mr. Wilson, but for the professional man like myself, there is nothing unusual about it at all. Terry has regressed to an earlier, more acceptable behavior in the belief that it will ultimately help her suppress an emotional experience that was too shocking for her mind to accept. Her flight from reality is nothing more than an escape, a relief valve for her mind." The doctor went on, trying to explain it in the most comprehensible way possible. "My biggest problem is trying to get her to overcome this fear of hers for needles."

"When she stayed with us, she wasn't afraid of any needles," her father said. "Why, she used to give her mother insulin shots."

"Yes, I remember your wife telling me this earlier when I talked to her." The doctor stopped and lit a cigarette. "Her fear is deeply rooted in her subconscious, her awareness of participating in causing the condition that she ultimately deplores. While she was using drugs, she had reached the stage of addiction. She attempted to maintain herself in equilibrium by taking adequate doses of heroin at set intervals, not disdaining the orgasmic kick associated with intravenous administration of the drug but aiming mainly at the avoidance of withdrawal symptoms."

The doctor caught himself. He was getting beyond the realm of what his listener could understand. "I'm sorry, Mr. Wilson, sometimes I get carried away with myself." He stared at the older man. "Have faith, Mr. Wilson. I don't want to build your hopes up, but I do believe in my heart that one day you will see your daughter walk out of here just as she was before this terrible thing happened to her."

Mr. Wilson stood on the pathway and watched the doctor walk away. Faith, yes, he would have faith, and a little more. He would pray, and with the help of God, one day he would truly see his little girl walk away from here. He turned and walked back toward the hospital, his step firmer than it had been before. There was no more doubt in his heart now. It was just a matter of time.

# 21

The sun was a blazing ball of fire in the sky; heat waves bounced off the pavement in a continuous pattern of heat. Porky wiped the sweat off his face and continued to gaze out the open window. "This is just about the hottest goddamn summer I've ever seen," he muttered, not really speaking to anyone in the room.

His apartment was full of young addicts. Many of the older faces were gone, not to be seen again. Gee Gee had been buried for over a month now— an overdose, so all the addicts thought, to Porky's satisfaction.

He didn't have but two doormen left now, Big Ed and Dave, but they would do. Since the death of Bear and Lennie, plus Teddy, he didn't have any fear of being stuck up again.

Suddenly a convertible pulled up in front of his house and stopped. The driver jumped out of the car. Porky grinned. Young Ronald was coming back for the second time that day to cop.

He stared at the two young girls still sitting in the car. From his window they didn't look to be over fifteen years old, but that was the way it was now. The new addicts were all young. That suited Porky just fine. He stared at the young girls, and when one of them looked up in his direction, he stuck his tongue out.

She turned her head quickly, causing him to laugh. He grinned, as Ronald knocked on the door. As soon as Ronald became strung out enough, the girls would follow.

It would come to pass as sure as night turned into day, and he would be there to see it happen. It was a game of life that he played with all the junkies, only the cards were stacked against the junkies and he was the dealer.

He stared around his house of horror at all the players. Tess was there with a new girlfriend, and Tess's girlfriend didn't look to be over seventeen. With all these young kids starting to use dope, this promised to be a beautiful year.

Some of the dopefiends stared back at Porky insolently.

He laughed loudly, brutally, in their faces. Some of them looked up from their nods and stared at him as though he was losing his mind.

He leered at them knowingly; he knew he was holding the winning hand in the game.

He didn't use—no, of all his faults, that was one he didn't have. Porky was not a dopefiend.

If you enjoyed *Dopefiend,* don't miss
# *Whoreson*

Available in March 2012 at your local bookstore

Here's an excerpt from *Whoreson* . . .

# 1
---

From what I have been told it is easy to imagine the cold, bleak day when I was born into this world. It was December 10, 1940, and the snow had been falling continuously in Detroit all that day. The cars moved slowly up and down Hastings Street, turning the white flakes into slippery slush. Whenever a car stopped in the middle of the street, a prostitute would get out of it or a whore would dart from one of the darkened door-ways and get into the car.

Jessie, a tall black woman with high, narrow cheekbones, stepped from a trick's car holding her stomach. Her dark piercing eyes were flashing with anger. She began cursing the driver, using the vilest language imaginable about his parents and the nature of his birth. The driver, blushing with shame, drove away, leaving her behind in the falling snow. Slush from the spinning tires spattered her as she held onto a parked car for support. She unconsciously rubbed her hand across her face to wipe away the tears that mingled with the snowflakes.

Two prostitutes standing across the street in the Silver-line doorway, an old dilapidated bar that catered to hustling girls, watched her curiously.

Before she could move, another car stopped behind her. She turned and stared at the white face leering over the steering wheel. The driver noticed as she turned that her stomach was exceptionally large. Guessing her condition, he drove on. She stood holding her stomach and watching the car move down the street until it stopped near a group of women in front of a bar. She started to move towards the sidewalk, but her legs gave out on her, and she fell into the slush in the street.

From the darkened doorways, prostitutes of various complexions ran to the stricken woman's aid. Before, where there had been closed windows, there now appeared heads of different shapes and sizes.

"Bring that crazy whore up here," a stout woman yelled from a second-story window. While four women half carried and half dragged Jessie up the stairs, a young girl, still in her teens, yelled to the woman in the window, "I think she goin' have that damn baby, Big Mama."

The large woman in the window looked down at the girl, amused. "It's about time she had it, gal. Seems she's been sticking out for a whole year." Big Mama started to close the window, then added, "You run down the street and get that nigger doctor, gal, and don't stop for no tricks."

The young girl started off for the doctor, muttering under her breath. She ducked her head and pulled up her collar in an attempt to cut off the chilling wind. When a car stopped and the driver blew his horn, she ignored the call for business and continued on her errand.

Big Mama's living room was full of prostitutes sitting and standing around, gossiping. It was rare for a woman to have a baby on the streets; also, it gave them an excuse to come in out of the snow.

"What the hell Jessie working out in this kind of weather for? Ain't she and her man saved no money?" a short, brown-skinned, dimpled woman asked. The room became quiet until another woman spoke up.

"You know goddam well that black ass bastard she had for a pimp run off last week with some white whore," she said harshly. "He jumped on Jessie and took all the money she been saving to get in the hospital with, too."

This comment started up gossip on the merits of various pimps—then suddenly a slap and the sound of a baby yelling came to them, and everyone became silent.

Big Mama put out the few girls who had remained in the bedroom, then took the baby from the doctor and carried it towards the bed. Her large face was aglow with happiness as she smiled at the woman lying in her bed.

"You can be glad of one thing, Jessie, this baby don't belong to that nigger of yours that's gone," she said while turning the baby around so the mother could see it. "Looks like you done went and got you a trick baby, honey, but for a child as black as you, I sure don't see how you got one this light."

Jessie raised herself and stared at the bundle Big Mama held. "Oh my God," she cried and fell back onto the bed. Big Mama stepped back from the bed, shocked, and held the baby tighter. Her dark face, just a shade lighter than Jessie's, was filled with concern. She had never had a child of her own. Like many women who have been denied offspring, she had an overwhelming love for children. Her voice took on a tone that all of the prostitutes working out of her house respected. When she spoke this way they listened, perhaps because she weighed over three hundred pounds and had been known to knock down men with one swing of her huge hands. She spoke and only her voice could be heard in the house.

"If you don't want this baby, Jessie, I'll take him." Her eyes were full of tears as she looked down at the tiny bundle in her arms. "You can damn well bet he'll have good taking care of, too."

The small, elderly, balding doctor cleared his

throat. He held out a birth certificate. "I'll have to get on to my other calls, so please give me a name for the little fat fellow."

Jessie stared at the bundle Big Mama held. All the black curls covering the baby's head only inflamed her anger. Her eyes were filled with blind rage as she turned and stared at the doctor. He stepped back unconsciously. Here, he thought, was a woman who had been badly misused by some man. He hoped that he would never again see such hate in a woman's eyes.

Jessie laughed suddenly, a cold, nerve-tingling sound. Big Mama shivered with fear, not for herself, but for the tiny life she held in her arms.

"Well, Mrs. Jones," the doctor inquired, "have you decided on what to call your baby?"

"Of course, doc, I've got just the name for the little sonofabitch—Whoreson, Whoreson Jones."

The doctor looked as if he had been struck by lightning. His mouth gaped, and he stared at her dumbfounded.

Big Mama was the first to recover. "You can't do that, Jessie. Give the child a good Christian name."

"Christian name hell!" Jessie replied sharply. "I'm naming my son just what he is. I'm a whore and he's my son. If he grows up ashamed of me, the hell with him. That's what I'm wantin' to name him, and that's what it's goin to be. Whoreson!"

In De'nesha Diamond's explosive series, the fiercest ride-or-die chicks in Memphis are battling alongside—and against—their ruthless men, to be the last diva standing . . .

Don't miss

## *Street Divas*

Available now at your local bookstore

Here's an excerpt from *Street Divas* . . .

## ON SALE NOW

*Street Divas*

by De'nesha Diamond

Welcome back to Memphis, where when the sun goes down, shit starts popping off. The three major female gangs ruling the gritty Mid-South are the Queen Gs, who keep it hood for the Black Gangster Disciples; the Flowers, who rule with the Vice Lords; and the Cripettes, mistresses of the Crips.

The stakes are higher now, but the rules never change in a city where blood paints the concrete. Surviving is not guaranteed, even if you drop your head and mind your own business. Memphis's street divas are as hard and ruthless as the men they hold down. Their biggest mistakes happen when they fall in love.

# 1

## MELANIE

*Pow! Pow! Pow!*
Python ducks and twists away from the bedroom door before Fat Ace's bullets tear huge chunks out of the door frame. Unfortunately, that leaves me in Python's direct line of vision. Time crawls the second our gazes connect, while death skips down my spine and wraps itself around my heart.

"No, Python. Wait," I beg. I even foolishly lift my hands like a stop sign, as if that's really going to force a time-out. Python's black, empty, soulless eyes narrow. At this fucking moment, I'm no different from any other nigga on the street: disposable. I'm already dead to him, and my tears are nothing but water.

Fat Ace squeezes off another round.
*Pow! Pow! Pow!*

Wood splinters from the door frame inches above Python's head, but that doesn't stop him

from lifting his Glock and aiming that muthafucka straight at me. I'm a cop, and I'm used to plunging headlong into danger, but I don't have a badge pinned to my titties right now, and my courage is pissing out in between my legs.

Python returns fire.

*Pow! Pow!*

Fat Ace misses again.

"Please. I'm carrying your baby." I clutch the small mound below my breasts as a desperate act, and I succeed in getting his eyes to drop to my belly.

To my left, Fat Ace's head whips in my direction. His voice booms like a clap of thunder.

"What the fuck?"

I spin my head back toward Fat Ace. Why does it look like this muthafucka suddenly can pass for Python's twin? Anger rises off of him like steam. I open my mouth, but my brain shuts down. It doesn't matter. There are no words that can save me.

"You fucking lying bitch!" Fat Ace's gun swings away from Python and toward me, while Python's gat turns toward Fat Ace. Both pull the trigger at the same time.

*Pow! Pow!*

*Pow! Pow!*

The bullets feel like two heat-seeking missiles slamming into me. I fall backward; my head hits the wall first.

De'nesha Diamond

Across the room, Python's bullets slam into Fat Ace's right side, but the nigga remains on his feet and squeezes out a few more rounds.

I'm in shock, and it takes a full second before the pain in my chest and left side has a chance to fully register. When it does, it's like nothing I've ever felt before. Blood gushes out of my body as I slowly slide down the wall and plop onto the floor.

*Pow! Pow!*

Python shoots the gun out of Fat Ace's hand.

*Pow! Pow! Pow!*

"What, nigga? What?" Python roars.

Fat Ace clutches his bleeding hand but then charges toward Python real low and manages to tackle him to the floor before he is able to squeeze off another shot. They hit the hardwood with a loud *thump,* and Python's gun is knocked out of his hand.

I need to get help. There's way too much blood pooling around me. *I'm dying. Me and my baby.*

"Is that all you got, nigga?" Fat Ace jams a fist in the center of Python's face. Blood bursts from Python's thick lips and big nose like a red geyser.

Tears rush down my face like a fucking waterfall. *I'm sorry, baby. I'm so sorry.* It's all I can tell my unborn child, other than I'm sorry that his mother is a complete fuckup.

"Your ass gonna die tonight, you punk-ass bitch," Python growls, slamming his fist across Fat Ace's jaw.

*Christopher!*

My head snaps up. My son, Christopher, is in the other room. How can he sleep through all this noise? An image of Christopher curled up in the bottom of his closet, trembling and crying, springs to my mind. *I have to get to my baby.*

I slump over from the wall but lack the strength to stop my upper body's falling momentum. My face crashes into the hard floor, and I can feel a tooth floating in blood in my mouth.

Covered in sweat and blood, Python and Fat Ace continue wrestling on the floor. Fat Ace, still naked, gets the upper hand for a second and sends a crushing blow across Python's jaw. A distinguishable *crack* reverberates in the room. To my ears, the muthafucka should be broken, but Python ain't no ordinary nigga. And sure enough, in the next second Python retaliates, landing one vicious blow after another. A tight swing lands below Fat Ace's rib cage. Not only does its force cause another *crack*, but it also lifts Fat Ace up at least half a foot in the air and gives Python the edge in repositioning himself.

The punches flow harder and faster. The floor trembles, as if we're in the middle of an earthquake. Python is shoved against the side of the bed, and the damn thing flies toward my head. Lacking the energy to get out of the way, all I can do is close my eyes and prepare for the impact. The bed's metal leg slams into the center of my forehead with a sickening *thud*, and a million stars explode behind my eyes.

The scuffling on the other side of the bed continues; more bone crushes bone. When I finally manage to open my eyes, Python is trying to stretch his hand far enough to reach for a gun, but it is a few inches too far. Fat Ace is doing all he can to make sure that shit doesn't happen.

Watching all this go down, I realize that I don't give a fuck if they kill each other. Why should I? I'm already sentenced to death. I can feel its cold fingers settling into my bones.

More tears flow as I have my last pity party. It's true what they say. Your life does flash before your eyes. But it's not the good parts. It's all the fucked-up shit that you've done. Now that judgment is seconds away, I don't have a clue what I'm going to tell the man upstairs. That's a good sign that my ass is going straight to hell.

*I have to say good-bye to Christopher.*

Sucking in a breath, I dig deep for some reserved strength. Determined, I drag my body across the floor, crawling with my forearms.

*Pow!*

To my right, the bedroom window explodes, and shards of glass stab parts of my body.

Python and Fat Ace wrestle for control of the gun.

"Fuck you, muthafucka," one of them growls.

Still, I'm not concerned about their dumb

asses. I need to see my baby one more time. However, I get only about half a foot before sweat breaks out across my brow and then rolls down the side of my face. How in the hell can I be cold and sweating at the same time?

*Pow! Pow! Pow!*

More glass shatters. I turn my head in time to see Fat Ace's large, muscled ass dive out of the window. Python runs up to the muthafucka and proceeds to empty his magazine out the broken glass.

"Crabby Muthafucka!" Python reaches into his back pocket and produces another clip. He peers out into the darkness for a minute. "I'ma get his punk ass," he says and then turns and races out of the bedroom in hot pursuit, nearly kicking me in the head as he passes.

Relieved that he's gone, I drag myself another inch before my arms wobble and threaten to collapse. I need to catch my breath.

*Pow! Pow! Pow!*

The shooting continues outside. In the distance, I hear police sirens. Then again, it could be wishful thinking. It's not like the department would respond this fuckin' fast.

*Christopher. I gotta get to my baby.*

Convinced that I've caught my second wind, I attempt to drag myself again. I try and I try, but I can't move another inch. A sob lodges in my throat as I hear the sound of footsteps. *Christopher!* He must've gotten the courage to come see if I'm all right. "Baby, is that you?" Damn. That one question leaves me breathless. I'm panting so hard, I sound like I ran a damn marathon.

The slow, steady footsteps draw closer.

"Baby?" I stretch out a blood-covered hand. When I see it, I'm suddenly worried about what Christopher will think seeing me like this. Shakily, I look around. I'm practically swimming in my own piss and blood. It could scare the shit out of him, scar him for life.

He's almost at the door.

*Tell him not to come in here!*

"Baby, uh—"

"Your fuckin' baby is gone."

Python's rumbling baritone fills my bedroom and freezes what blood I have left in my veins. My head creeps back around, and I'm stuck looking at the bottom of a pair of black jeans and shit kickers. More tears rush my eyes. This nigga is probably going to stomp my ass into the hardwood floors.

"You're one slick, muthafuckin' bitch, you know that?"

"Python—"

"How long you been fuckin' that crab, huh?"

My brain scrambles, but I can't think of a goddamn thing to say.

"What? Cat got your tongue?" The more he talks, the deeper his voice gets. The sob that's been stuck in the middle of my throat now feels like a fucking boulder, blocking off my windpipe.

Python squats down. I avoid making eye contact because I'm more concerned about the Glock dangling in his hand. My heart should be hammering, but instead I don't think the muthafucka is working.

The gun moves toward me until the barrel is shoved underneath my chin, forcing my head up. Now it doesn't seem possible that I've spent so many years loving this nigga. How does a woman fall in love with death?

Python is not easy on the eyes, and his snake-forked tongue doesn't help. Big and bulky, his body is covered with tats of pythons, teardrops, names of fallen street soldiers, but more importantly, a big six-pointed star that represents the Black Gangster Disciples. He's not just a member. In this shitty town, he's the head nigga in charge—and my dumb ass crossed him.

"Look at me," he commands.

My gaze crashes into his inky black eyes, where I stare into a bottomless pit.

"You know you fucked up, right?"

I whimper and try to plea with my eyes. It's all I can do.

Muscles twitch along Python's jawline as he shakes his head. Then I see some shit that I ain't never seen before from this nigga: tears. They gloss his eyes, but they don't roll down his face. He ain't that kind of nigga.

"You fuckin' betrayed me. Out of all the niggas

that you could've fucked, you pick that greasy muthafucka?"

"P-p-p . . ."

"Shut the fuck up! I don't wanna hear your ass beggin' for shit. Your life is a wrap. Believe that!" He stares into my eyes and shakes his head. "What? You thought your pussy was so damn good that I was going to let this shit slide? I got streetwalkers who can pop pussy better than you. You ain't got a pot of gold buried up in that ass. I kept your triflin' ass around because I thought . . ." He shakes his head again, and the tears dry up— or had I imagined those muthafuckas?

*Sirens.* I'm sure this time. The police are coming.

He chuckles. "What? You think the brothas and sistas in blue are about to save your monkey ass? Sheeiiit. That ain't how this is going down."

So many tears are rolling out my eyes, I can barely see him now. I want to beg again, but I know it's useless. Time to buck up. Face this shit head-on.

"I can't believe that I *ever* thought you were my rib. You ain't good enough to wipe the shit out the crack of my ass," he sneers, releasing my chin and standing up.

The next thing I hear is the unzipping of his black jeans.

"You wanna live, bitch? Hmm?"

I nod, but he still grabs a fistful of my hair and

yanks me up. Next thing I know, his fat cock is slapping me in the face.

"Suck that shit. Show me how much you wanna fuckin' live, bitch. You fuck this shit up and I'll blast your goddamn brains all over this fuckin' floor. You got that?"

I try to nod again, but the shit is impossible. Python's dick is so hard when he shoves that muthafucka into my mouth that he takes out another fuckin' tooth. I can't even say that I'm sucking his shit as much as I'm bleeding and choking on it.

This nigga don't give a shit. He's cramming his dick so far past my tonsils; the only thing he cares about is that tight squeeze at the back of my throat.

"Work that shit, bitch. You want to live, you better make my ass nut." Python's grip tightens, and I'm sure any second he's going to pull all my hair out by its roots.

Sweet blackness starts closing in on me. There's hardly any air getting past his cock's incredibly thick head.

"Ssssssss." He grinds his hips and then keeps hammering away. "C'mon, pig. Get this nut."

I don't know how in the hell I remain conscious, but I do, hoping this nigga will come sooner than later. But when Python's dick does spring out of my mouth, I'm not blasted with a warm load of salty cum, but with a hot stream of nasty-ass piss. I close my mouth and try to turn my head away, but this nigga holds me still and tries to drown my ass.

"Open up, bitch. Open the fuck up!"

Crying, I open my mouth.

"Yeah. That's right. Drink this shit up. This is the kind of nut you deserve!"

By the time he lets my head go, I'm drenched from head to goddamn toe, but still sobbing and trying to cling to life.

Python stuffs his still rock-hard dick back into his pants and zips up. "Fuckin' pathetic. That had to be the worst head I ever had."

My eyes drop to the space in between his legs. There I see my seven-year-old baby, Christopher. He stands in his pajamas, clutching his beloved teddy bear. "I'm so sorry," I whisper.

Christopher's eyes round with absolute horror.

*He's going to watch me die.*

"You're a fuckin' waste of space, bitch. Go suck the devil's dick," Python hisses and then plants his gun in the back of my head and pulls the trigger.